The Danzig Corridor

Paul R. E. Jarvis

1

Having witnessed the city of Danzig descend into sectarianism, Viktor feared for his family's safety. His wife, Zofia, was pregnant and their two boys, Peter and Niklos, had begun to ask awkward questions about why their friends had left. Leaving behind the family home was never going to be easy, but now it was a matter of survival. The German Army was coming. It was only a question of when.

Most of the night, Viktor hovered in the no-man's land between anxious consciousness and disturbed dreaming. His mind was racing; he couldn't sleep. The braces of his trousers hung loosely at his hips as he crept downstairs. He stopped in front of the mirror. A tall man, broad in the shoulders, Viktor looked like a Polish Clark Gable—Zofia always said. He adjusted his swept-back, brown hair with a comb from his pocket, flattening an awkward tuft on the side with a dab of saliva.

Downstairs, moonlight filtered through the shopfront, casting long shadows across the bakery. The chill of the tiled floor under his bare feet a stark reminder that today would be the first day he could remember when the ovens would not be lit. An army of around a hundred policemen marched past his shop, taking him by surprise. Dressed in their characteristic dark blue overcoats and ostentatious, black shako caps, they strode along the cobbles. Solemn-faced, their eyes were fixed on the road ahead. *Where were they heading?*

Outside, the bitter morning air made Viktor shiver. His beloved horse, Miedziak, protruded its head over the stable door to see who had ventured into the courtyard so early in the day. The old boy snorted, ejecting two plumes of steam which swiftly evaporated. Viktor patted the animal's long neck while feeding him oats from a nosebag which hung from a nail.

The wooden delivery cart occupied the centre of the cobbled yard. Peeling back the grey tarpaulin covering, he swept the flour from its slatted floor. There would be no space for luxuries on this journey, just the essentials. Stowing three bottles of water and a couple of blankets, he headed inside for some much-valued chocolate. This was an essential item, to be only used strategically for cheering up the boys when nothing else worked.

Viktor crept upstairs to their bedroom where his wife still slept. He watched her sleep from the end of the bed, a smile involuntarily curling his lips. He loved everything about her, even after ten years of marriage. Her looks, her personality, and even her moodiness, he was just drawn to her. They had been childhood sweethearts and he had been too shy to ask her out at first, so he relied on one of his friends to do it for him. In his world, she was everything. Viktor bent down and kissed her soft cheek, causing her to stir. The enormity of the day flooded back as quickly as the haziness drifted away.

'Morning, gorgeous,' she said, her eyes still closed.

'Morning, love,' he replied. 'It's time to get up.'

'What time is it?'

'Just after four.'

'Are the boys awake?' she asked, stifling a yawn.

'No, they're still asleep.'

'Good,' she said. 'They'll need their rest.'

'Things look bad! The police are out on the streets. They must know something.'

'We'd better go,' she said, now fully awake. 'You get the boys ready and let's skip breakfast. We can eat while we're travelling.'

'When do you think we should tell them we're going to Olsztyn?'

'Now,' she replied, starting to dress. 'Try not to worry them, though. Today is going to be hard enough without them being upset.'

'Hey! I'm just going to tell them we're off to visit my parents,' he said. 'You know what they're like. They'll be so excited they won't think anything of it.'

'Are you sure we should go to Olsztyn? There are many more Germans there than there are here.'

'Where else could we go?' he asked, searching for an answer. 'We can't go west, because we'd end up in Germany. The rest of Poland is likely to be just as bad as here. The only other possibility would be to head for Russia, and I really don't trust Stalin. He'd sell his own grandmother if he thought it would give him more power. Trust me, my parent's farm is the safest option.'

'It's a bit of a gamble, don't you think?'

'I agree it's risky heading into East Prussia, but I can't imagine there's going to be much fighting there. If we can cross the border before it kicks off, we'll be fine.'

'I hope you're right,' she said, knowing what he was like once he had made up his mind.

The contrast between the two children was astounding. Niklos was five and slept amidst a heap of tangled bedclothes. It looked as if he had been doing somersaults throughout the night. Conversely, Peter, three years his elder, lay with the bedding arranged neatly. If he had not created an impression on the pillow, it would have been hard to tell the bed had been occupied. These differences summed up their contrasting personalities.

5

Niklos was full of energy, similar to his mother. From the moment he opened his eyes in the morning to last thing at night, he was continually moving. Peter was much more like Viktor, serious and much more restrained.

'It's time to wake up, lads,' Viktor announced from their bedroom doorway.

By the time the two boys had made their way downstairs, he had already drained his first coffee cup.

'I have some good news,' he said with an upbeat tone. They appeared uninterested by their father's proclamation, primarily because his usual announcements resulted in the two of them having to wash the dishes for their mother. 'We're going to visit Grandma and Grandpa for a couple of days.'

'Really?' said Niklos.

Viktor nodded, resulting in broad-beaming grins across their young faces.

'When do we leave?' Peter asked excitedly.

'Once we've loaded the cart. So, hurry upstairs and grab your favourite toys to show Grandma.'

No more words were necessary. The two boys ran out of the kitchen, jostling each other as they raced up the stairs.

'I told you it wouldn't be a problem,' he said, cuddling his wife while she stood at the sink.

Viktor admired his wife's figure as she scraped back her shoulder-length, curly hair, before covering it with a brown headscarf, knotted under the chin. She was a pleasing mixture of skinny and shapely, with an appealing face to match. He crept up behind her, giving her a hug. A warm glow appeared in her blue, almond-shaped eyes, the corner of her lips curling upwards. Lingering for as long as possible, husband and wife embraced before facing the journey ahead.

After a quick run around the house, looking for things they may have forgotten, Zofia locked the back door and then hurried the children into the heavily laden cart. The boys clambered among their belongings and settled wherever they could find space. With a brisk shake of the reins, Miedziak reluctantly ventured onto the uneven cobbles of the narrow alleyway. Zofia secured the gates with a sturdy padlock before joining her husband on the bench behind the horse. As they joined Hucisko Street, a tear ran down her left cheek. Everything was happening so fast. She pulled her scarf tight, attempting to hide her sobbing. *Would she ever see her home again?*

Victor glanced at her, putting his hand on her thigh. 'We'll be back by Christmas,' he said, trying to reassure her.

She stared straight ahead, blinking back the tears.

Danzig had once been a jewel of the Prussian Empire, but Germany had been carved in two at the end of the Great War, creating a new state, East Prussia, which now sat like a German island amongst Poland and the Baltic states. The city of Danzig, sandwiched between East Prussia and what remained of Germany, became a free state to allow Poland access to the Baltic Sea, loosening the Poles' dependency on Germany and allowing them to trade with the rest of the world. Isolated, the predominantly German population in the city had rallied behind the leader of the regional Nazi Party who had promised re-annexation. The Nazi Party had started agitating the German population in 1936, causing cultural tensions to soar. Three years later, war in the region now seemed inevitable, prompting many of the city's Polish residents to leave, while the German families waited impatiently for reunification.

A handful of Polish men, calling themselves 'The Militia,' had elected to remain in the city. Viktor had received many invites to join them but had always declined. For the last few days, he had seen them busily barricading the streets in readiness to defend their homes. Many roads and key defensive positions were blocked with sandbags, occupied by groups of three or four men with only one rifle between them.

Over the last week, the atmosphere had deteriorated further. A German battleship, the *Schleswig-Holstein*, had moored off the Westerplatte peninsula in one of the city's harbour channels. Crowds of chattering schoolboys had hurried past Viktor's shop, eager to catch a glimpse of the gun-metal grey vessel. The city no longer felt safe; they had to leave. Viktor decided they should head for his parents' farm near Olsztyn, about a hundred miles to the east. They had made the journey many times without incident, but their destination was in East Prussia. German territory.

Suddenly, two deafening booms rocked the cart, followed by a high-pitched screech overhead. One of the boys let out a scream. Two further explosions shook the ground, provoking the horse to rear up wildly. Viktor redistributed his weight to prevent them from tipping. Slowly, he brought the frightened animal under control while Zofia gathered her children in her arms. She hugged them tightly, spreading her cloak around their shoulders.

The massive guns fired again. Each shockwave pounding deep in his chest, prompting Viktor to spur Miedziak onwards. The grey sky roared, heralding a trio of German dive-bombers. They were flying so low he could see the black insignia on their wings. Rifle shots rang out from an alleyway as the militia fired at the planes. One of the aircraft broke from formation, arced around, and then strafed the alley. Mud and grit were thrown into the air, causing the terrified boys to shriek A prolonged sequence of loud detonations followed, punctuated by bursts of machine gun fire. The tremendous noise echoed off the nearby buildings, exacerbating the confusion. He glanced across at Zofia; the look of horror on her face said it all.

A few blocks behind them, a tall building took a direct hit. Large pieces of masonry were hurled into the street, producing further chaos. Volleys of retaliatory rifle fire could occasionally be heard but were soon swamped by the well-orchestrated fire from the advancing German troops.

An aircraft dived directly above them, the shrill howl of its siren generating panic. Viktor watched in horror as the plane released a bomb immediately before pulling into a steep climb. The bomb's trajectory carried it over a row of houses towards the harbour before it exploded. Acrid clouds billowed across the road, stinging their throats. The two boys quaked as they clung to their helpless mother.

Viktor, with his face set like flint, jerked the reins, urging the horse to go faster. He had stopped caring about the pedestrians around him; they had to get far away from the port. After forty-five minutes, they reached the checkpoint on the bridge at Wyspa Spichrzów. The official who was meant to oversee it had fled long ago. The barrier lay broken on the ground, trampled underfoot by the long line of desperate people clambering along the river crossing. Sporadic scuffles had erupted as people tried to push past each other. Meanwhile, an old lady wailed to the sky, disbelief etched on her face.

More planes screamed overhead, stirring the oppressive air as they headed towards Westerplatte. Another series of blasts forced the crowd closer together. With a groan, one of the buildings began to wobble, weakened by the numerous explosions. The wall collapsed, spewing the building's content into the street. The people in front of them buckled to avoid the falling debris. Viktor saw his opportunity. He pushed Miedziak even harder, provoking angry cries from those around him. The cart ploughed over the bridge, mounting the kerb. It did not matter anymore; they had to get out of the city.

2

Sixteen hundred miles from the horrors in Danzig, a truck carrying men from the Second Battalion of the Hampshire Regiment hurtled along a country lane, deep in the English countryside. Their overnight triumph had fuelled some raucous singing, pushing tiredness to the back of their minds.

They passed through the barrier at the entrance of Aldershot barracks, before pulling onto the parade ground. As soon as the wheels stopped turning, Corporal Henry Taylor jumped down onto the asphalt, weary from the night's exercise. His lower legs were caked in mud, a prominent smear decorating the left side of his uniform jacket. His narrow eyes, acknowledged the driver before he trudged towards his dormitory, dragging his equipment behind him.

'Well done, 'Enry,' Alan Phillips said, patting his colleague on the back.

'Thanks,' he replied, he said, his smile still warm despite his exhaustion.

'Did you see that Grenadier sergeant's face when the exercise ended? He was furious.'

Henry nodded, dumping his kit on the floor, next to

his bunk.

'Sarge, it's a shame you weren't there,' Phillips shouted across the room. 'We showed those Grenadiers a thing or two. Henry masterminded the whole thing. His plan worked like a dream.'

Sergeant Midgley stood next to the window, watching other trucks park up. A sling supported his left arm, the result of a training accident the previous day.

'When do you think you'll be fit to return to duty, Sarge?' Henry asked.

'Oh, the medic said I should be fine by the end of next week. But I'm not so sure.'

Henry grabbed an early morning edition of a newspaper which lay on the table in the centre of the room and launched himself up onto his bunk, still wearing his grubby uniform.

'Germany invades Poland,' he read out loud, his muddy boots hanging over the edge. 'I guess we're going to be shipped out in the next couple of days.'

'Sarge, do you think your injury will stop you coming with us?' Phillips asked.

'Don't worry, lad, wild horses couldn't stop me coming with you.'

'If you ask me, it goes to show you can't trust politicians,' said Phillips. 'Peace in our time, I ask you. The prime minister couldn't guarantee peace in a cemetery.'

'What do you think?' Henry asked, looking at Ed, sitting below, cleaning his boots.

'We'll get our marching orders before long. It can't come soon enough for me.'

'I have always thought that Chamberlain and his government were spineless,' Phillips said, walking to the shower block with a towel around his waist. 'If you ask me, we should have invaded Germany months ago. That would've stopped this nonsense getting out of hand.'

'If Britain gets involved, I wonder where they'll send us?' Ed asked. 'Poland sounds very cold, doesn't it?'

'We won't be going to Poland, lad. It's too far away,' Midgley said. 'Think about it—Britain's not threatened by war there. The bigger danger lies with Germany.'

'They tried to conquer Europe twenty years ago,' said Phillips. 'I wouldn't put it past them to try again. They've got unfinished business.'

'If we go anywhere it'll be somewhere like France or Belgium, you mark my words,' Midgely added.

The news of the events in Central Europe had spread around the base. The reactions within the different barracks varied. Some men were chattering excitedly; others were more reflective, quietly writing letters to their loved ones. Henry was feeling quite melancholic. Sitting on his bunk, legs hanging down, he thumbed through some faded photographs of his parents which he kept next to his pillow. Both were long dead, but he continued to miss them. Seven years ago, his father had passed away from tuberculosis. The slow, painful decline of the man he admired most in the world still haunted Henry. It had been horrible. His father had fought in the trenches of Northern France, yet this disease had reduced him to a frail shell, stripping him of all its dignity. Just prior to his death, he had been totally dependent on others for the simplest of tasks. If he were honest, his father's decline had been the reason he had escaped to the army.

His parents had met during the last war. Henry's father had been based in the north of France. His mother, the daughter of the local magistrate. She only spoke a little English. Consequently, Henry grew up bilingual. Unfortunately, she had died during childbirth, when he was just seven years old. His only sibling, David, had survived the ordeal and was now a private with the Welsh Guards, currently stationed in Gibraltar. It had been several weeks since Henry had written to him, but they hadn't seen each other for more than a year. They were not good at keeping in touch. It was not because Henry did not get on with him. Far from it. He just never seemed to get around to it. Henry wondered what the impending war had in store for him and his brother.

Having spent the early hours of the morning engineering his unit's success on the mock battlefield, he now felt jaded. With Midgley's shoulder injury forcing him out of action, Henry had been asked to take charge, and it had gone well. Far better than he had expected. Pleasingly, the unit had followed his instructions correctly. He hoped his superiors had realised what he was capable of.

Despite it being late in the morning, Henry tried to sleep before the game arranged for that afternoon. The regimental rugby match had become an annual event. They were often tough affairs, and when the players took to the field, the privileges of rank were forgotten. It was usually held in October, but with the increasing likelihood of war, the date had been hurried forward. He needed to be fresh for the encounter, so he kicked off his boots, stretched out on his bunk, and was soon asleep.

Henry woke with a jolt; he was soaked. Ed Jones stood over him waving an empty, enamel mug in his hand.

'Sorry, 'Enry, but you wouldn't wake up,' Jonesy laughed. 'You have to be on the field in three-quarters of an hour.'

Henry leapt down to chase him, but Ed, surrounded by laughing co-conspirators, taunted him from the other side of the room before Henry had even reached the floor. In a state of semi-amused shock, He dried himself and then rummaged through his locker, looking for his rugby kit.

The officers were already on the pitch, heckling, as the men of the Hampshire Regiment walked out. Major Winston, an allegedly neutral referee from the Grenadier Guards, stood on the halfway line, incongruous in his desert uniform on an overcast day in southern England. The choice of Winston was disappointing. He had refereed the same fixture the previous year and had shown a great deal of favouritism towards the officers. Henry was especially concerned after his victory over Winston's beloved Grenadier Guards the night before.

The team captains shook hands and chose ends. As Henry took up his position, Mac Williams, a captain in the regiment, started taunting him.

'Taylor, I hope you're going to be gentle with us.'

Henry smiled back politely and then jogged away.

The match was a melee of hard-hitting tackles and clandestine punches. When Major Winston blew the final whistle, the officers had won by fourteen points to twelve. Henry had sustained a blow to the face during one of the mauls and could feel it beginning to swell. As the teams walked off, Captain Williams caught up with him.

'You chaps showed some spirit.'

'Thank you, Sir.'

Plastered with mud, Henry fought his way through the crowd towards the changing room. Standing at the door was the tall, willowy figure of Julian Fosdyke, a major from the Hampshires. Henry assumed the major must be in his early fifties from the crow's feet which had started to form at the corner of his eyes, but the bushy black moustache, which seemed to occupy his entire face, showed no sign of greying.

'Good show, Taylor. That was one of the best matches we've had for a few years.

'Thank you, Sir.'

'Mind you, your eye looks quite nasty,' Fosdyke commented, pointing with his pace stick. 'You should have one of the medics take a look at it.'

'Yes, Sir. I will, Sir.'

'Taylor, I want to see you in my office in half an hour,' the major said, his tone taking on a more official air. 'There's something I would like to discuss with you.'

'Sir, yes, Sir,' he said, now more than a little worried.

With that, Fosdyke turned and walked away briskly.

The colour drained from his face, a gnawing heaviness developing rapidly in his stomach. *Had the major seen some of the punches thrown during the game? Henry smiled wryly to himself. Typical. Only he could be court-martialled before he had gone off to war.*

In the changing room, he kicked off his boots, stripped off, then headed to the shower. He stood under the ice-cold water letting his aching body become accustomed to the temperature. *Assaulting an officer was a serious offence. Surely, they would not court-martial him for what happened during a rugby match. Would they?*

Back in the dormitory, he slipped on a clean uniform. The medic had appeared unimpressed with his injury. The only advice he had been given was to put some ice on it to reduce the swelling. Henry examined his face in the mirror inside his locker door. He always considered his steely blue eyes as his best feature, but the left one was now almost entirely closed by the swelling. Nonetheless, he scrutinised his appearance closely. If he was going to be disciplined, he was going to do it in style. His blond hair was clipped closely on the sides, the fair stubble giving it a faint grey appearance. The top was combed over to the right with a strand flopping onto his forehead. Perfect for hiding under a beret. He dry-shaved for the second time that day, making sure his appearance was as faultless as it could be.

His boots glistened in the autumn sun as he strode across the parade ground towards Major Fosdyke's office. His stomach churned nervously as he climbed the stairs to the first floor. When he knocked on the glass-panelled door, he developed palpitations and broke into a cold sweat. Inside, a busty, blonde girl looked up from behind her clattering typewriter. Her short, wavy hair fashionably sculpted into a centre parting beneath a khaki uniform hat. He guessed she must be in her mid-twenties.

'You must be Corporal Taylor,' she said sweetly, greeting him with a pleasant smile.

'Yes, ma'am,' he said.

'Go through. The major's expecting you.'

She gestured towards a door to the side of her desk. Henry took a deep breath and then knocked. A gruff voice from inside bellowed, 'Come!'

Shutting the door behind him, he stood to attention and saluted. To his surprise, the small room was crowded. Major Fosdyke was seated behind a large, mahogany desk. Behind him was Colonel Prentice, another of the regiment's top brass. Henry barely knew him but was aware he had a reputation for being fierce. Worryingly, Mac Williams stood next to the window. Slightly taller than Henry, the handsome captain looked intimidating as he leant against the wall. Henry's pulse was audible inside his head, pounding faster than he ever thought possible. *I've had it now.*

After returning Henry's salute, Major Fosdyke said, 'Stand at ease, corporal.'

Henry adjusted his stance accordingly as Williams began speaking, 'It was a good game today, Taylor! Well played.'

'Thank you, Sir,' he said, expecting a sucker punch to follow.

'Sorry about the black eye. You know, the heat of the battle, and all that.'

So, it had been Williams who had punched him. That answered the question, but why was an officer apologising to a corporal? All kinds of irrational scenarios raced through Henry's head, his anxiety giving way to panic.

The grey-haired colonel cleared his throat. 'Corporal Taylor, we've been watching you closely.'

Henry swallowed hard. *Here it comes.*

'As you're probably aware, we live in uncertain times. More than ever before, we need good men like you,' he paused, habitually stroking his unkempt eyebrows. 'Today, at sixteen hundred hours, the secretary of state for Defence is going to declare general mobilisation. In other words, the British Army is preparing for war.'

Henry nodded. *Where is this going?*

'We've examined your service record, and I must say it is excellent,' the major said. 'Following discussions within the regiment and our observations, I have the great pleasure of informing you of your promotion to sergeant. It will take effect immediately.'

Henry's nerves abated, but his expression remained stone-like.

'Do you understand, Taylor?' Major Fosdyke asked after a few seconds of silence, his moustache twitching as he spoke.

'Yes, Sir. Thank you, Sir.'

'You should be grateful to Sergeant Midgley. It was his letter of recommendation which brought you to our attention,' the major said.

'Thank you, Sir.'

'Sergeant Taylor. Unless Hitler performs a rapid U-turn, Britain is going to war,' the colonel said gravely. No one is sure where this will end. In the next twenty-four hours, most of us will be shipped overseas to fight and, sadly, many will not come back. You don't need me to tell you, the very nature of war makes it dangerous, but sometimes we have to face danger head-on. As I said, we've been watching you for the last few months, and you have impressed us. We would like you to stay behind when the regiment is deployed overseas. I can't tell you much else, other than there is something important planned for you. You are being transferred to a newly formed unit, which is affiliated with the Intelligence Corps. I want you to report here the day after tomorrow at midday. We'll discuss your new role then.'

Henry nodded, struggling to absorb what he had heard.

'Once again, congratulations, Sergeant Taylor,' said the Colonel. 'Dismissed!'

Henry saluted, turned, and marched out.

The secretary looked up and gave him a flirtatious

wink before returning her attention to her typing.

During Henry's absence, the announcement of general mobilisation had been made. The dormitory was frantic as the men packed their belongings in preparation for their departure. His old unit was leaving in the second wave, which meant he had one last day with them. There were many rumours about their potential destination. Everyone's friend seemed to know for certain it was going to be one country or another. Most people suspected they would be going to France, which caused great excitement. Talk of French women and the nightlife in 'Gay Paris' filled the air. He looked on glumly, knowing he would not be leaving with them.

'Is everything all right, old chap?' Jonesy asked, noticing Henry was not his usual self,

'Na, not really!' he said solemnly.

'A penny for them?'

'Yeah, but let's go outside.'

The two of them had joined up together at the age of seventeen. Jones, slightly shorter than Henry, had dark hair which sat untidily above a round face with piggy eyes—a stark contrast to Henry's fair, handsome looks. They had become best friends during basic training and knew each other's lives inside out. Jonesy sat on the wall, while his best friend continued to stand, clearly anxious about something. Henry started to explain about his promotion.

'You're a sergeant, 'Enry?' Jones patted him on the back. 'Well done.'

'Thanks, but I'm letting the lads down, aren't I?'

'How?'

'It looks like I'm being left behind to take up some desk job, while you guys see the real action.'

'You'd be letting us down if you don't take it,' Jonesy said flatly. 'You have shown them hard work and dedication gets you somewhere. Anyway, if you ask me, it makes perfect sense. You don't want to be stuck in some muddy, foreign hole, do you?'

18

'I suppose you're right, but I'm a soldier, not an office clerk,' he said, letting his exasperation boil over.

'It sounds to me you're the lucky one. We're being shipped out in the second wave to God knows where, and you get to stay home with more money and less likelihood of being shot. I would swap places with you in a heartbeat.'

Henry forced a smile.

After chatting for over thirty minutes, the two men returned to the dormitory to find a sing-song had started. Several soldiers from different regiments had gathered in their room and were having a great time. United by their camaraderie and uncertainty about their future, they were having one last laugh together before they were deployed throughout Europe.

For the first time since he had joined the Army, Henry felt like an outsider. His promotion had come with one perk, though; he no longer had to sleep in the same room as the other men. Instead, he had his own room. He unloaded the contents of his locker onto his bunk and then, in two trips, transferred all his earthly goods into his new quarters.

At lights-out Henry stood outside his door, listening to the excited whispering from the main dormitory. The chatter made him realise how much he was going to miss being one of the lads.

The next morning passed slowly. Henry tried to keep himself busy while his old comrades made their final preparations. The first of the troops left the base that afternoon, heading for ports on the south coast. From there they would be ferried to the continent. Most were displaying false bravado, but some were clearly anxious.

As a final farewell, Henry spent the evening with his old unit in the local pub, standing around a piano, singing merrily and harassing the overworked barmaid.

The following morning, the British government sent Germany an ultimatum. If their troops were not withdrawn from Poland, then Britain would be at war once again. Hitler was given a two-hour period within which to respond, but there had been no reply when the deadline passed at eleven o'clock.

At a quarter past eleven, the Right Honourable Neville Chamberlain gave the most important speech of his life. All over the country, people huddled around wireless sets, trying to listen to the prime minister. Unlike his usual statements to the house, Chamberlain's words captivated the nation. After fifteen minutes, he concluded by saying, 'I have to tell you now; this country is at war with Germany.'

As he finished, he let out a deep breath and took his seat. The whole United Kingdom fell silent with him.

At the same time as Chamberlain was making his announcement to the British people, the camp at Aldershot was a hive of activity. Tens of trucks waited on the parade ground. The regimental bands played morale-boosting favourites, as senior officers and men located their designated vehicles.

Henry and a couple of his close friends walked among the crowd, trying to locate the other men from the Second Hampshires.

'Well, this is it, 'Enry,' Jonesy said reluctantly. 'Give 'em hell.'

'Don't worry, mate. I will.'

'You too, Alan,' he said, embracing his friend.

A hush descended as an Army padre, wearing a long purple stole, gave a solemn blessing into a microphone. Henry threw his best friend's kitbag onto the back of the truck while Ed clambered aboard. The band struck up again, blaring out a fanfare as the convoy with its human cargo set off for the south coast. Once the last of the vehicles had disappeared, he glanced at his wristwatch.

'Damn!' he muttered to himself. He only had ten minutes to get ready for the meeting with Fosdyke.

3

Henry buffed his boots until he could see his face in them, then changed into his smartest uniform. After straightening his tie in the mirror, he dashed back across the parade ground towards the major's office. The same secretary sat behind the desk, busily scribbling on a notepad. She looked up, recognising Henry instantly.

'Sergeant Taylor, it seems you can't stay away from me!' she said playfully, causing him to blush.

He enquired about his appointment, trying hard not to appear thrown by her comment.

'Oh, they're meeting in the lecture theatre down the corridor.'

He thanked her, accidentally slamming the door on his way out.

Unsure he was in the correct place, Henry took a seat in the back row next to the door. Six other soldiers were dotted around the room. It felt like his first day at school; no one spoke, and, like Henry, everyone was dressed immaculately.

Shortly, Major Fosdyke, followed by Captain Williams, entered the room. Everyone sprang to attention as the two officers proceeded up the aisle onto the stage.

'Please be seated, gentlemen. We have much to discuss,' the moustachioed Fosdyke said, stepping onto the platform at the front of the room. 'Each one of you has been selected, based on recommendations from your commanding officers. So, congratulations to all of you. Although we are few, we aim to achieve great things. I am pleased to inform you, you are now members of Bravo Section, which is affiliated with the Intelligence Corps. Do not think this is a soft option—what lies ahead will require a lot of hard work and much danger.'

Henry shuffled in his seat as Captain Williams, with his more relaxed demeanour, took centre stage.

'Our unit is unlike any other. As far as the rest of the armed forces and civilian society are concerned, we simply do not exist,' he said, prowling back and forth on the platform.

Henry's ears pricked up.

'So, irrespective of which regiment you are currently enrolled in, from this moment forward, you are a member of Bravo Section,' the major stated. 'Of course, if any of you wishes to leave before we get started, then you may do so now,' said the athletic-looking captain, his usually cheery face taking on an uncharacteristic seriousness.

No one moved.

'Thank you, gentlemen,' he said, making his way behind the podium.

'Your official transfer papers will be with you in the next few weeks. I am sure you fully understand, whatever is said in this room must stay in this room. Quite frankly, your survival depends on your discretion.'

'The formation of this unit was instructed by the government,' Williams said. 'It is the brainchild of the prime minister. He wants to strike at the heart of our enemies. Our main aim is to reduce the effectiveness of the German forces on the front line. Now, this will be achieved by a variety of measures, but primarily our efforts will be aimed at destroying their military and logistic infrastructure. You will work as a small, isolated team in very hostile territory. You are Hitler's worst nightmare, gentlemen. You are the unseen saboteurs.'

Henry liked what he was hearing and quickly forgot the preconceived ideas he had before the meeting.

'However, there is one downside,' the major said. 'As individuals, we can never take any credit for what we have done, because officially we do not exist. Those who need to know will be aware of our successes, but the public and the rest of the armed forces will be unaware of your exploits.

'So, we won't see your ugly mugs in the newspapers,' Williams said with a smile.

Henry studied the room. The other men were sitting forward on their seats, looking eager and enthusiastic. He readily anticipated working with them. Leaning back, he was sure he had not met any of them previously. This troubled him as he had no idea of their strengths or weaknesses. How would they react under pressure? Who could he rely on to get out of a scrape?

'So, gentlemen,' said Williams. 'One by one, please stand and introduce yourselves. Let's start with you at the back, Sergeant.'

'Sergeant Henry Taylor, Second Hampshire,' he said, rising to his feet.

He felt everyone in the room staring at him, his black eye making him feel even more self-conscious.

'Sergeant Taylor will be the section leader,' Captain Williams said. 'In other words, during operations, he is in charge. So, try and keep in his good books!'

Each of the men introduced themselves before Fosdyke stood up again.

'Right, gentlemen. We have precious little time for you to get acquainted,' the captain said. 'You fly in less than thirty-six hours on your first mission. So, we had better get cracking.'

Audible gasps erupted around the room. *We leave the*

day after tomorrow? Henry's stomach knotted at the thought of it.

'Right, lads,' Williams said. 'Lunch has been provided in the room next door.'

As everyone rose to leave, the major beckoned Henry over.

'Well, what do you think?' Fosdyke asked as he approached.

'It sounds intriguing, Sir' he commented.

'Sorry, about all this cloak and dagger stuff, but we had to ensure word didn't get out. The very existence of this unit is classified. The only way for us to be certain about secrecy was to wait until general mobilisation before we got you guys together,' Williams explained. 'Other than a few of the top brass, the only people who know about us are based in Whitehall.'

'These are some of the most talented soldiers in the British Army, and with your leadership, I believe you can achieve anything,' Fosdyke added.

'So, we need to optimise our use of the time we have,' Williams said. 'It must be a little daunting, but once you've put your lads through their paces and they have shown what they are capable of, you'll feel a whole lot better.'

Henry nodded but was not reassured.

'The files for all the men are in my office,' said Major Fosdyke, sensing the sergeant's uncertainty. 'Pop by later. I'll let my secretary know you're going to drop in. From what I can gather, she's taken a bit of a shine to you.'

Lunch was an awkward affair, a mixture of polite conversation and niceties, but anxiety and anticipation bubbled under the surface. Tommy Rogers, one of the corporals in the group, tried to relieve the awkwardness by asking Henry how he'd obtained his black eye. He paused before replying, 'Oh, some woman in a pub. You know how it is.'

His comment was met with wolf whistles and table slapping from the small audience, lightening the mood slightly.

After lunch, the newly formed Bravo Section had their first fieldcraft exercise. Decked in full kit and camouflage, Henry and his men were taken via truck to Wanborough Woods, the site of Henry's victory over the Grenadier Guards. He had ascertained he had two corporals under his command: Tommy Rogers, who appeared to be keen and enthusiastic, and Robert Scott, an excellent linguist, who was quite handy with a Lee-Enfield rifle. Then there was the medic, Patrick O'Shea, the explosives expert; Alf Morrison; and two infantrymen, Joe Mayberry and Malcolm Porter.

Henry felt self-conscious giving orders to his men under the scrutiny of the major. Dividing the unit into two teams, each led by one of the corporals, they took turns defending a hill from the onslaught from the other team. Both groups performed well, and Henry's anxieties were swiftly dissipating. Being 'in charge' still felt strange, although, to be fair, his orders were obeyed without question. The two corporals, Tommy Rogers, with his blond floppy-locks, and the lanky Robert Scott interacted well. What Henry found most challenging was being called 'Sarge.' He kept looking over his shoulder to see if there was someone more important standing behind him.

That evening, the team moved into their new dormitory, down the corridor from Henry's new room. As they were soon leaving on an operation, the unit was now required to stay in the barracks. This was a shame, as Henry thought a trip to the local pub would have been a worthwhile team-building experience. Another sign of their impending mission was the presence of armed guards. They stood silently outside the dormitory door, preventing unauthorised people entering or the men inside from leaving. Despite their apparent incarceration, the usual lighthearted chitchat of soldiers continued to fill the air. On several occasions, they asked Henry about the destination of their imminent mission, but he had to admit he did not know.

'What? They haven't even told you?' Mayberry asked.

'Nope, I'm just as much in the dark as you guys are,' he said honestly.

'I reckon they'll send us to Berlin to kill Hitler,' one of the others hypothesised.

Henry hoped not. That would be a tough destination for their first mission. The chances of success would be next to nothing.

The following morning was dull and overcast. Henry walked across the parade ground under the watchful eyes of their guards, his sleep-deprived thoughts continuing to buzz around his head. He was the first to arrive in the lecture room, and he started pacing back and forth nervously. Slowly, the other men of the Bravo Section trickled in.

Captain Williams entered the room at precisely zero eight hundred hours.

'Good morning, gentlemen!' he said.

'You are all probably wondering about the nature of tomorrow's mission and, indeed, you will find out in due course. What I can tell you is you will be parachuting into enemy territory in the early hours of tomorrow morning. Now, British armed forces have never parachuted into a war zone before. So, you, gentlemen, will be lucky enough to be the first. I am aware none of you has any jump experience, so we will practice this morning.'

Henry felt sick at the thought of flying, let alone jumping from a plane several thousand feet up. He did not like heights but was going to have to hide this from the others.

After being suspended feet above the floor in parachute harnesses, he and his men spent forty-five minutes in the gymnasium learning how to land safely on a giant mat without injuring themselves. Next, they were taught how to use the various toggles and pull cords. Henry had especially disliked the teaching on what to do if your parachute did not open. Still, at least he now knew what to do if this situation arose.

As the truck trundled towards the airstrip, an uncomfortable nervousness gripped the group. The bravado and banter had disappeared. Instead, each man stared at their feet, avoiding eye contact.

The seven of them boarded a small, twin-propeller plane through a hatch in its underside. Wearing full jump-kit, they were crammed into the carcass of the aircraft, followed by the jump-master who was coordinating the occasion. He instructed them to clip their parachutes onto the static line, then to sit on the floor between the legs of the man behind.

The propellers started with a jolt, and soon the plane was taxiing along the airstrip. Henry's anxiety, together with the erratic motion, made him feel queasy. They slowed and turned through one hundred and eighty degrees before coming to a standstill at the end of the runway.

The hold of the craft was unlit. Henry felt the pilot increase the throttle, making the engines roar. There was a clunk as the brakes were released and the aircraft began to speed along. After fifteen to twenty seconds, they lurched into the air. The whole plane rattled momentarily before banking steeply to the left. Henry swallowed hard to stop acid rising into his mouth.

After what felt like an eternity, the tone of the engine changed. A red light came on, casting a strange glow over the men. This was the signal for each man to check the kit of the man in front of him.

'Number one, okay,' shouted Malcolm Porter, trying to make himself heard above the external noise.

'Number two, okay,' bellowed Tommy Rogers as the cry passed down the line.

The shouts continued along the length of the aircraft. Once everyone's equipment had been checked, the jump-master opened the hatch, filling the plane with daylight.

The wind howled through the open door with a deafening roar, causing the straps on Henry's goggles to flap painfully against his face.

The red light changed to green, and the jump-master shouted, 'GO, GO, GO!'

With a brief moment of hesitation, Malcolm Porter launched himself from the plane. From the back of the queue, Henry watched his men jump through the door into the grey sky beyond. His heart raced as he edged nearer the door. Finally, it was his turn. Standing at the door, he could see the chutes hanging below him. He took a deep breath, then jumped.

The next few moments were a blur. As Henry left the plane, a blast of cold air winded him, making him forget his training. The jolt of the parachute opening brought him to his senses. Looking up, he was thankful his canopy was open and nicely rounded. Relieved, he hung there, suspended in tranquility above the beautiful Hampshire countryside. Below, the observers were tracking the jumpers with binoculars. Henry was reassured by their presence, although, not entirely sure what they could do if he got into difficulty.

The ground was approaching at a fair rate of knots. Henry brought his knees up in anticipation for the impact. As he landed, he rolled onto his side, and his canopy settled loosely on top of him. With a feeling of elation, he jumped to his feet and unclipped his chute. Around him, men were cheering and leaping around in celebration. He walked over to one of the observers.

'Is everyone down?' Henry asked.

'All the chutes opened, but we've lost Mayberry. He's floated off towards Farnham. We'll have to send someone to pick him up.'

The jump-master was the last to land. After he had unclipped himself from his harness, he walked from man to man, congratulating them on their successful landings. With no time to rest, they were given another parachute and told to board the plane again for another jump. Thankfully, Henry's second attempt was straightforward. This time, he remembered to count his descent, and his landing was perfect.

Unfortunately, Malcolm Porter landed heavily, injuring his left ankle. Other than that, the rest of the men were down, except Mayberry, who had still not been located from the previous jump. Jubilant at their parachuting success, they were loaded onto a truck and taken back to their barracks. Meanwhile, Porter was transferred to the medical station for a doctor to examine his rapidly swelling ankle.

In sharp contrast to the journey out to the airstrip, the trip home contained much more noise and laughter. Almost all of the jokes were about the unfortunate Mayberry who was still missing. Henry thought the young man had better be prepared for some extensive ridiculing when he was located.

As soon as they had climbed down from the truck, they were ushered into the mess hall, where afternoon tea was waiting for them. They sat down and tucked in. Half an hour later, as the men of the unit were finishing their meal, Mayberry entered the room to rapturous applause and cheers. He took a seat at the end of the table, like a triumphant king returning from conquest.

Captain Williams appeared in the doorway and waved Henry over.

'I have some bad news,' he said in hushed tones, standing in the corridor. 'Porter has broken his ankle. He won't be fit to go with you tonight.'

'That leaves us a man down, doesn't it?' Henry asked.

'Kind of. As you know, all the troops have been shipped overseas. The only men available are those in sickbay.'

Henry looked at him curiously.

'Look, there's one chap who's well enough to go with you,' Williams said awkwardly. 'His name's Travers. He's just getting over chickenpox. The doctor says he's no longer contagious.'

'Are you sure that's a good idea? Can't the operation be postponed until a suitable replacement can be found?'

'The mission must go ahead as planned,' the captain insisted.

'Does he have any parachute experience?' Henry asked, knowing what the answer was likely to be.

'No, but if you're happy for us to proceed, we can fit in some jump-training for him now.'

'If that's the only alternative, then I guess we ought to take him.'

'It's your call,' said Williams. 'I'll understand your decision either way.'

Henry followed the captain into an office. Sitting on a chair was a lad in his late teens, his face still peppered with a few crusted spots. The youth appeared pleasant enough, but he did not look old enough to even shave, let alone fight on the front lines. What would the other men in the unit think?

'Let's go and meet the others,' he said.

Henry walked into the mess hall with the lad trailing behind him.

'May I have your attention, please?' said Henry, raising his voice. 'I'm afraid Porter's broken his ankle.'

Audible groans came from the men around the table.

'So, we have a new member for our team.' Henry froze, unable to remember the lad's name. 'Why don't you introduce yourself?'

'Hello! I'm Terry Travers,' the teenager mumbled, clearly intimidated.

The group of men looked on, no one speaking.

'Have you eaten, son?' said Robert Scott, breaking the awkward silence.

The lad shook his head.

'Well, come and sit here,' Scotty smiled. 'There's enough to go around.'

The unit introduced themselves to their newest member; Mayberry and Travers shared a common friend, helping to break the ice.

Over the next couple of hours, some of the men shared their expertise in workshops. Alf Morrison talked about explosives, Tommy Rogers taught man-to-man combat techniques, and O'Shea demonstrated life-saving battlefield medicine procedures.

The final session of the afternoon was spent on the rifle range. Robert Scott showed off his advanced marksmanship skills, giving a breathtaking demonstration of long-range shooting, and explained the mysteries of the telescopic sight.

The unit then practised, aiming at paper targets pinned to straw bales positioned at various distances from the firing line. To everyone's surprise, Travers made the highest score of the afternoon. Henry congratulated the teenager before a few of the men hoisted the young lad onto their shoulders and carried him around.

At the end of a long day, dinner was served in the mess hall with Captain Williams and the major joining them. At the end of the meal, Fosdyke scraped back his chair and addressed the unit.

'It is eighteen hundred hours. For you gentlemen, the next two hours are free,' he said. 'I suggest you get some rest. The mission briefing will start at twenty hundred hours in the lecture theatre.'

4

The secretary stood as he entered the room.

'The major said I could view the files of the other soldiers,' Henry said.

'Why, of course, Sergeant,' she said playfully.

She opened the top drawer of the filing cabinet and rummaged around for a few seconds before slamming it shut.

'I have the keys to the office opposite if you want somewhere to study them,' she said.

'Yes, that's very kind of you,' he replied, slightly flustered.

She held out a bundle of manila folders which Henry gathered awkwardly.

'My name's Susan, by the way,' she said, turning on the light in the small room. 'If you want anything, just ask.'

'Thank you, Susan,' he said. 'But I think I'm fine for the moment.'

With that, she left, leaving him to thumb through the folders.

After reading for over an hour, Henry could not believe his eyes. Understandably, there was no folder on Travers, but the rest of the men in the unit seemed outstanding. He was surprised that Alf Morrison had worked for the foreign office as a freelance German interpreter before joining the Army. Mayberry had graduated top of his year when he completed basic training. They all had commendations and exemplary records of achievement. With all these accolades, Henry started to feel rather inadequate.

'They're not a bad bunch of lads, are they?' said the major from the door. 'Normally, we don't let sergeants look at these folders. But, you've had very little time to prepare, so we thought you'd better have all the information available to you.'

'Thank you, Sir,' he said, startled by the voice. 'They've performed well today, haven't they? I was impressed.'

'Yes, it was quite encouraging, but you'll need to keep an eye on them over the next few days. They may be excellent individuals, but they're not yet used to working together as a team,' Fosdyke replied.

'I have one other concern, Sir.'

The major raised an eyebrow inquisitively.

'It's Travers, Sir. He's a little bit inexperienced, don't you think?'

'After watching him today, I think he'll be just fine. Your corporals appear to be taking him under their wings.'

'But he's had no parachute practice.'

'He managed one jump. The jump-master was satisfied, but I agree, it's far from ideal. Nonetheless, we must make the most of the situations we find ourselves in, don't you think, Taylor? Now, shall we go to the briefing?'

Without another word, he bundled the folders together and returned them to Susan in the office opposite, before following the major towards the lecture theatre.

Captain Williams was waiting for the men to assemble. Once everyone was inside, their ubiquitous armed guards locked them in the room.

'Right, gentlemen,' Williams began. 'As you are aware, Germany invaded Poland and the Army is rapidly advancing across the country with unprecedented speed. We need to do all we can to slow their advance. So, in the early hours of the morning, you will be flying out to Poland with the sole intention of restricting their capability in the area. You will be dropped a few miles south of Danzig at around zero six hundred hours. Now, worryingly, intelligence tells us that the German Fourth Army currently occupies the city and the surrounding region. This will make your job a little bit harder. At the moment they're busy trying to contain the local militia and what's left of the Polish Resistance. So, if we strike now, we can achieve our objective and get out before they know what's happened.'

'So, you can see why we have emphasised the importance of secrecy,' Fosdyke said. 'I know you chaps have not had as long as you would have liked to prepare for this mission, but for it to be a success we had to ensure the element of surprise. If the Germans get the slightest whiff of this, then your safety will be in jeopardy.'

Henry looked around the room. Everyone was deeply engrossed in what was being said, their eyes fixed on the speakers. Taking out a small book from his jacket pocket, he jotted down a few notes.

Captain Williams pointed with a stick towards a pull-down chart containing a map of the Baltic coast. 'The Pomorze industrial region lies twenty-five miles south of Danzig. This area is vitally important to Germany because it needs the steel it produces to make weapons. Also, vast quantities of coal and oil are transported by numerous barges along the Vistula River to the port in the city. These are vital resources the Germans require to support their war effort. If we can disrupt the production and transportation of these valuable commodities, then we can cut off the supply in the region, causing the German forces to grind to a halt.'

Fosdyke stepped forward, flicking a switch which turned off the overhead lights and started a projector. A black-and-white aerial reconnaissance photograph appeared on the screen in the centre of the stage.

'As you can see, the industrial complex is built on the flood plains of the Vistula River. The surrounding area receives all its electricity from this large hydroelectric dam.'

He circled it with his stick before advancing to the next slide.

'The dam contains a canal-style lock system which allows barges to ferry their cargoes up and down the river.'

A third slide appeared which showed a barge navigating the locks. Henry was amazed at the quality of the images being displayed, making him wonder how far in advance this mission had been planned.

'Gentlemen, your only objective is to destroy this dam,' the major said sternly. 'The flooding and subsequent damage will paralyse the whole region.'

Captain Williams addressed the small group again. 'From the drop zone, here…' He pointed once more at the map. '…you will have to cover the ten miles to the industrial complex on foot. Bear in mind there are only seven of you, so engagements with the enemy should be kept to a minimum. You don't want to become involved in an extensive firefight, because you'll be rapidly outnumbered. The last thing you need is a full-scale engagement with the main body of the German Fourth Army. Consequently, keep a low profile at all times. Is that clear?'

Everyone nodded.

'The trickiest area will be around the dam itself. This is where we predict you will experience the most opposition. At present, only a few maintenance staff work there, but due to its strategic importance, we expect a garrison to be stationed there at some point in the next few days.'

Henry nodded, jotting down the details.

'Irrespective of whether the mission has been successful, you must be at the designated rendezvous site at twenty-three hundred hours on the eighth of September,' Fosdyke said, circling a further area on the map.

Immediately, Robert Scott thrust his hand in the air, 'Sir, it's not going to take seventy-two hours to knock out that dam. Why do we have to wait?'

Captain Williams was surprised by the directness of the question, 'Unfortunately, the weather forecast prevents us from sending a retrieval flight until then. So, you will have to keep a low profile.'

'We're anticipating you'll take the dam on the night of the sixth. That gives you two days to reach the extraction point and be ready for extraction,' Fosdyke commented.

'Sir, what happens if we don't make the pickup?' Mayberry asked.

'Well, officially, this mission, like this unit, does not exist,' Fosdyke said openly. 'Your success or failure will not make tomorrow's headlines. So, if you miss the rendezvous, you will, unfortunately, be on your own. We will not be sending other troops to find you if you go missing. So, if the worst happens and you become isolated, you will have to make your own way back to Britain.'

Instantly, the atmosphere in the room changed. The cavalier attitude which had been building up over the past couple of days disappeared. Much whispering could be heard around the lecture room. The major returned to the pull-down map and tried to settle the group.

'If you find yourselves isolated, then, sadly, there are not too many safe routes out of Poland. To the west lies Germany. Clearly, this is not a sensible route home. Czechoslovakia and Hungary are to the south, but German forces occupy both. Consequently, neither is really viable. To the east is Russia. Up until a few weeks ago, I would have suggested this would be your best way out, and probably still is. But, we suspect the Russians have made a deal with Germany over this invasion.'

'We're not sure what kind of reception you would get if you arrived in Moscow,' said Williams.

'They might hand you immediately over to the Germans,' Fosdyke explained. 'As far as we can see, the only other viable possibility is to head north, into Danzig itself. The port is very busy with both commercial as well as naval traffic. If you are separated from the rest of the unit, you could board a ship bound for a friendlier country.'

'Sir, isn't Danzig full of Germans?' Scotty asked directly.

'Yes,' said the major, trying hard to hide his irritation from the direct question. 'Gentlemen, the bottom line is, there is no particularly safe alternative to the designated rendezvous.'

'So, there can only be one rendezvous. If you don't make it, we will assume the mission has been compromised, and you have fallen into enemy hands. The Germans are continually pushing troops into Poland, as we speak. If they know you're in the area, they will increase the troop numbers even further. To attempt a rescue in those situations would be suicide for both the team on the ground and the aircrew. So, you have one chance and one chance only.

The meeting continued for another forty-five minutes. Slides, taken from the air of the rendezvous point, were shown. The exact location for the pickup was demonstrated, and Henry carefully wrote down every detail and even made a sketch in his notebook. Many more questions were raised and answered, and many technical aspects were covered.

After the briefing, they were hurried into the stores of the quartermaster. In the room was a circle of trestle tables. At each 'station,' Henry was issued different pieces of equipment. First, he received his new uniform. Then, the archetypal Brodie helmet worn by all British soldiers.

Captain Williams was behind the next table, with a large clipboard in front of him.

'Write the name and address of your next of kin on this card for me, please, Sergeant.'

Henry paused for a second, then wrote 'Private David J. Taylor, First Battalion Welsh Guards.' Feeling unnerved, he moved on where he was provided with an empty backpack and the webbing to be worn over his uniform jacket. At the last table, he was given his entrenchment tool and mess tins. Struggling with the weight of his equipment, he headed for his room, supervised continuously by his armed escorts.

Looking in the mirror, Henry pulled on his uniform, admiring the symbol of his new unit, a swooping silver eagle, which adorned the right arm of his jacket.

He wandered through to the dormitory. Patrick O'Shea sat on his bunk, looking tense as he waited for the others. In addition to their usual equipment, he wore a green canvas haversack over his left shoulder containing all of his medical equipment.

The seven of them walked silently across the parade ground towards a squat, concrete building under the watchful eyes of their armed guards. He arrived to find two further soldiers standing either side of door. Inside, he strode up to a counter on the ground floor.

'Name, rank, and number?' an officer asked from behind a grill.

'Henry Taylor, Sergeant, six-four-two-three-five, Sir.'

The uniformed man checked Henry's name against a list.

'Sign here.'

A clipboard was thrust under the grill, Henry's hand shaking as he scribbled his signature. Following an instruction from the clerk, a guard standing to Henry's left opened a steel door and ushered him through to another room.

The small, dingy space was poorly lit by a solitary, unshaded bulb hanging from the ceiling. Another officer stood behind a counter that contained various items of equipment and weaponry. Henry gathered his kit before being handed a Lee-Enfield bolt-action rifle and several clips of ammunition. Finally, he was given one explosive device, similar in size to a football. They were deceptively heavier than they looked. He had no idea where to put these, so he decided to stuff it into the top of his backpack and then forced it shut. The extra weight meant he had even more difficulty standing up and fought his way towards the door.

'Not that way, sergeant,' the guard said. 'Major Fosdyke wishes to speak with you.'

The grim-faced guard showed Henry through a door into a small anteroom. The major was sitting on the edge of a large oak desk, waiting for him.

'Okay, Taylor! It's nearly time for you chaps to get airborne,' he said, handing him a faded map which Henry tucked it into his top-left jacket pocket.

'Whatever happens, you and your men must be at the rendezvous at twenty-three hundred hours, on September the eighth,' he said.

'We'll be there, Sir. Don't worry,' he said confidently.

'I pray that you are, Taylor. I pray that you are.'

The major wished Henry luck before proceeding through the rabbit warren-like complex of the sprawling building. The other men of Bravo Section were standing in a chilly courtyard, busily blackening their faces as a tin of camouflage paint was being handed around.

A transport truck pulled up next to them, and they slowly struggled aboard. Alf Morrison was most encumbered, carrying a Bren machine gun across the top of his rucksack, adding an extra twenty-three pounds to his misery. He required three of his comrades to heave him into the vehicle before their armed escort nimbly jumped up and sat beside them. Looking at how uncomfortable all was lugging around all that weight, Henry could not help thinking the Bren was an inappropriate weapon for this kind of mission, but the top brass had insisted they took some extra fire power with them.

***

The cold Polish night had taken hold. Viktor shivered, as he continued to steer the horse along the deserted road. Struggling to see the edges in the darkness, he used the reassuring noise of the horse's hooves on the hard surface to direct them. Zofia was resting in the back of the cart, huddled under a blanket with the two boys beside her.

They had not stopped the previous night because he had wanted to be as far away from the city as possible. Now, he was exhausted, with only the adrenaline keeping him going.

The cart briefly mounted the grass on the side of the road, waking Zofia from her light slumber. She sat up carefully, trying not to disturb the children sleeping next to her. Wrapping her arms around her husband, she squeezed him tight.

'Where are we?' she whispered.

'I'm not sure,' he said, startled by the movement behind him. 'We're safe for the time being.'

The cart continued while Zofia snuggled into her husband's neck.

'You're frozen,' she said, her nose touching his skin. 'Let's stop here for the night. You need warming up.'

'No!' said Viktor forcibly. 'We have to get as far away from Danzig as we can.'

'There's no one else around,' she said. 'We'll be safe here. Listen, I can hear running water over there. Why don't we stop? You need to rest. We can get going again at first light.'

Reluctantly, Viktor brought them to a standstill on the grass verge. He unhitched the horse, leading it down to the water where it drank thirstily. After securing it firmly to a tree, he gave the horse some oats before crawling alongside Zofia on the cart. He pulled the shared blanket over himself and soon dozed off.

5

The men stood in a draughty hangar, chatting nervously while they waited for takeoff. Henry glanced at his wristwatch—almost midnight.

'Right, lads!' he said, only because the conversation had petered out. 'We've a big day ahead of us, so is everyone happy with the plan?'

'I was wondering, Sarge. How long's the flight?' Travers asked.

'Between five and six hours,' Henry said, trying hard to recall the details from the briefing.

'I have a question about the pickup,' Mayberry piped up. 'How far is the walk to the dam?

'Oh! Um! I can't remember exactly, but it's quite a way,' he said, stalling for time as he thumbed through his notes. 'But, we should easily be able to cover it in a day.'
Before he could find what he was looking for, a door slammed, causing the group to turn around. The jump-master, Sergeant Miles Halstead, came out of his office at the far end of the hangar.

'Listen up!' he bellowed after introducing himself to Henry. 'We're going to take off in approximately fifteen minutes. For those of you who are interested, the flight is going to take us over the North Sea. We'll fly around the northern tip of Denmark before landing at Copenhagen to refuel.

'From there, we'll have a short hop across the Baltic, towards Danzig. Now, once we're over Poland, we'll be in enemy airspace. So, we won't be hanging around. I need you all to be ready when we're ten minutes from the drop zone. We can't afford any hesitation at the door, so when I say jump, you jump, okay?'

The group nodded.

'Don't worry—if you don't, I'll be right behind you to offer a helping hand,' he said bluntly.

Pointing to rows of parachutes laid out along the hangar floor, he said, 'Now, you'll need to put on your main and reserve chutes. Pair off and help each other get ready.'

Robert Scott was paired with Henry. Scotty fussed with the straps and buckles on his parachute. The corporal towered head and shoulders above anyone else in the group, but his manner was very gentle.

Halstead helped Travers initially, then wandered among the other members of the unit, checking that the rest of their parachutes had been fitted correctly. As the jump-master checked Mayberry's parachute, he said, 'When you jump, make sure your rifle is across your chest rather than over your shoulder. You probably think it is easier carrying your weapon that way, but, if you do that, the butt will hit the ground when you land, forcing the barrel into your face.'

Without further comment, they adjusted the position of their weapons. Next, Halstead handed out small, folded squares of paper. Inside was a single, scored white tablet.

'These are anti-emetics,' he said, prompting a sea of blank faces to look back at him.

'They'll stop you from getting airsick,' O'Shea whispered to Henry.

'Please take them,' said the jump-master. 'It'll mean I

won't have to clean the plane on the way home.'

Everyone laughed at the graphic image, as they washed down their tablets with a swig of water from a canteen being handed round.

After a few final safety tips, the men walked outside onto the airstrip. As they emerged from the hangar, a black squad car pulled up alongside them. Its rear window slowly wound down to reveal the cheery face of Captain Williams.

'Stand easy, men. I thought I'd come and wish you fellows luck,' said Williams jovially.

'Thank you, Sir,' said Henry.

'We're expecting great things from you chaps,' the captain said.

The car sped off, parking on a grass verge at the edge of the runway, giving its occupants a vantage point from which to observe the unit leaving on its first mission.

In front of them stood a huge transport plane on the tarmac. Henry was shocked at how much bigger this model looked, compared with the one they had used for the practice jumps the day before. Sergeant Halstead expertly pulled himself into the entrance hatch behind the wing. Henry tried to follow, but the weight of his kit hindered him. After two failed attempts, the jump-master reached out, grabbed Henry by his shoulder straps then unceremoniously heaved him into the aircraft. Slightly embarrassed, he squeezed down to the back and sat on one of the parallel benches running along the internal walls of the plane.

Once everyone was seated, Halstead closed the door, shutting out the lights from the airstrip, plunging the interior into darkness. In the gloom, the men started cracking jokes to calm their nerves, as they waited. The starboard engine choked into action, causing the plane to judder. When the propeller reached its maximum pitch, the aircraft rocked again as the port engine kicked in.

The noise was immense. So much so that Henry could not hear what Patrick O'Shea was saying from the bench opposite, so he just smiled back. They started to crawl along the runway until it was positioned for takeoff. The pilot increased the throttle further, causing the aircraft to vibrate vigorously, as the extra power of the engines fought against the brakes on the undercarriage. The noise grew louder and louder until the brakes were released with an audible clunk.

The aircraft rocketed down the runway before finally lifting into the night sky. At 3,500 feet, the plane levelled out, then banked to take up a northeasterly heading. The combination of the gloom and the tablet caused Henry to quickly drift off to sleep.

***

Viktor woke with a start as a solitary fighter roared overhead. To his surprise, it was already morning, though it felt as if he had only been asleep for a few moments. He felt Zofia wriggle next to him and realised the two boys were beginning to stir too. He reached inside his jacket and checked his fob watch—it was twenty past five; time to get going. He made sure everyone was awake, then set about preparing for the day ahead. Niklos and Peter helped their mother untie the horse from the tree before leading it down to the water where it drank thirstily.

After it had drunk its fill, they led Miedziak back up the bank and hitched him to the cart. Meanwhile, Viktor wandered down to the stream to wash his hands and face. The initial shock of the ice-cold water on his skin made him flinch, removing any trace of sleepiness. He filled several green bottles with water to replace those which had been drunk during the previous two days. He walked wearily back to the cart and stretched his aching limbs before climbing onto his seat. With a brief look over his shoulder, they set off on the next leg of their journey.

The two boys played with some large pieces of bark they had found by the stream. Niklos moved them through the air as if they were an airplane. Peter made noises like a machine gun and snapped Niklos' 'plane' unfairly with his fingers, causing his younger brother to cry.

'Enough!' Viktor said, his harsh tone causing both boys to start bawling.

Zofia snatched the bark from the children and cuddled them into her.

'Look, I know it's hard, but you have to hold it together,' she scowled at her husband.

'You're scaring them. Look at it from their perspective. We left without an explanation, we drag them through a battle, and now you shout at them for playing?'

'Hold it together? You want me to hold it together?' he ranted. 'Unless it's escaped your attention, we've just abandoned our home and our business.'

Viktor paused and let out an angry sigh.

'Is this easy for you?' he snapped back at her.

'Of course not—don't be so ridiculous,' she retorted.

'I'm just saying, we're all finding it difficult, that's all,' he said after a few further moments of silence.

'I know,' she said as she leant over and kissed him on the cheek. 'I know.'

***

Like most of the men, Henry drifted in and out of sleep for the first couple of hours, and only woke when Halstead returned from the cockpit.

'How far have we got?' he asked as the jump-master approached.

'We're about to begin our descent into Copenhagen,' said the jump-master, before taking his seat and fastened his seatbelt in preparation for landing. Henry did the same, gesturing for Alf to pass the message along the lines.

The plane hit turbulence as it descended through the clouds before making a heavy touchdown on the tarmac in a damp Copenhagen. Through the small window next to him, Henry watched a bowser draw alongside the aircraft and then commence filling the fuel tanks.

'Does the Danish government know the purpose of this trip?' Henry asked Halstead.

'No, they wouldn't have given us clearance. The flight manifest describes it as a routine RAF flight to Stockholm,' said the jump-master with a smile. 'Ultimately, we're going to land there after we've dropped you guys off, so our story will check out. We'll be a little later than we've predicted, but we can blame that on bad weather.'

After ten minutes, they were ready to go again. Copenhagen shrank away as the aircraft ascended. All the men were awake, except Scotty, who slept in a particularly uncomfortable-looking position. Once they had levelled out again, Halstead unfastened his seatbelt, rising to his feet.

'We're now crossing the Baltic Sea,' he said, waking Scotty. 'We'll be entering enemy airspace in less than an hour. After that, there will be about another thirty minutes flying before we're in the drop zone.'

Henry nodded, his stomach churning, more from anxiety than the turbulence.

Robert Scott suffered the most in the cramped

conditions. Jammed on either side by the relatively bulky frames of Alf Morrison and Joe Mayberry, his long legs were bent up, almost to his shoulders.

Scanning their faces, his new unit clearly contained several interesting characters. O'Shea, the scouse medic, seemed a pleasant enough chap but appeared incredibly jumpy. Henry worried it would rub off on the others in the group. It was clear, Pat clung to his Irish-Catholic upbringing, especially at times of severe stress. No more so than in the hangar, before takeoff. The sight of him clutching his rosary as he whispered a few 'Hail Marys' had unsettled Travers.

In contrast, Tommy Rogers appeared to be a hard man. No matter what was thrown at him, nothing fazed him. This was not surprising, as he had seen action in the trenches towards the end of the First World War, as a consequence of lying about his age when he enlisted. Henry realised, for the mission to be a success, he would have to draw on Tommy's extensive experience. As he looked around at his men, Henry's only real concern was Travers. The young lad had the potential to be a remarkable soldier, but his immaturity could be a problem.

6

With twenty minutes to go, Halstead asked the men to clip their parachutes onto the static line above their heads. At the back of the plane, Henry was the first to struggle to his feet.

'Right, chaps, this is what we've been training for,' he shouted enthusiastically, motivating his men. 'As soon as you're down, remember to roll up your chute and then form a perimeter. Don't forget we're deep in enemy territory, so keep your eyes peeled.'

All seven men rose reluctantly to their feet, some of them yawning.

The shouts continued down the line as they checked their equipment:

'One...okay.'

'Two...okay.'

'Three...okay.'

The plane banked steeply, throwing them around like peas in a drum. The aircraft plunged as a machine gun resonated outside. Squinting through the circular transparent panel in the hatch door, Tommy tried hard to ascertain what was going on.

'A fighter! It's a German fighter!' he hollered,

triggering nervous shrieks amongst the men.

'Okay, focus,' Henry yelled, his own pulse racing.

Another burst of fire raked them, leaving a row of holes in the fuselage above Robert Scott's head.

'Sheesh! That was close,' the corporal gasped as he adjusted his helmet.

'Everyone get down!' Halstead instructed. 'C'mon, face down on the floor, now!'

His tone left no one in any doubt; this was not a request. They lowered themselves as the pilot performed stomach-wrenching acrobatics. Out of the corner of his eye, Henry saw a momentary flash, followed shortly by an ear-splitting bang. Through the glass, yellow flames licked around the trailing edge of the port wing. The aircraft shook violently, accompanied by a change in the tone of the engines. A few seconds later, the red jump light illuminated.

'Come on, let's be quick, gentlemen. We don't have long,' Halstead said, his voice faltering slightly.

He wrenched open the hatch, letting in a blast of cold air heavy with smoke. Travers started to hyperventilate, looking around for reassurance from his colleagues, but it was not forthcoming.

'I have a bad feeling about this,' O'Shea said, clutching his rosary to his lips.

The haze inside the aircraft changed to an eerie green as the jump light came on.

'This is it, gentlemen,' said Halstead, barely audible above the noise of the wind whistling through the plane. 'Okay, number one, Go, Go, GO!'

Alf Morrison stepped out without looking back. One by one, the men of Bravo Section followed him, glad to leave the stricken aircraft. Henry was the last man to the door. After wishing Halstead good luck, he launched himself through the door.

'One hundred thousand, two hundred thousand,' he counted as he plummeted downwards.

On the count of three, Henry's parachute opened, jerking him upwards. The straps around his chest tightened, squeezing the air out of his lungs. It took him a few seconds to catch his breath before he remembered to look up. Thankfully, the voluminous, white canopy floated above him.

The aircraft was some distance behind him, moving awkwardly, like a sick bird with black smoke belching from under one of its wings. The engines emitted a horrifying whine as the pilot fought to regain altitude. Meanwhile, the tenacious German fighter continued to fire at the ailing plane. He hoped to God that Halstead and the rest of the crew would make it out alive.

Bullets fizzed past him, appearing to come from the ground. Some of his men were nearly down, drawing the majority of the enemy's fire. He watched helplessly as groups of men in grey uniforms converged on his unit's positions below.

Henry spied a clearing in the trees, so he tried to manoeuvre himself towards it. Despite wriggling in his harness, the parachute did not move as much as he wanted, directing him to a bank of trees. Expecting his canopy to become snagged at any minute, he closed his eyes.

As he made contact with the ground, he rolled onto his side before springing to his feet and unclipping his chute. He cocked the bolt on his weapon, searching for cover. *So much for forming a defensive perimeter.* Machine gun fire erupted over to his left. He dropped to his knees, clutching his rifle.

Travers emerged from the foliage. 'What do we do? What do we do?' the teenager cried frantically.

'Come on, stay calm,' Henry said, trying to get his bearings. 'How many of them are there?'

'I don't know. I've seen two or three, I think. I definitely hit one in the shoulder.'

'Good lad! Now, have you seen any of the others?'

Travers shook his head as another burst of gunfire peppered the tree they were using for cover.

'Okay, it's just the two of us for now,' he said, attempting to sound upbeat.

'Return fire while I look around.'

After taking a deep breath, the teenager fired a few rounds, doing little more than disturbing the birds in the trees. Silhouettes moved within the forest, but it was unclear whether they were friendly.

Bullets shook the tree again, forcing them to keep their heads down. Henry attempted to look out but was pinned.

'Terry, aim towards that ash tree over there,' he said.

As soon as the next burst finished, Travers unleashed a quick volley, allowing Henry to set off, crawling through the carpet of leaves. He clambered over several low-hanging branches before finally taking cover next to a rocky outcrop. Up ahead, amidst the undergrowth, a Wehrmacht soldier crouched on the forest floor. Intermittently, his grey uniform was illuminated by the flash of his weapon's muzzle. Henry unclipped a grenade from his webbing and then removed the pin. Clutching it tightly, he waited for Travers to fire again. When the shots rang out, he lobbed it at the enemy position. There was a momentary cacophony of white noise, followed by a shrill, high-pitched whine and then total deafness. Henry nervously scanned his surroundings, pushing his back against the rock.

Cordite-tainted smoke swirled in the autumn breeze as his hearing began to return. Travers crawled across the forest floor, Henry waving the teenager forward.

Every so often, he could see Travers' uniform amongst the greenery, before disappearing completely. A couple of shots rang out, causing Henry's pulse to race. For a while, there was no movement at all, then Travers reappeared on an embankment, beckoning him over.

Brushing through the leaves, he found two dead

German soldiers lying beside their damaged MG-08. One had a shrapnel injury to his chest, presumably from his grenade. The other had a blast injury to his right leg, and an ugly entry wound in the centre of his forehead.

'He went for his rifle, Sarge,' Travers said. 'I had to shoot him.'

'Don't worry, lad,' said Henry. 'You've done well. Now, stay vigilant. There's bound to be others.'

Cautiously, Travers scanned the bushes around them while Henry examined the bodies for any intelligence. He found very little, except for a leather wallet full of German banknotes and some personal photographs. Behind them, a twig snapped. Henry raised his weapon and was about to pull the trigger when the unmistakable figure of Alf Morrison clambered through the trees.

'Whoa! It's me!' he said, fighting his way through the greenery.

'You idiot,' grumbled the sergeant. 'I almost unloaded this rifle into you."

'Sorry, Sarge,' Alf said. 'I was pleased to see someone I recognised. Have you guys seen any of the others?'

'No,' said Travers, before Henry had a chance to speak.

'How many of the enemy have you seen?' the sergeant asked.

'Only those two,' Morrison said, pointing to the dead soldiers at their feet. 'I landed miles away.'

'Well, you're here now; that's the main thing,' Henry said, relieved to be slipping off his backpack. 'You'd better set up the Bren. I don't suppose they're the only two.'

Infrequent bursts of rifle fire erupted from their right. A British soldier ran through the trees, but Henry could not work out who it was.

Travers whistled to direct the fleeing man.

'Quiet!' chastised Henry in a forced whisper. 'Don't give away our position.'

Four Wehrmacht infantrymen pursued the soldier,

who frantically dodged bullets as he weaved through the trees. Alf squeezed the trigger once the chased man had passed. The 'pinking' noise of the machine gun echoed through the forest, only easing off when all of the pursuing guards had been mown down. Henry jogged forward to make sure they were dead.

'Am I glad to see you guys!' Mayberry said, breathing hard. 'I thought I was a goner.'

'Any sign of the others?' Travers asked.

Mayberry shook his head grimly.

As the adrenaline wore off, Henry began to think more clearly. He took the map from his jacket pocket and unfolded it. It was futile; they could literally be anywhere in Poland. He had to work out where they were and, more importantly, find the other members of Bravo Section.

Patrick O'Shea found his four comrades easily. The unmistakable sound of the Bren had directed him to their location, and he had heard them whispering long before he had seen them. Embarrassed by their lack of professionalism, Henry shook Pat's hand.

'Are you okay?' he asked.

'A bit shaken,' O'Shea said, sitting down on an upturned tree bough.

'Have you seen any of the others?'

'Yeah, I landed not far from Scotty.'

'Scotty? Where is he?' Travers asked.

'He's dead. His 'chute snagged in the trees as he came down. I tried to help him down, but a German patrol appeared from nowhere. I ducked into the undergrowth and hid from view. I heard him shouting, then some shots were fired. After that, it went quiet.'

'How awful,' Henry said.

'They started spreading out to find the rest of us, so I didn't hang around. I just ran.'

'How many were there?' asked Alf glumly.

'Ten or eleven.'

'Well, they're still in the forest,' Henry said. 'We'd

better get moving.'

'What about Tommy?' Mayberry asked. 'Has anyone seen him?'

Everyone shook their heads.

The five men retraced Mayberry's steps until they found the corporal suspended from a tree; a small pool of blood had collected beneath his feet. Mayberry climbed up and cut the gangly corpse from its harness, causing the body to slump to the ground. Pulling the identity tags from around Scotty's neck, Henry placed them in one of the pouches in his webbing.

The other men dug a shallow grave with their entrenchment tools while he stripped the ammunition and any other useful equipment from the corpse. Once finished, they heaved the body into the freshly dug pit along with their reserve chutes to lighten their loads.

Alf and Mayberry started to fill the hole, as the others kept a lookout. Being the only religious man in the group, O'Shea whispered a brief prayer for their fallen comrade. Henry felt numb. It was his first mission as a sergeant, and already, one of his corporals was dead and the other missing.

They spent the next half-hour searching for Tommy but could find no trace of him. Not even his parachute.

'This is like looking for a needle in a haystack,' Alf grumbled.

'We need to keep looking for him. He's around here somewhere, I know he is,' Travers persisted.

'How long must we do this?' Morrison muttered. 'He's not here.'

'Would you like it if we left you for dead?' Travers snarled.

'Will you two keep it down?' Henry scolded, looking up from his map. 'We're going to have to leave without him. We can't afford to spend any more time here.'

Everyone nodded except the teenager.

'Hopefully, Tommy is okay, just separated from us,'

the sergeant said. 'He knows where the rendezvous is going to be. He'll have to make his own way there. If anyone can get out of here, it's him. In the meantime, I suggest we head north.'

'North?' asked Mayberry incredulously. 'Towards Danzig? Are you mad? The Fourth Army occupies the city. Do you really want to waltz in and thumb a ride home?'

'Take it easy, Private,' warned Henry, quickly losing his patience. 'As I see it, we don't really have many other options. We don't know where we are. If we travel north for long enough, we'll reach the coast. If you remember our briefing, the dam was not far from Danzig. We're likely to end up further away from our target if we head in any other direction.'

'Yeah, I agree,' said O'Shea, who had remained quiet during the heated exchanges. 'When we make it to Danzig, we might be able to commandeer a vehicle. That would make life a bit easier, wouldn't it?'

'If you ask me, if we do that we'll end up in front of a firing squad,' said Mayberry petulantly.

'Thankfully, no one asked you,' Henry said pointedly. 'I know heading towards Danzig is risky, but right now we've no other option.'

7

The road had been virtually clear since they set off earlier that morning. They pulled up in the small village of Ryszca to collect some provisions for the days ahead. The Vistula River wound its way through the heart of the settlement, dividing it in two. A rickety, wooden bridge, barely wide enough to let the cart across, was the only link between the two sides. Other than a few farms, an inn, a general store, and a handful of ramshackle cottages, there was little else.

Zofia sought out the village shop, while Viktor took the two boys down to the water's edge, to see the barges travelling up and down the river. A fisherman sat on a narrow jetty, silently watching his line in the water. The gentle breeze ruffling his sparse grey hair which poked out from under his black, peaked cap.

'Any luck?' he asked.

'No, my friend, the fish are not biting today,' the angler replied, shaking his round head.

Viktor glanced over his shoulder. Niklos and Peter hared around, screeching as they played. As he lit his pipe, Viktor's attention returned to the fisherman's float being tossed by the wash from the passing barges.

The fisherman twitched as the float dipped briefly

under the surface, lowering the tip of his rod. He wound the reel a little, reducing the slack in the line. The float bobbed again before disappearing completely. He leapt to his feet and pulled back on the rod viciously, causing it to arch and dance. Viktor peered over the edge and caught a glimpse of a silvery-grey fish opposing the angler's actions.

Once unhooked, the friendly angler studied his catch as it convulsed on the jetty. After a few moments of contemplation, the fisherman gently reintroduced it to the water with calm words of reassurance. This puzzled Viktor. After waiting all day for a fish, you threw it back as soon as you catch one. Fishing seemed pointless.

From behind him came a loud scream, followed by a splash. He spun around to see Peter yelling and pointing at Niklos, who had fallen into the river. A sickening feeling came over Viktor as the young boy drifted away. Viktor shouted desperately, but the boy did not respond.

He shed his jacket and shoes and leapt in. The shock of the cold water took his breath away, as he frantically started to swim. He yelled to Niklos again. The child gasped before dipping below the surface as he thrashed to stay afloat. Viktor stretched to reach him, but his fingertips only brushed the boy's clothes. Fighting against the current, his efforts only pushed Niklos away.

Viktor made a bold lunge, managing to grab hold of the collar of Niklos' jacket and pulling the child close. The boy writhed in terror, accidentally kicking his father multiple times. Holding the child's head above the fast-flowing water, Viktor propelled himself towards the bank using his legs. Water splashed into Niklos' face, causing him to panic. The child thrashed out, struggling to keep his face from being submerged, winding Viktor. He wriggled from his father's grip and was dragged away by the current.

A hand reached from above, lifting the child out of the river onto the jetty. The fisherman handed the screaming boy to a woman in the group of onlookers.

Zofia sauntered out of the shop, carrying several bags

of groceries. Seeing the crowd on the riverbank, she wandered towards them, wondering what spectacle had attracted them. Expecting to see a fisherman with a big fish or a street performer, she was horrified to see Niklos soaked through and in some distress. Zofia dropped her shopping and fought her way through the crowd.

Gathering her youngest son into her arms, she looked around for an explanation.

'What happened?' she screamed over the distraught cries of the young boy.

'He fell in,' Viktor tried to explain. 'I thought he was dead.'

'Where's Peter?' she demanded.

Unable to prevent his teeth from chattering, he spied his elder son sitting some distance away on the riverbank.

'I didn't mean for him to fall in, Dad,' the boy sobbed as his father sat next to him on the riverbank. 'He's going to be okay, isn't he?'

'He's going to be fine,' Viktor reassured Peter, putting his wet arm around him.

'Will Mum be cross with me?' Peter asked, looking up at his father.

'Nobody's angry with anyone,' he said, knowing full well Zofia was furious with him for not supervising the children properly.

'Are we still going to see Grandma and Grandpa?'

'Of course,' he said reassuringly.

'Now, give your dad a hug and let's go and see how your brother is doing.'

Viktor held Peter's hand as they trudged across the riverbank towards the jetty.

'This man saved his life,' Viktor said, introducing the rugged fisherman.

'I don't know how I can ever thank you,' she said genuinely, still cradling the young boy. The man shrugged bashfully.

'Let me buy you a drink,' Viktor suggested, wanting

to avoid his wife.

'It was no trouble, honestly,' replied the angler modestly. 'I'm just glad he's okay.'

'Please, I insist,' he persisted, trying to avoid spending time with Zofia until she had calmed down. Finally, the fisherman conceded.

Viktor went back to the cart and changed out of his wet clothes, using the large blanket they slept under to preserve his modesty. By the time he returned, an arthritic, older woman had ushered the rest of his family into her cottage a few yards from the riverbank.

Niklos' clothes dried in front of the fire while the family ate hot vegetable soup accompanied by freshly baked bread rolls at a circular table.

'He's a fortunate boy,' Mrs Szewska said, looking down at Niklos as he slept cuddled up to his mother in the rocking chair.

'Thank you for all this,' said Zofia. 'You've been very kind.'

'I'm glad the lad's not come to any harm,' the old lady said, sinking into the armchair next to the fireplace. 'I don't recognise you. You're not from around here. Where are you from?'

'Danzig,' Zofia said politely. 'We left when the invasion started. We're heading for Olsztyn.'

'Olsztyn? You have a long way to go. Why would you want to go there? It's full of Germans.'

'It's where Viktor's parents live. We think it'll be much safer than staying in Danzig.'

'True enough,' Mrs Szewska said.

The single-roomed cottage was lit by the orange glow emanating from the hearth. Mrs Szewska monopolised the conversation, which ranged from the outbreak of war to the children's eating habits. The old lady's soft tone and the warmth of the fire was causing Zofia to feel sleepy. She suppressed a yawn as the old lady continued to talk.

Viktor and the fisherman had enjoyed a meal of

locally made sausage, washed down with many glasses of illicit vodka. Unfortunately, there had been more drinks than Viktor cared to remember, and now he was slightly unsteady on his feet.

'We had better be going,' he said, his voice a little slurred.

'Can't we stay a little longer?' Zofia asked, worrying about Viktor's inebriation. 'The boys have been through so much today. I'm sure they'll have a room at the inn.'

'No, we are grateful to Mrs Szewska,' Viktor said, turning to the old lady. 'But we have a long journey ahead of us.'

'You're in no state to take charge of yourself, let alone a horse and cart,' Zofia said firmly as they walked to the door. 'And don't think I have forgiven you for earlier either.'

Viktor frowned.

Zofia knew better than to persist when Viktor had been drinking. Without another word, she helped a sleepy Niklos into his dry coat before thanking the widow for her hospitality again.

'Please call in again if you're passing,' the old lady shouted.

Waving as they left, the four of them set off again towards Olsztyn.

***

The forest was a dense mixture of towering oaks and elegant pines. It felt like such a dark and secretive place. Periodically, Henry glanced at his compass to make sure they were not veering too far from their northerly course. Every once in a while, he would have to set them on a new heading. A few trees had fallen and now lay at awkward angles on the ground. Clambering over one such obstacle, he quickly looked back to see if Tommy Rogers was behind them, but there was nothing. He knew the chances of seeing him again were dwindling.

They were well behind schedule. Consequently, Henry was pushing the men hard to make up for lost time. Everyone was jumpy, severely shaken by the events earlier that morning. He feared he was pushing them too much and hoped it would not exacerbate their anxiety further.

At the head of the patrol, Joe Mayberry walked down a grassy incline, then suddenly dropped to his knees. The rest of the group stopped and crouched slowly. After checking that all was clear at the rear, Henry crawled forward to where Mayberry squatted. Through the leaves, he could see a small timber hut at the bottom of an embankment and a road leading away through the forest. It was no more than a hundred yards in front of them.

A metal chimney on top of the hut sent spirals of grey smoke into the cold air. Ahead, a makeshift barrier spanned the road, and next to it stood two Wehrmacht soldiers, chatting idly. Henry listened as they talked in German. From their tone, he could tell his unit's approach had not been detected.

'What are they talking about, Alf?' he whispered, not taking his eyes off the guards below.

'Girlfriends back in Hamburg,' Morrison said with a smile.

Should they pass by quietly and aim to reach Danzig with as little contact as possible? Or, should they assault the roadblock? The major had instructed them to refrain from engaging the enemy, but the hut would provide some well-needed shelter from the drizzle which was falling and an opportunity to regroup. Henry was about to suggest they should avoid an engagement when he saw something which changed his mind.

Between the trees, he could see a grey army truck, emblazoned with German insignia. *What a prize that would be!* If they could capture a vehicle, then everything would change. Morale would rise, and their journey time would be considerably reduced. Henry told Alf to set up the Bren and briefed the other men on his plan.

Henry crouched in front of his small squad, speaking in a calm whisper. His words were accompanied by some reassuring nods from the rest of the group, which calmed his own anxiety.

The five remaining members of Bravo Section crept stealthily through the dense foliage until they were nearer to the barrier. They slipped off their backpacks, signalling to each other when they were ready. Henry took up a concealed position which provided a good view of the whole area. He lobbed a grenade through the trees, remembering to cover his ears. After a few seconds, an earth-shattering explosion knocked the two Wehrmacht sentries to the floor.

Alf Morrison, opened up with the machine gun, while Mayberry and Travers set off. The noise of the machine gun drew two other German guards from out of the hut, struggling into their uniform jackets. Alf saw them too and directed his fire towards them.

From his elevated position, Henry could see the two sentries who had previously been standing next to the barrier. One, who had sustained a leg wound, lay prone on the road. Despite his injuries, he returned fire blindly into the treeline. The other squatted with his back against the hut's wall, trying to assess the situation. Henry cocked the bolt on his rifle and peered down the barrel. He took a second to line up the sight with his target and then squeezed the trigger. Instantly, the Wehrmacht soldier by the hut slumped after being hit in the chest, leaving a spray of blood on the wall behind him. Frustratingly, Henry's view of the other sentry was obscured, so he knelt and waited patiently.

Alf pivoted the Bren and fired again. Small clods of earth were thrown into the air as he walked the rounds towards the other sentry. The German soldier scrambled awkwardly towards the relative cover of the barrier's supporting pillar.

The wounded soldier started returning fire, forcing Henry to retreat to the safety of an ash tree as Mayberry and Travers emerged from their leafy hiding place. Mayberry led the way, deftly firing while running, releasing an impressive shot which killed the cowering sentry.

As the two British soldiers approached the other side of the road, Henry heard an engine start. His heart sank as the truck pulled away. Travers and Mayberry chased after it, but despite their best efforts, it escaped along the road. Reluctantly, they separated and circled the hut in opposite directions.

Shortly afterwards, another Wehrmacht soldier emerged from the hut. Henry was about to take a shot when Travers crept across his field of view. Afraid of hitting him, Henry refrained from squeezing the trigger as the young lad and German soldier edged around the building towards each other.

As Travers turned the corner, he spotted the Wehrmacht soldier a fraction of a second quicker than his adversary. To Henry's relief, the enemy guard was dispatched with machine-like efficiency, causing a warm swell of pride to rise up inside him. The young lad continued to perform well. Much better than he had expected.

Another two soldiers cowered inside. Travers fired several rounds through the open door while Alf and Henry watched nervously from the other side of the road. After reloading, Travers waved Henry over. Disappointingly, the hut was bare except for an enclosed coal stove and a small table draped with a navy-blue tablecloth. Several chairs lay scattered along with the remains of a card game. Assisted by Travers, Henry dragged the two dead soldiers outside, then checked them for any intelligence. Nothing. The truck had gone, and the hut was empty. It had all been pointless.

8

Kneeling next to the muddy tyre tracks, Henry rubbed the disturbed ground with his hand, contemplating the lost opportunity. If only they had managed to capture the truck. Something moved in his peripheral vision, prompting him to raise his rifle.

Joe Mayberry was sitting against the back wall of the hut with a dead German unteroffizier lying in front of him.

'Sarge, I'm sorry,' Mayberry said.

'What do you mean, sorry?' Henry asked. 'I'm sure you and Travers tried your hardest to catch the truck. There's not a lot we can do about it now.'

'No, I'm afraid I've messed up,' he apologised excessively.

The soldier lowered his arms to reveal a rapidly expanding blood-stained oval on his shirt, immediately below his collarbone. Henry leapt to his feet, scrambling across the rough ground between them.

'Don't worry, son,' he said, trying hard to reassure him. 'You'll be fine.'

With the injured man's arm around his shoulder, Henry dragged the injured soldier around the corner to the hut.

'O'Shea!' he screamed.

'How bad is it?' Mayberry asked as he laid him on the table.

'It's only a scratch,' he lied unconvincingly.

'Am I going to die?'

Henry paused, slightly too long.

'Oh my God, I'm going to die! I'm going to die!' Mayberry yelled.

'Don't be daft. Calm down. You're going to be okay,' Travers said with a firm reassurance as he appeared in the doorway. He squeezed past Henry and crouched at Mayberry's shoulder, offering him a few further words of comfort which seemed to be working.

An expanding pool of blood collected under Mayberry. He writhed around on the uneven table, causing it to bang on the floorboards. O'Shea arrived, perspiring and panting hard. On seeing the stricken soldier, he muttered a swear word under his breath. He applied pressure to the bleeding wound before starting his initial assessment, counting the respiratory rate and checking the pulse.

Mayberry was becoming increasingly short of breath from a combination of anxiety and blood loss. The medic tore open the front of the soldier's uniform to reveal a small puncture wound on the left side of his chest. It was oozing a little and bubbled with every breath. A look of alarm came over O'Shea. With help from Travers, he rolled Mayberry onto his side and lifted the back of the blood-soaked shirt. O'Shea's worst fears were confirmed. A fist-sized hole occupied the space between his shoulder blades. It was bleeding torrentially, prompting the medic to work faster. He hurriedly emptied the contents of his haversack and quickly sorted through the items.

Picking up a large battlefield dressing, he bound it around Mayberry's torso, instructing Travers to apply as much pressure as possible. The medic placed another over the smaller frontal wound, securing it on three sides.

Standing back, O'Shea caught Henry's eye, and the two of them walked outside. Henry lit a cigarette, shook out the match, then took a long drag.

'How bad is it?'

'Not good,' the medic said, shaking his head. 'He has a sucking chest wound.'

'A what?' asked Henry, hearing a foreign language.

'A sucking chest wound,' the medic repeated. Henry remained baffled. 'Look, every time he takes a breath, the air goes into his chest cavity through the bullet hole, rather than down his windpipe. As a result, he's not getting enough air into his lungs.'

'You mean he's suffocating, despite breathing.'

'Essentially,' O'Shea nodded.

'So, what can we do for him?'

'Not a lot here,' the medic muttered. 'I've dressed the wounds which will help, and I can give him some fluid. But I'm only buying him time. He's going to die unless he gets surgery in the next hour or so.'

'You're kidding? Are things really that bleak?' Henry asked. 'I mean, he didn't seem too bad when I found him.'

'It doesn't get much more serious than this,' said O'Shea grimly.

'Are you sure we can't do anything else for him here?'

'No! I have no way of telling what else the round may have damaged as it's travelled through his chest. From the way the wound is bleeding, the bullet's nicked something important.'

'Hell!' cursed Henry. 'I imagine the nearest hospital's in Danzig.'

'He'd be dead before we got there,' said O'Shea bluntly. 'You're not going to like what I'm going to say, but we're going to have to leave him here. His only chance is for him to be found by a German patrol and they transport him to one of their field hospitals.'

'They're not likely to go to that amount of trouble for a British soldier, are they?'

O'Shea wandered back into the hut. The young private was now sweating profusely and crying out incoherently. The medic retrieved a white box from his pile of equipment and took out a syrette of morphine. After snapping off the cap, he jabbed it into the muscle of the stricken soldier's thigh, squeezing the contents of the tube. Worryingly, Mayberry barely moved despite the pain it must have caused.

Over the next few minutes, Mayberry's cries became quieter and less agitated. The colour had drained from Mayberry's face, his complexion waxy. O'Shea reached up to the neck and felt for a pulse. It was difficult to find, racing and thready. The medic pulled at the skin below the injured soldier's right eye, causing his eyelid to pucker. The usually red area of flesh inside was practically white.

Muttering to himself, O'Shea produced a needle from his bag. In one deft movement, he inserted it into a large vein in the crook of Mayberry's arm, prompting Travers to look away. Removing a bottle of fluid from his haversack, O'Shea connected it to the needle with some rubber tubing.

'How long will that take?' Henry asked, standing in the doorway.

'Around twenty minutes,' said O'Shea, who was mopping beads of sweat from Mayberry's forehead.

'Be ready to go as soon as the fluid has run through.'

Alf reviewed how much ammo they had left. Between them, they had nineteen clips, twenty-one grenades, and several magazines for the Bren.

'If we continue to use bullets at this rate, we'll have to assault the dam with pointy sticks,' Henry chuckled to himself, trying to lighten the sombre mood.

He thought for a minute before throwing his cigarette butt to the ground.

'Right, you two, gather up all the ammo and guns from the Wehrmacht soldiers and let's see what we have."

Travers and Alf had the unenviable task of prising

weapons from the hands of the corpses and searching their uniforms for clips of ammunition. They ended up with four German MP-38 machine pistols and more than fifty magazines.

Henry held one of the German weapons in his hands. It felt better made and sturdier than the Lee-Enfield. Besides, they were much lighter, more compact, and fully automatic. More importantly, they possessed much more ammunition for the MP-38 than they had for their British weapons. An idea struck him. He gave the order for Alf and Travers to dig their second pit of the day. Morrison glanced at Henry as if he had gone mad but said nothing as the two of them started digging.

The earth was hard and rocky, making their job all the more difficult. Once finished, Henry caused further dissent by asking them to throw their rifles and ammunition into the pit. The two bemused soldiers followed the order, whispering disgruntledly as they completed the task.

'Why are we doing this, boss?' asked Alf.

'We've not got enough ammo to continue with these,' he replied, throwing his rifle into the hole.

He handed out an MP-38 to each man. 'We're going to use these instead,' he said.

'It'll sure beat lugging that monstrous Bren around,' Alf said.

As Travers and Morrison were looking at their new weapons, O'Shea came out of the hut and walked over to Henry.

'I've taken the drip out. There is nothing else I can do for him here,' O'Shea said frankly. 'I'm trying to keep him comfortable.'

'You're doing a good job, Pat,' Henry said reassuringly. 'Okay, listen up!' he said, turning his attention to the whole group. We're moving out in five minutes.'

'What about Mayberry?' Travers asked.

'He's staying here,' Henry said reluctantly.

'We can't leave him here,' the teenager protested.

'He'll die.'

'Ssh! Terry,' Alf urged. 'He's more likely to die if we take him with us.'

Travers bit his lip and kept quiet.

'Terry, go and undress the body of the German officer behind the hut and swap his uniform with Mayberry's,' Henry ordered.

'What? That's a bit weird, isn't it?' said Travers.

Henry let out an exasperated sigh but tried not to lose his temper with the young soldier. 'Look, if the Germans find a wounded British soldier they'll either let him die or shoot him. They're not going to care what happens to him. However, if they think he's one of theirs, they'll do all they can to save him.'

'Fair enough, Sarge,' Travers said. 'Sorry!'

Henry forced a smile. 'Just make sure you dress the unteroffizier carefully in Mayberry's uniform. They must not suspect anything if he's to stand any chance. Alf, can you give him a hand?'

After the morphine and the intravenous infusion of fluid, Mayberry looked a little better. Worryingly, he did not stir when they struggled to dress him in the unteroffizier's uniform. O'Shea tried reassuring Travers this was most likely due to the large dose of medication.

Henry redistributed the remaining German weaponry, grenades, and ammunition amongst his men.

'There will be a strange sense of irony if we shoot them with their own guns,' O'Shea said, rinsing the blood off his hands with water from his canteen.

'No more than they deserve if you ask me,' Travers mumbled to himself.

Henry gave the order to move out, despite Travers being unsettled by the decision to leave Mayberry behind. When they were three-quarters of the way towards the top of the embankment, Henry picked up a German stick grenade from out of the pit. He unscrewed the cap at the bottom of the hollow handle, revealing the detonator cord.

Pulling it hard, he lobbed it on top of the pile of weapons before sprinting towards his colleagues. As he clambered up the bank, there was the first of many explosions as the grenade and, subsequently, the other ammunition detonated.

'What did you do that for?' Travers asked, as they set off. 'Couldn't we have just buried them?'

Henry smiled. Although this young lad was learning fast, he had failed to grasp the bigger picture.

'The noise and the clouds of smoke will attract any nearby German units. Hopefully, they'll find Mayberry and think he's a wounded comrade. It's his best hope. So, we need to get as far away from here as possible before they show up.'

9

General Günter von Kluge sat behind the desk in his newly acquired office on the second floor of Danzig's civic hall. Short in stature, he always carried himself with a gravitas which demanded deference. Outside, the strong winds forced the swastika to dance around its flagpole. Its ropes clanking periodically in the breeze, a rhythmical accompaniment for his ponderings as he absentmindedly played with a smudged telegram from the Führer, congratulating him on his success.

A few days before, the Fourth Army, under von Kluge's leadership, had crossed Germany's border with Poland and captured the city of Danzig against relatively little opposition. Earlier that morning, his tanks and troops had paraded through the streets in a ceremony to celebrate the city's liberation. He felt an immense swell of pride; genuine exultation visible on the faces of the crowd.

The inhabitants had much to rejoice about. No longer abandoned by the Fatherland, the day they had dreamt of had finally come. Once again, Danzig was now part of the mighty Third Reich. Despite the congratulations from the euphoric citizens, the remaining small pockets of Polish resistance continued to irritate him.

The German High Command considered von Kluge to be a maverick. It had only been a year since he had been forced into retirement after protesting the aggressive foreign policy of the Nazi Party. So, a telephone call from General Jodl, the chief of operations, inviting him back to the Wehrmacht, had taken him by surprise.

Jodl's offer had created a difficult dilemma. Von Kluge hated civilian life—it lacked purpose and order— but returning to the army carried significant personal risk. Those who openly opposed the Führer had a tendency to disappear or die in mysterious circumstances. To persuade him, Jodl had offered the command of his beloved Fourth Army, which he accepted after much consideration. For the moment, the Wehrmacht needed him, but it had been made perfectly clear: his actions were being scrutinised.

His musings were brought to an abrupt end by a knock at the door. The general turned in his leather chair as his adjutant entered.

'Heil   Hitler!'   Lieutenant   Kathofer   said enthusiastically.

'Heil Hitler,' replied von Kluge, raising his arm but remaining in his seat.

'Sir, I have some news. It relates to the men who barricaded themselves in the post office.'

'Spit it out, Kathofer.'

'I'm pleased to report most of the defenders are in custody. The area is now secure.'

'Good,' von Kluge nodded. 'Hang on, you said most? How many escaped?'

'Four,' the lieutenant said. 'But, I do not anticipate any further trouble, Herr General. We have identified the ringleaders. Let's just say they have been taken care of.'

'Anything   else,   Lieutenant?'   the   general   asked eventually, as Kathofer hovered anxiously.

'Sir, one of our fighters encountered a British transport plane about sixty miles southwest of Danzig.'

'A British plane?'

'Yes, Sir. It was downed, but our pilot says some of the crew bailed out.'

'How many parachutes did he see?'

'He wasn't certain, Sir.'

'Have they been rounded up?' von Kluge asked eagerly.

'Not quite, Sir.'

The general scowled.

'We have managed to apprehend one of them. He is being held in the cells at the police station. We will keep him there until an interrogator arrives from Berlin.'

'Has he said anything of interest so far?'

'No, Sir.'

'Oh, well. I'm sure he'll talk when the interrogators get here.'

'Unfortunately, we've just received reports of an attack on one of our roadblocks near Kwktzyń in the Malbork region. It's close to where the British plane was sighted.'

The general placed a pair of silver-framed pince-nes onto his angular nose and studied a map on the desk in front of him. 'The logical conclusion is the two things, the plane and the roadblock, are connected,' he commented.

'The driver of the truck transporting the British soldier says he barely escaped with his life.'

'Where is he now?' von Kluge mulled over the information. 'How many enemy soldiers did he see?'

'He's writing a statement for the interrogators. I'm afraid he's not sure.'

'Typical,' said the general, annoyed that his day had been ruined so soon. 'Berlin would be impressed if this little problem was resolved quickly. He would now have to settle the matter before any criticism could be levelled at him. 'I do hope we've sent reinforcements.'

'The SS have already left with around fifty men, Sir.'

'*What?*' erupted von Kluge. 'Who asked for them to get involved? Danzig is under the Wehrmacht's jurisdiction, not theirs. We should be dealing with it ourselves, not the Führer's glamour boys.'

'Sir, it was a direct order from Berlin,' Kathofer apologised. 'They seemed to know about it before we did.'

'That doesn't surprise me, Lieutenant. They have eyes and ears everywhere.'

Kathofer nodded.

'Out of interest, which SS officer is it?'

'Hauptmann Roehm, Sir.'

'Roehm? Andreas Roehm?' His face paled. 'That's a name I haven't heard for some time. I knew his uncle Ernst. It must be five years or more since he died.'

'Sadly, I never met him, Sir,' Lieutenant Kathofer said.

'Don't believe the rumours, Lieutenant,' the general said forcibly. 'Ernst Roehm's murder was a huge cover-up by the Chancellery. The last time I saw Andreas, he was wearing lederhosen and riding on his father's shoulders, and now you tell me he's made the rank of hauptmann. Incredible. He must have rocketed through the ranks, just like his uncle before him. I hope he stays on the good side of the Führer, for his sake.'

Preoccupied, von Kluge walked over to the window, gazing across the city. Kathofer stood awkwardly until the general spoke again.

'Keep an eye on what the SS are up to and please inform me of any progress they make.'

'Of course, Herr General.'

'By the way, have the Wehrmacht Headquarters in Malbork been made aware of this incident?' von Kluge asked.

'Yes, Sir.'

'Could you ask their commanding officer to keep me informed?'

'Of course, Sir,' said Kathofer.

'That'll be all, Lieutenant.'

With that, Kathofer clicked his heels, turned, and left,

leaving von Kluge staring across the city. The mention of Roehm's name had unsettled him. An anger rose up inside him which had been buried for many years. Ernst Roehm had been a senior aide to Hitler, the commander of the Nazis' paramilitary wing and, at one time, Hitler's closest confidant. However, a power struggle had ensued, and Roehm, a heavy-handed thug, had fallen out of favour with the Führer. Ultimately, this led to his assassination. No one ever spoke of it, but everyone knew the truth. Hearing the name of Ernst Roehm reminded him of his own vulnerability, especially if he continued to swim against the tide of party opinion.

He returned to his desk and poured some iced water from a decanter into a glass. *What would happen when the Führer had no use for him?* He shook his head, trying to clear his mind. He had more a pressing issue. *What were the British up to?*

***

Walking at the rear of the patrol, Henry silently chastised himself over what had happened to Mayberry. Thoughts raced around his head. *What had he done wrong? Was he to blame?* The longer he thought about it, the fewer answers he had, and he had become thoroughly despondent. Raising his hand, O'Shea stopped the unit. Edging forward, he could see a small town at the bottom of the valley through the trees.

'Well, that's a darn sight better than another German patrol,' Henry whispered to O'Shea.

He pulled out his map, attempting to identify their location, but it could be any town along the course of one of the many rivers in the region.

'What shall we do, Sarge?' Alf asked.

Henry was unsure. *Should they skirt around the town and*

continue towards Danzig on foot? Or, should they creep down and search for another way out of this mess? The latter strategy carried a much higher risk of them being spotted, but the clock was ticking. They had to complete their objective in time to make the pickup.

Henry spoke to the others and explained the options. O'Shea piped up, oblivious to Henry's indecision.

'I think we should go down there. We can have a root around and hopefully find out where we are.'

'Sarge, I agree with Pat,' said Alf. 'Maybe we could look for a vehicle or something. Otherwise, we might end up stuck in this God-forsaken forest forever.'

'Good, that's settled,' said Henry without having to issue an order. 'One of us will go into the town and scout around while the rest of us stay here.'

'One of us?' O'Shea asked. 'That goes against everything we've ever been taught. We always work in pairs. That was what we were told during basic.'

'Keep your voice down,' Henry said calmly. 'I know it's not ideal, but look around you, we don't have the manpower. One person can slip in and out of a town much easier than two can.'

'I'll go,' Travers said. He adjusted his helmet, leaving a smear of mud on his forehead.

'No, lad. I think it'll be better if I go,' Alf said. 'I know I can't speak Polish, but I can hold a conversation in German. Most of the people around here are bilingual, so I should get by.'

O'Shea suggested drawing lots, but Morrison was adamant he was going. Frankly, Henry did not care whether Morrison or the medic went, but Travers was definitely not going on his own. The teenager was far too inexperienced to do something like this on his own.

'Leave your weapons behind. You'll look conspicuous with them strung across your chest. You'd better take this,' Henry said, handing him his pistol.

'Thanks, Sarge.'

'You know if you're caught with this, they will execute you. So only use it if you really have to, and try and stay as inconspicuous as you can.'

Alf nodded, then struggled out of his backpack and webbing.

He took off his uniform jacket and stood, then unwound his puttees from his ankles and let his trousers hang freely.

'I'll warm up as soon as I get moving,' he said nonchalantly, forcing it into his pocket.

Giving his helmet to Travers for safekeeping, Alf started removing the camouflage paint from his face. Within a few minutes, he looked much less formidable and was ready to go. The others shook his hand, wishing him luck.

'This'll make things seem a little better,' O'Shea said, standing up from a billycan resting over a spirit burner.

In his hand, he held an enamel mug of piping hot tea. Henry nodded his appreciation and warmed his frozen hands. The two men sat on the forest floor, side by side with their backs to the fallen log while Travers stood watch. Henry sipped tentatively. The liquid burnt a little as it swilled around his mouth.

'Never underestimate the power of a hot drink,' the medic said philosophically. 'They're excellent at focusing the mind.'

'Well, things are not going to plan, Pat,' Henry admitted, cradling the mug.

'Nah, we've had a few setbacks,' O'Shea said. 'But now we're heading in the right direction.'

Henry smiled falsely. Discovering the town had given the group something to focus on, and it seemed to have lifted everyone's spirits slightly.

***

Alf was a mule of a man; he was five and a half feet tall and just as broad. His stocky build and swarthy complexion meant Alf bore a striking resemblance to the local Polish population. From that perspective, he was quite confident about blending in. His first priority was locating some more suitable attire.

Since leaving Mayberry behind, the atmosphere in the group had become incredibly tense. Alf was glad to be on his own; having a few hours away from the others would improve his mood.

Having plodded down the valley for around thirty minutes, the land opened out into a large clearing. Alf stepped through an iron gate onto a narrow path flanked by long grass. He moved swiftly, meandering across several fields, only breaking cover when there was no other option. The path disappeared between two wooden barns, and as he approached, Alf could hear the low-pitched chatter of two Polish farmers as they went about their work. Ducking under a small window, he scurried past on his hands and knees undetected.

Self-conscious about what he was wearing, Alf worried the people in the town might raise the alarm. If they did, with only a pistol to defend himself, he would not last long.

As farmland gave way to houses, Alf could see the town square, full of makeshift stalls surrounded by a morass of people. Beyond the shoppers and traders stood several rows of rundown dwellings. It was clearly the poorer part of town, although from what he had seen so far, there did not appear to be a wealthy one. Small children played noisily with a ball. They ignored Alf, and he did the same to them.

Between the second and third rows, a washing line spanned the street between the two houses, containing several items of clothing blowing in the breeze. His eyes scanned the contents for something appropriate to wear. To his disappointment, most of the items were ladies' garments, dresses and overalls, but in the middle hung a gentleman's overcoat which weighed down the line. So much so, some of the clothes scraped the floor. Perfect. He walked alongside it and, in one swift movement, grabbed the coat and pulled hard. The pegs holding it in place pinged off, and he bundled it under his arm without breaking his stride.

At the far end of the road, Alf sheltered in the shade of a tall, brick building which dwarfed everything else in that part of town. He examined his prize. The overcoat was made from a coarse, dark-brown tweed. Alf tried it on and attempted to fasten the buttons. It was tight across his shoulders, but the length was okay. Disappointingly, the sleeves stopped some considerable distance beyond his fingertips. It was a little damp, but he did not mind, just grateful to have another layer to wear on this chilly autumnal morning.

10

Hindered by an icy wind, Alf strolled across the market amidst a scrum of shoppers. Through the crowd, he spied several tables and chairs positioned around a ferociously burning brazier outside a cafe. He needed some respite from the cold, and the wavy, heat haze appeared very inviting. Two older men chatted as they huddled close to the fire. The two men looked at him as he sat on an unsteady seat adjacent to the brazier. He smiled politely, and they promptly returned to their conversation. Reclining in his chair, he lifted the front legs off the ground and placed his hands behind his head while he surveyed the market.

A high-pitched bell tinkled as the shop door opened. Alf returned the four legs to the floor as he rehearsed what he was going to say. A waiter stepped out and muttered something at him in Polish. He ordered a coffee in German, trying to hide his accent. The waiter looked him up and down, sighing disappointedly before briskly walking away. Feeling very conspicuous, Alf pulled up the collar on his coat and fiddled absentmindedly with a pepper pot from the table next to him.

In the market, old ladies wearing brightly coloured

headscarves barged their way through the crowd, while groups of menfolk stood around chatting. Reassuringly, several people had walked past him but none had given him a second glance.

The waiter returned with a tray and placed down a steaming cup of coffee in front of Alf. He slid a small paper receipt under the saucer before hurrying back indoors. Morrison gazed at the steam rising before lifting the drink to his lips. The villagers appeared to be going about their business as usual despite the war. After taking a mouthful, he placed the cup down, appreciating the warmth which lingered in his fingers.

A few dogs ran past before darting randomly into the crowd. Alf thumbed the small receipt which the waiter had left. Disappointingly, it only had the price of his coffee scribbled in blue ink, giving no clue to which town this was. The heat from the nearby fire started to permeate his clothing, making him much more comfortable. He would have liked to stay longer but knew he should explore some more.

The coffee had become lukewarm, and he grimaced as he took another slurp. He chose not to drink the rest and returned the quarter-full cup to the table. After placing the lowest value note he had under the saucer, he pushed back his chair and disappeared into the crowd.

Deep in thought, he turned a corner, bumping into two Wehrmacht soldiers, both of whom were carrying submachine guns. One started shouting, calling him an ignorant peasant. Not wanting to speak, Alf shrugged his shoulders and walked on with his head bowed.

He was no more than fifty yards away when one of the soldiers called after him. Alf's pulse quickened and he began to sweat. With his head down, he carried on, pretending not to hear them. The two soldiers pursued him, continuing to call out, but Alf ignored them. At the first available opportunity, he walked down a sideroad and increased his pace, trying to lose them. His eyes darted from building to building, desperately looking for somewhere to hide, but there was nowhere.

They were now close behind him. Alf started to panic and considered using his pistol, but quickly realised it was a bad idea. He chose to walk up the front path of the nearest house and mimed searching for his keys. The pair of soldiers stopped at the end of the alley. Again, they shouted for him to come over. With few other options, he walked towards them.

They spoke to him in German, but he pretended not to understand. After a few minutes, the taller of the two became frustrated by Alf's apparent lack of understanding. The soldier held out the wallet he had been carrying. A wave of relief surged through his body. They were not after him, after all. He must have dropped it when he collided with them in the alley. Nodding and smiling his thanks, he pocketed it, having to stop himself from saying thank you in English. With that, they headed towards the market, talking to each other as they went. That had been close. Too close.

Relieved, he retraced his steps before passing a row of shops he had not seen in his earlier haste. Crossing the road opposite a colourful orthodox church, he walked through an otherwise drab residential area.

As he proceeded along the pavement, he heard an irritating, low-level noise. The sound was familiar, but he could not place it. It continued to grow louder. Then, it dawned on him, just as a company of Wehrmacht soldiers turned the corner at the far end of the street and began marching towards him.

Once again, Alf searched around for somewhere to hide, but there was nowhere. He felt like a rat in a maze; whichever way he turned there they were. He continued walking, trying to blend in with the locals. To turn around and walk the other way, or even worse, run, would have been too suspicious.

From the other side of the road came a barrage of

abusive shouts. An officer at the front of the parade bellowed a command, bringing the column to a halt. The immaculately dressed infantrymen stood bolt upright, expressionless and unflinching. He strode over to the young Polish man who had been shouting obscenities at the soldiers. The youth continued his tirade. Without warning, the German officer lashed out. A single punch to the abdomen made the young Pole double over, then the officer followed with a kick to the back of the head, leaving him motionless on the pavement. On witnessing this, mothers dragged their children off the street and pedestrians melted into the background, allowing Alf to slip away unnoticed. After the events of the morning, they would be looking for him and his colleagues. He could not afford to stay here much longer. It had already been more than two hours since he had left the others. They would be wondering where he was.

It had begun to rain heavily, so Alf ducked into the nearest doorway to keep dry. From his surroundings, he could tell he was now in a business district of the town as the buildings were mainly made from brick rather than wood. As he sheltered, a piercing shriek filled the air, making him jump.

**

The fine drizzle, which had plagued them for most of the morning, had become a steady downpour. Fed up with waiting, Henry stood up and stretched his legs.

'Pat, can you and Travers see if you can find us somewhere to get out of the rain? We can't stay out in this; we'll catch pneumonia.'

'By the look of those dark clouds, it's going to empty down,' O'Shea said. 'I'll see if we can reserve a suite at the Dorchester.'

'I'll settle for the Ritz if they're full. Take your weapons,' he added, adopting a more serious tone. 'Be back here in twenty.'

O'Shea nodded, then woke Travers, who slept against the fallen log.

Pat's nerves were on edge; every shadow and every rock could conceal a German soldier. He slipped the safety off his machine pistol and held his finger over the trigger. Out of the corner of his eye, he saw Travers yawn and stretch silently. The sudden movement made O'Shea turn and level his weapon at his comrade.

'Easy,' said Travers. 'I'm on your side.'

'Sorry,' he replied, smiling nervously. 'This place just makes me jumpy.'

'What are we looking for, anyway?'

'Somewhere for us to shelter?'

'Well, I think it's stupid. There's not likely to be anything around here. We're in the middle of nowhere.'

There was the subtle click of a twig breaking. Both men dropped to their knees instinctively, raising their weapons. Travers stayed where he was as O'Shea crawled forward on his belly for a closer look.

***

They had made this journey many times in the past. Sleeping under the stars used to be magical. However, this trip could not be further from Zofia's rose-tinted memories. She longed to feel the way she did when Viktor locked up the shop and the children were in bed. Typically, they would chat about their day, along with the usual run-of-the-mill chitchat. There was safety in the familiarity of everyday life.

The boys played in the back of the cart as if the day's events had never happened. Considering what they had been through during the last forty-eight hours, they were coping surprisingly well. However, the children were not the problem; Viktor was. He usually clammed up when something was bothering him, and he had been silent since leaving Ryszca.

Viktor was hungry and longed for a warm meal and a cosy bed while his wife sat stony-faced, staring into the distance. He was afraid to engage her in conversation. She looked different, older somehow. More lines had appeared on her face, even since leaving Danzig. *When would this all be over?*

The horse continued to plod onwards, labouring up a steep hill. The children, under the supervision of Zofia, were running alongside the cart in an attempt to make the horse's job easier. A cyclical rumble filled the air, prompting him to scan for more aircraft, but the overcast sky was empty, apart from the occasional bird. He glanced over his shoulder to see how far they had come. A cloud of dust hung in the distance. Uncertain of what he was looking at, he kept looking back momentarily.

'Zofia! Take the boys and hide over in those trees,' he shouted.

She immediately gathered the children in front of her and then ran with them towards a shrub oak. He anxiously fed Miedziak a couple of carrots as the dust cloud moved nearer.

The ground started to vibrate. At less than two hundred yards away, he could discern three large troop carriers and a field ambulance approaching. He tried not to stare but found his eyes wandering towards them as they approached. The vehicles came to an abrupt stop next to the cart. An officer wearing a distinctive black uniform leapt down from the cab of the lead vehicle. Two other soldiers, bearing arms, joined him.

'I'm Hauptmann Andreas Roehm of the SS. May I ask who you are?'

Before Viktor could answer, the officer nodded to the other two guards. They set about searching through their belongings, unloading the cart roughly onto the ground. He tried to speak, but his mouth had become dry with fright.

'What is your business here?' Roehm barked

'Parents! I'm going to visit my parents,' he said, blurting out the information like a tap under pressure.

Roehm nodded. 'So where are you heading?'

'Allenstein,' he said, using the German name for Olsztyn, hoping to curry some favour.

Roehm smiled.

'Are they children of the Reich? For today, they should be rejoicing.'

Viktor nodded, imagining what the officer's response would be if he had said his parents were Poles.

Roehm wandered around the cart, turning his attention towards Miedziak.

'This is a fine beast. A good working horse,' the hauptmann said, patting its neck.

Viktor walked around to where the German officer was now standing.

'Have you seen any other soldiers on your travels?'

'N-n-no,' stuttered Viktor, 'not since leaving Danzig.'

Roehm listened, removing his pistol from a shoulder holster before holding the barrel against the horse's head.

'Are you sure?' he said, clicking off the safety.

'Certain,' Viktor said, accompanied by a desperate, exaggerated nod.

'I wouldn't want you to lie to me.'

'I'm not, Sir. I swear. You are the first soldiers I have seen.'

'Tell me, why did you leave Danzig?'

'I was worried about my parents. They're getting on a bit. I wanted to be near them, what with the war and everything.'

'War? There is no war,' Roehm said. 'We're liberators. We've returned Danzig to the Fatherland. They should understand that.'

Viktor smiled, saying nothing, knowing whatever else he said would cause him grief. The officer slipped the pistol back into his holster before walking away.

Breathing a sigh of relief, he patted the horse again. Suddenly, Roehm grabbed Viktor by his scarf, twisted it, forcing him to his knees. The pressure compressed Viktor's windpipe, causing him to struggle for breath.

'You'd better not be lying!' he said firmly.

Viktor shook his head, now unable to speak. Roehm's grip tightened further and he stared menacingly with his silvery-grey eyes. Viktor's face turned redder as the scarf dug into his neck, his vision starting to blur. Just as he was about to black out, Roehm finally let go, sending the Pole to the floor in a crumpled heap.

'If you see anything of note, remember me to report it,' he said sternly.

Viktor watched as the officer climbed back into the cab of the lead truck, slamming the door behind him. The two guards dropped their boxes, then rejoined one of the troop carriers.

The vehicles drove off, leaving Viktor kneeling next to the horse, gasping for breath. Once the dust cloud was no more than a blur on the horizon, he waved Zofia and the kids over.

'Are you all right?' Zofia screamed, running towards him.

'I'm fine,' he said, straightening his tie.

'What was that all about?'

'I don't know,' he said. 'Something about British soldiers.'

'What? That makes no sense.'

'I know.'

He dusted himself down, then set about reloading the cart.

11

A relentless drizzle continued to plague them as the day dragged on. Zofia was so cold, her bones ached and she found herself fantasising about a taking hot bath. In her imagination, she could almost feel the warm water lapping around her, and writing with her finger in the condensation on the mirror. She dreamt of using the expensive soap Viktor had given her the previous Christmas. Having kept it for when she really needed pampering, she had only used it once. This was undoubtedly one of those occasions. The more she thought about submerging her aching body, the worse she began to feel.

With her head in her hands, Zofia sobbed quietly, hoping no one would notice. In a rare demonstration of affection, Viktor put his arm around her shoulders while shaking the reins, encouraging the horse to move faster.

By the side of the road, a couple of hundred yards ahead, Zofia spotted a large building. She wiped her eyes for a better look.

'Is that an inn on the left?' she asked.

Viktor squinted as the rain blew into his eye. Without speaking, he brought the cart to a standstill outside the building. He handed the reins to Zofia for safekeeping before wearily climbing down.

No lights were on, so he rapped on the door. To his surprise, it opened with a creak. He called out, but the inn remained silent. Tentatively stepping inside, he walked along a short passageway into the bar area. Viktor shouted again, but no one answered.

The wide, dreary room was dominated by a mahogany counter that over the years must have seen many glasses of ale slide over its surface. The rest of the room contained several haphazardly arranged tables, each with a couple of chairs. A fireplace occupied the far wall, full of ash from a long-forgotten fire, and the furniture was covered with a thin layer of dust. The inn appeared to have been abandoned many months ago. Perhaps its owners fled when the first rumours of the war started.

Beyond the counter was a small kitchen. It was particularly messy; whoever lived here had left in a hurry. Numerous empty cardboard boxes littered the floor, and a cast-iron stove had been upended, preventing the rear door of the property from being opened. Viktor wandered through the other rooms, but no one was around. This was the perfect place to spend the night.

With help from the two boys, Zofia led the horse to the back of the building so they could not be seen from the road. They unhitched Miedziak, tethering him to a nearby fence amidst an overgrown wasteland of weeds. Lifting up her skirt, she climbed onto the cart and started unloading the various bags and boxes they had packed for the journey.

Upstairs, the rooms were in a worse state of repair. Wallpaper was peeling off the walls, and telltale black mould marked the course of rainwater percolating down from the roof. Despite this, Viktor was happy. Several bare mattresses had been left behind. He was under no illusions. The night was not going to be luxurious, but it would be considerably better than another night squashed amongst their belongings on the cart.

He found Zofia in the bar, on her hands and knees, trying to light a fire in the grate.

'Viktor, go and see if you can find a stream. We need some water for dinner,' she said without looking up.

'But there's a hand pump in the kitchen.'

'It's broken,' she said. 'Go on, be a love.'

He was too tired to protest. All he wanted was to collapse into bed, but he knew the quickest way to achieve this was to do as she said.

'Okay,' he said in a falsely cheery tone, before calling the two boys who were exploring upstairs.

Not only would the three of them be able to carry more water than he could on his own, but it would also give their mother some time to herself, which she clearly needed. After locating appropriate vessels, they set off in search of water.

The drizzle was stopping with the sky threatening to restart at any moment. The wind blew hard, whistling through the long grass which towered over Niklos' head. The ground behind the inn was an unkempt wilderness. Viktor told the boys to stay where they were until he had made sure the wasteland held no nasty surprises. He stumbled his way across the uneven surface, sometimes in grass up to his waist. Suddenly, Viktor slipped down a muddy bank landing on his back, ending up like some ailing insect. The two young boys ran over to help him, trying to stifle their laughter as their muddied father struggled back to his feet.

Peter, the elder boy, stared at his father, gauging whether they would be in trouble for laughing, bracing himself for a telling off. As Viktor reached the top of the bank, his frown broke into a huge beaming grin. They laughed together for the first time since leaving Danzig. After a very muddy cuddle, they recommenced their search for water.

A quarter of an hour of searching was ended by Peter

shouting, 'Over here! Over here!'

Viktor scurried over to the child, who was leaning against an old well. A sprawling hawthorn bush partially obscuring it from view.

Among the weeds lay an old bucket. Despite it being rusty, there were no holes in it. When he tried to attach it to the well's spindle, Viktor found the rope was missing. The three of them could only find a few frayed inches of old cord strewn on the ground. Certainly not enough to reach the water. He looked to the sky and muttered to himself before sending Peter to fetch the rope they used to tether Miedziak.

'Niklos, find me a stone,' he said.

The young lad scoured the wasteland, returning with a round, grey pebble in his hands. Viktor held it over the well while his youngest son eyed him suspiciously.

'What are you doing that for?'

'When I let go, I want you to count out loud.'

Viktor released his grip, and the stone disappeared down the well.

'One.'

'Two.'

'Three.'

Splash!

Viktor let out a celebratory cheer.

'What does it mean, Dad?' Niklos asked, slightly confused.

'It means the well has not dried up,' he said.

Niklos cheered but was unsure why.

Peter returned with the bundle of rope strung over his shoulder. He was surprised to see his father and brother celebrating.

'What's making you two so happy?' Peter asked, worrying if he was the subject of a secret joke.'

"There's water in the well,' Viktor said triumphantly as he eagerly took the rope from his son.

The notion there might not have been water had not

occurred to Peter, leaving him puzzled.

'Don't worry about it—I'll explain later,' said Viktor.

Viktor tied the bucket to one end of the rope, making the two boys play a game of 'tug of war' with the line to ensure it would not come loose when laden with water. Once he was sure they were not going to lose it down the well, he fastened the free end to the spindle.

The children started to turn the iron handle, finding it difficult at first but slowly building up speed. After a few winds of the handle, the rope went slack.

'Okay,' said Viktor. 'That means it's reached the water. Give it time to fill.'

They waited patiently before rewinding the handle. Crystal-clear water slopped over the bucket sides as it reappeared.

'Perfect,' Viktor said, after tasting it cautiously. 'Now let's fill up those bowls.'

It took three further buckets to fill all their pots and pans. They carefully staggered back towards the inn. With only a couple of minor spillages en route, they walked into the bar to find a fire blazing in the grate. Zofia was sitting at one of the tables chopping vegetables.

'Well done. Put those pots on that table,' she said to the boys. 'Now, take off those wet things before you catch your death of cold.'

She stripped the two boys down to their underwear, placing their soggy clothes over the table nearest to the fire while Viktor bolted the inn's front door, securing them for the night.

***

The rain was falling hard. Henry was very wet and hated being on his own. He had too much time in which to think. Sending the entire squad away meant he was isolated and vulnerable. Crass decisions like this had gotten Mayberry killed. His thoughts turned to the soldier they had left behind. He did not know for sure if Joe was dead, but the severity of his injuries suggested his chances of survival were negligible. In contrast, he was not too self-critical when it came to Robert Scott's death. That had been unfortunate, but out of his control.

He heard footsteps behind him. Using a log for cover, he lay on the ground, releasing the safety from his weapon. His breathing quickened as his eyes darted from tree to tree. Some leaves rustled to his right, his finger trembling on the trigger. To his relief, Alf Morrison emerged from the foliage, followed promptly by O' Shea and Travers. The three men walked over to Henry, still lying on his belly in the mud.

'Are you all right, Sarge?' Morrison asked jovially.

'Just relaxing,' he laughed, clicking the safety back on before rising to his feet.

'We found this one wandering back up the hill,' said the teenager, pointing at Alf.

'Anything of interest in the town?'

'I've loads to tell you,' Morrison said mysteriously.

'Excellent,' Henry said. 'Did you find us anywhere to shelter?' He turned his attention to Travers and O'Shea.

'There's a small hunting cabin over that ridge,' the medic said proudly.

'Great,' said Henry emphatically. 'Let's get out of this weather, then Alf can tell us about what he's found.'

Pat led them along an indistinct animal track, then through a thicket of trees. Its location was perfect, a secluded cabin deep in the forest, but the rugged, wooden structure was tiny. With barely enough room to close the door, the four soldiers sat on the floor amongst their equipment. At least they were dry and out of the unpleasant autumnal wind. Henry immediately knuckled down to business.

'I'm glad you made it back safely,' he said, rather too

formally. 'Now Alf, what can you tell us about the town?'

'Well, this snazzy coat was my best find,' he said, trying to mimic a catwalk model in the cramped space.

'Oh, very nice,' said O'Shea in an exaggerated camp manner.

Henry started to lose his patience. They did not have time for this clowning around.

'Oh, yes! I forgot to mention,' Morrison said, noticing his sergeant's frustration. 'I now know where we are.'

Finally, a smile broke across Henry's face. The others leaned forward, giving Morrison their full attention.

'Are you sure?'

'Yep, quite sure,' said Alf confidently. 'The town in the valley is called Prabuty,' Morrison said.

The four men huddled around the broad sheet of paper in the evening light coming through the cabin's only window.

'Don't ask me to pronounce it correctly, but we are here,' Alf said, pointing at the map.

'So, you think we are in this forest to the south of the town?' Henry asked, his finger resting on their location.

Alf nodded.

'That's about seventy miles south-southeast of Danzig,' he estimated.

'So, does that mean we don't have to go all the way into Danzig anymore?' Travers asked.

'I guess not,' Henry said. 'Now, we are here, and this is where the dam is situated. We don't have enough time to travel this distance and make the rendezvous.'

'Well, there's something else I haven't told you,' Alf said with a smile. 'It is not shown on this old map, but Prabuty has a railway station.'

'I don't know where the MOD find their maps, but they're missing some crucial information, don't you think?' O'Shea said.

'I have more good news,' Morrison said. 'The train from Prabuty travels north to Elblag. From there, the line heads towards Danzig. The last one leaves at twenty-two thirty hours.'

'How did you find out all this?' Henry asked curiously. 'I hope you didn't make yourself too obvious.'

'Nope, I sat in the bushes next to the track. Luckily, the station master was showing a Wehrmacht officer around.'

'Germans!' O' Shea exclaimed, more loudly than he meant.

'The town's absolutely crawling with them,' Alf said sternly. 'There were a few narrow escapes, but don't worry, I wasn't compromised.'

'Are you sure you weren't followed?' the sergeant asked, glancing nervously out of the window.

'Yes, quite sure,' he said. 'I watched the path for half an hour before coming back up the hill.'

'Good,' said Henry.

'So, what do you think we should do?' Travers asked.

Henry held up his map. 'The train will help us regain some of the time we've lost,' he said, formulating the plan.

'Won't that be a little risky?' asked Travers. 'It sounds as if they're using the station to move in troops.'

'There was always going to be danger,' Henry said. 'We knew it would be risky, long before we ever set foot in Poland. We're going to have to take some chances if we're going to complete our mission and get out.'

'Can I say something, Sarge?' O'Shea asked.

'Of course.'

'In my opinion, we should use the train.'

'The Germans know we're in the area, and you can be sure they'll be looking for us. If we sneak out of here, they'll be focussing their resources in the wrong place.'

'I couldn't say it better myself,' Henry commented. 'I suggest we go tonight before any more troops are brought in.'

Everyone nodded.

'Alf, you've been to the station. Do you think we'll be

able to board a train without being spotted?'

Morrison paused for a while as he considered the layout of the station. 'Yes, it is possible,' he said, drawing the outline on the floor. 'There's a central platform which has a railway line on either side. There were several German guards positioned on the platform. But, I think we can get to the train from the other side, staying out of sight.'

'Are you sure we can do it?' asked Henry.

Alf nodded.

'From the contours, the railway should run parallel with the main Danzig to Elblag Road,' Henry said.

'Where will we get off?' Travers asked.

'If you look here, thirty miles to the west of the Elblag, the road crosses a tributary of the Vistula,' Henry said. 'I suggest we leave at this point. From there, we can try to commandeer a boat and sail towards the dam. Do you remember what the major said before we left? There's a high volume of traffic on the river, so it shouldn't be too difficult to find a vessel. But, if we can't, we'll have to cover this distance on foot.'

'Anyone disagree?'

The mood in the cramped hunting cabin changed. They momentarily forgot the difficulties of the past twenty-four hours, focusing entirely on the task at hand. They plotted and schemed until every small detail was finalised. Every possibility had been considered and appropriate contingencies discussed.

***

The murky evening sky cast a sinister shadow over the checkpoint. Confusion reigned. Roehm struggled to understand the scene in front of him. A tall pillar of smoke emanated from a hole containing the twisted remains of guns and ammunition. Many corpses littered the ground, their eyes still open, any signs of life long departed.

Inside the hut were further bodies; a British soldier and several Wehrmacht guards lay on the floor. An unteroffizier with a severe chest wound lay on a table. He had been patched up with bandages. Despite his horrific injuries, he was still alive. A weak pulse was palpable in his neck, but he looked awful. Roehm shook him, but he was scarcely rousable. Apart from a few incomprehensible sounds, the man was unable to speak.

A team of medics, travelling with Roehm's convoy, took over and inserted more intravenous lines and started running fluids into the ailing man, desperately trying to keep him alive until they could get him to an operating theatre in Danzig.

Despite it being late in the day, Roehm looked immaculate in his crisp SS uniform. He paced back and forth, trying to make sense of what they had discovered. Something was not right. If all the soldiers had been killed, then who had dressed the unconscious officer's wounds? It could have been one of the British soldiers, but why would they have wasted time and effort on a Wehrmacht officer who had injuries so severe he was likely to die anyway? Also, why had they attended to this soldier but none of the others? Some had wounds which would not have killed them outright, so why had they chosen to treat this man? Was it because of his rank? Roehm thought this was unlikely. So, was there anything special about him? He thought about contacting Wehrmacht Headquarters in Danzig, to find out all he could about this soldier. However, that would mean the SS asking them for help, which his superiors would frown upon.

Roehm's brain raced. This war was only three days old, and the British were already in Poland, despite no formal announcement of an invasion. That would suggest their mission had a clandestine nature. What could they want here? To the best of his knowledge, there was nothing of strategic importance in the area. What would warrant an operation of this level? Instinctively, Roehm knew he was missing something, but he could not put his finger on what.

Two stretcher bearers carried the critically injured officer towards the ambulance, with Roehm following closely behind. He sat on the hut's doorstep as they loaded the stretcher into the back of the vehicle. The night was drawing in. Half of his men were digging graves, while two moved from body to body, removing the personal effects from the dead. A couple of his guards were preparing to spend the next twelve hours at the checkpoint, manning the barrier. He knew they were going to have a long, cold night.

'Sir, we're ready to go,' his driver said.

'Thank you,' said Roehm, walking over to the guards who were going to be there overnight.

'Stay vigilant,' Roehm said. 'There are British soldiers in the area.'

'Yes, Sir,' they replied.

Climbing back into the cab of the truck, he gave the instruction for the small convoy to move out. The driver glanced in his mirrors, then set off along the bumpy road back towards Danzig.

12

By seven o'clock, it was pitch black outside—virtually no light remained inside the crowded cabin. Henry intuitively applied more camouflage paint to his face while the others groped around on the floor for any belongings they had not packed away.

Bitterly cold, the four British soldiers set off down the valley. Apart from the distant lights of Prabuty, they could see nothing. Alf led the way, retracing his steps from earlier in the day, the others following in single file.

The grass was damp. On several occasions, Henry's boots slipped from underneath him. He was not the only one. Every few steps, one of them would stumble in the darkness. Once they were off the hills, the terrain was much easier to negotiate. Nonetheless, they proceeded cautiously, using fences and trees as cover as they dashed from field to field.

At the southeastern edge of the town, they approached a squat, whitewashed farmhouse. A light emanated from the small, downstairs window. Instinctively, Henry put his finger to his lips unnecessarily. The fence posts stopped in front of the house, leaving a wide-open space for the men to cross without any cover.

Alf dashed across the open land first, hiding against the farmhouse wall. O'Shea was next, swiftly followed by Travers. Henry hovered nervously, waiting for his colleagues. He was about to set off when he heard a click from the latch on the farmhouse door. Dropping to the ground, he witnessed an old farmer amble out.

With a broken shotgun over his arm, the farmer sauntered towards him, causing Henry's stomach to knot. The old man rubbed his arms to keep warm. When he reached a point halfway from Henry's position and the house, the farmer stopped abruptly. Henry thought he had been spotted and expected the old man to raise his shotgun.

Unaware of his audience, the farmer reached down and unfastened his flies. Steam rose as the old man began to urinate into a clump of long grass. Henry froze, unsure what to do next. His training had not prepared him for this situation. It was clear he had not been seen, but any sudden movement might alert the old man, provoking him to shoot. Half crouching and half standing, Henry prayed he would not be noticed.

The old man corrected his dress, then headed back towards the farmhouse. His colleagues smiled with amusement as Henry's predicament unfolded, but Alf soon realised he and his two comrades would now be in the farmer's line of sight. With nowhere to hide, they would have to rely solely on the darkness to conceal them. Alf and the others lowered themselves to the floor, their bellies pressed hard against the cold earth.

The old man sauntered back, blissfully unaware his movements were being scrutinised so closely. When the door closed, Henry darted over to the other three men.

'That was close,' he said.

'Too close,' O'Shea added. 'I'm not sure I can take much more of this.'

'Nice view?' Alf asked glibly, causing Travers to snigger.

Henry raised his eyebrows, which said everything.

Three-quarters of an hour later, they had made their way to the railway track to the east of the city. Only a simple wooden fence separated the line from the field in which they were standing, and it provided little obstacle for the four of them. To avoid the sound of them walking on the rocky ballast, their successive steps had to land on sequential railway sleepers. Up ahead, a motionless steam locomotive straddled the track with the well-lit station on their right. In the shadow of the train was a thicket of leafy trees, almost encroaching upon the line. Perfect for concealing them.

From where they stood, they could see numerous guards in long, grey overcoats stationed at regular intervals along the platform. They remained motionless, while burly men in shirtsleeves heaved sacks and crates into the wagons.

A Wehrmacht guard strode past their hiding place, casting a long shadow over their position. No one had seen him approaching; the surprise almost caused O'Shea to yelp. The four men stood motionless, as the soldier continued along the track without breaking stride. After a few breathless minutes, the oblivious guard disappeared around the far side of the locomotive.

Henry's eyes flitted along the eight wagons behind the locomotive. The first was too close to the driver to be of any use to them. If they were spotted boarding the train, their mission would be over. The second carriage was an open-topped truck containing telegraph poles, so that was not appropriate. A considerable brass padlock secured the third wagon. The wooden-slatted doors of the fourth wagon were wide open, allowing Henry to see straight through to the platform beyond. Two German guards appeared to be looking directly at him, but neither of them moved while two red-faced workmen loaded the open wagon, hoisting cargo onto their shoulders and dumping it into the carriage.

As the sacks were being loaded, the pile nearest to Henry and his men capsized onto the ground between their position and the train. One of the previously motionless guards dashed forward and forcibly hit one of the workers with his rifle butt. Two further guards jumped from the platform and ran to the untidy heap which now littered the track.

The enemy guards were very close to their position. Henry observed them carefully as they worked with their rifles slung over their shoulders. Henry could hear their panting as they lifted the sacks back onto the train. Once everything had been reloaded, the heavy door was closed with a satisfying slam. The two guards walked back, taking up their original positions on the platform.

The thud of cargo being loaded into the other wagons lasted for another fifteen minutes before it fell quiet. The guard patrolling the station's perimeter passed by again as an ear-piercing shriek filled the air, a plume of steam escaping from the chimney atop the burly engine. Henry slipped off his backpack and weapon, handing them to Alf. A different whistle blew from the platform; it was time for the train to leave.

The four soldiers dashed from the shadows. Henry drew level with the fourth wagon, sliding open the giant door just enough for him to climb inside. He pulled himself up, landing heavily in the wagon's doorway. Not wasting any time, he turned around to assist the others as the train gathered speed. Next, Alf Morrison ran alongside the open door, struggling under the weight of his and Henry's equipment. He threw the two backpacks towards his sergeant, followed by the two weapons which Henry stowed behind him. Holding out his hand, he hoisted his colleague's hefty frame inside.

Travers was hot on his heels and was already running beside the door. He too bundled his equipment through the door before athletically launching himself inside without much effort.

The train was really gaining momentum, and O'Shea was struggling to keep up. He hurled his pack through the door and reached for Henry's hand. Pulling hard, he tried to drag him inside, but could not get an adequate hold. Pat stumbled, causing him to lose valuable ground and disappear from view. Straining every sinew, the medic sprinted as if his life depended on it. Without the extra weight of his equipment, he found an additional burst of speed and rapidly drew level again. The three men inside the train held out their hands for him to hold. Henry leant out and grabbed O'Shea under his left arm, managing to lift the medic's slight frame off the floor, while Travers and Alf bundled their flailing colleague into the wagon. With a collective sigh of relief, Henry slid the door shut.

They sat silently, catching their breath, as the train continued to accelerate. Henry offered around a pack of cigarettes and struck a match. The flickering orange glow lit the wagon's interior transiently before quickly fading.

'That was close,' O'Shea said, after taking a long inhalation.

'We're all safe now,' said Henry, trying to calm down the nervous medic.

'What landmarks are we looking for?' asked Travers, squinting between the slats of wood.

'Relax, we need to pass through Elblag before we have to jump,' the sergeant said. 'After that, we'll need to find a road bridge crossing the river about thirty miles the other side of the city. We've got plenty of time.'

'I don't mean to scare anyone, but isn't Elblag in East Prussia?' O'Shea said. 'It's a German city, isn't it?'

'Yep,' Henry said, playing down the significance of this revelation.

Despite the darkness, he sensed the concerns of his companions. Henry had hoped no one would realise they would have to cross the border.

'Nothing has changed. It makes no difference whether we're in German-occupied Poland or Prussia,' said Henry calmly.

O'Shea let out a nervous laugh.

'Look, keep focussed on the job at hand,' Henry said calmly. 'Once the train has passed through Elblag, it crosses back over the border and heads for Danzig. We'll only be in East Prussia for a few minutes. All we have to do is be ready to jump when we see the Vistula.'

'What do we do if there are no boats to take us up the Vistula?' Travers asked.

'Don't worry, there will be,' Henry said, not as certain as he sounded. 'And if there's not, we'll continue up the river on foot until we find one.'

'I don't know about you guys, but I'm concerned about jumping from a moving train,' said Pat. 'I hope getting off is going to be easier than getting on was.'

'You'll be fine. It'll be as easy as falling off a log,' Alf smirked wryly.

After a further forty-five minutes, they entered a built-up area. Between the wooden slats, Henry could see the silhouettes of houses, shops, and schools fly past. The locomotive began to slow as it approached the heart of the city. Suddenly, he realised the station at Elblag was on the opposite side to Prabuty, so the unlocked door of the wagon would be facing the platform.

'Quick!' said Henry in a loud whisper. 'Help me push these sacks over to this side of the train.'

O'Shea and Travers sprang into action when they heard the tone of Henry's voice.

'C'mon, stack them higher. We need to hide behind them,' Henry said, heaving a sack of flour across the carriage.

The four men worked busily in the darkness rearranging the sacks into neat piles. They lay on the floor and covered themselves and their equipment with more sacks, so they were hidden from view.

With a grating screech, they came to a juddering halt. The tallest stack toppled over, landing on Travers, pinning him against the wooden floor. They lay motionless, listening to the German voices talking on the platform. The air around them was thick with flour dust, and Henry found it hard to breathe.

Outside, he could hear someone checking the carriages, whistling while they walked. The door of their wagon screeched open, allowing a cold breeze to filter in. Henry tried to catch a glimpse of whoever was looking in, but it was too dark.

Although only a few minutes, it seemed like hours before the door was shut again. The train remained in the station for some time before it slowly surged forward.

'I'm not sure my nerves can handle much more of this,' Pat whispered his familiar insights.

'Yeah, I know what you mean,' said Alf. 'I could have sworn they were going to find us.'

'No use worrying about that now,' said Henry dismissively. 'We have to be ready to leave.'

'Can someone get me out of here?' Travers asked desperately. 'I can barely breathe.'

Alf and Henry rearranged the fallen sacks, before dragging the teenager back onto his feet.

'Are you okay?' O'Shea asked, watching the young lad rub the left side of his chest.

'Yeah, I'm all right. Just a bit bruised.'

'Right, make sure you're ready to go,' Henry said, picking up his backpack. 'Don't leave anything behind. I don't want anyone to know we've been here.'

The three other men nodded and set about gathering their equipment.

Henry grabbed the iron handle and slid the door open in preparation for a swift exit, but it only moved two inches before jamming. Presuming it had come off its runners, he shut the door and then rattled it briskly, trying to relocate it before trying again. Despite his best efforts, the door would not budge. To his horror, he spotted a large, steel padlock had been applied to the wagon's door.

'They've locked it!' he shouted. 'It must have happened when we were at the station. Quick! Try the other side. We can't miss the bridge.'

Alf clambered over the sacks and attempted to slide open the other door.

'This one's padlocked too,' he said.

Feeling like an animal trapped in a cage, Henry kicked the door hard, venting his anger. He tried to find something to lever the door with, but other than the sacks of flour, there was nothing else in the carriage. Alf and Travers put their combined weight behind it, but the door would still not move. Through the gap, Henry watched helplessly as the train passed the bridge over the river. He felt deflated. They had missed their destination and were now heading towards Danzig.

Out of desperation, O'Shea grabbed his weapon and forced the butt through the small opening between the door and its frame, then started striking the lock as hard as he could. First hit, nothing. Second, nothing. Third and fourth, nothing. Snatching the weapon, Alf hammered it into the lock. The first of Alf's blows caused it to buckle, but the door held fast. The second blow shattered the padlock, allowing O'Shea to open the door.

Henry immediately threw his backpack and weapon out of the wagon door and launched himself from the moving train. He hit the ground at speed and rolled several times. Finally coming to rest face down on a grassy verge next to the track. Slightly dazed, he clambered to his feet and set about finding his equipment. After searching more than a hundred yards of trackside, he found his backpack lying in a puddle, but his MP-38 was safe and dry. After ensuring everyone had managed to jump without serious injury, they headed back towards the bridge over the river.

After an hour's trudge, they arrived back at the spot where they had planned to leave the train. The Vistula glistened below them as the moon emerged from behind the dense cloud. If circumstances had been different,

109

Henry wished he could have spent time watching the light dance on the surface of the water, but they had a job to do. Alf set off down a steep bank which led down to the river.

The three of them waited at the foot of the embankment as Alf crept along looking for a craft to commandeer. Several barges were tethered close to one another, leaving a mass of tangled mooring ropes for him to negotiate. As it was late, there were no lights visible on any of them.

A little way downstream, one barge was tied to a jetty, set apart from the others. Typically, those in the river community were a social bunch. Most evenings, the families who lived and worked on the Vistula would congregate at a particular spot to share a communal meal before retiring for the night. Noticeably, this craft was some distance from the rest, suggesting its owners were not regulars on this stretch of the river, or perhaps it was empty.

The four men communicated with gestures and silently mouthed words. When everyone was happy with their roles, a nod from Henry set the men about their work. Three men boarded the barge while Travers stood on the bank keeping watch. Luckily, the door leading below deck was not locked. Alf, followed by Henry and O'Shea, disappeared down the steps.

Once inside, they turned on their torches, methodically sweeping the interior. The medic checked the toilet cubicle while Henry and Alf searched other cupboards and closets. The barge was empty.

Alf removed his uniform jacket and slipped on the overcoat he had squeezed into his backpack.

'Let's get underway before the owners return,' Henry said. 'Do you think you can steer this thing?'

'Of course,' said Alf. 'We'll be fine providing we can get it started.'

'C'mon then, let's get cracking.'

'Aye, aye, Cap'n!' Alf smiled, fastening the buttons on

the front of his coat.

With that, Alf disappeared up the three wooden steps onto the tiller platform at the stern. Travers, with one foot on the barge and the other on the riverbank, greeted Alf with a smile. The burly soldier set about starting the engine and could not believe his luck when he found the key was in the ignition. In a community where everyone knew everybody else, the thought of somebody tampering with, let alone stealing, someone else's barge was unthinkable.

Alf pushed any thought of the owners to the back of his mind. He made sure no one was coming before he turned the key. The engine spluttered temporarily before it stalled. After another turn of the key and a little more throttle, the engine ticked over with a regular vibration. Travers gathered in the rope from the bank and then pushed the barge away with his foot as they pulled away.

13

Andreas Roehm had spent the entire evening at the hospital in Danzig, and it was now well into the small hours. By some miracle, the unconscious officer had survived the bumpy journey from the checkpoint and had undergone surgery to clamp off a bleeding artery in his chest. According to the surgeon, it was a miracle the patient had lived this long. Nonetheless, a couple of things continued to puzzle Roehm. Why had this officer's wounds been treated and who was responsible?

Sitting at the soldier's bedside, Roehm waited impatiently for him to wake up. Although he had no medical knowledge, he knew the young officer was improving. The soldier now appeared a warm pink colour, rather than the languid yellow complexion he had demonstrated earlier. Encouragingly, his breathing no longer seemed laboured. Roehm became mesmerised by the blood dripping into the man's forearm from a glass bottle hanging on a stand.

He glanced at his watch. Was it only five minutes since he had last looked? When the officer woke up, he would have some questions for him. What had actually happened at the checkpoint? Had he been working with the British? Had the surgeons worked all night to save a spy? There were so many things Roehm wanted to ask, but the doctor had been rather unhelpful as to when the officer would regain consciousness. He would have to wait. He hated waiting.

As he sat on the uncomfortably hard stool next to the bed, another thought hit him. Absorbed in the mystery of the wounded soldier, Roehm had overlooked another critical issue. Why were British soldiers in Poland? There had been no reports of any other enemy contact in the region, so what were they up to?

A pretty nurse rose from behind a desk at the far end of the ward to commence her evening rounds. Under her hat, her red hair scraped back into a ponytail which swung from side to side as she walked. After reviewing a couple of patients, she arrived at the young officer bedside. She bent over him to check his blood pressure. Roehm noticed the first two buttons of her uniform were unfastened, and he could not help his eyes from wandering. When he looked up, she was staring straight at him.

'His blood pressure's okay,' she said with a smile.

Somewhat embarrassed, Roehm tried to appear unflustered. 'Any idea when he'll wake up?'

'When he's ready,' she said. 'He's been through a lot. It's best he sleeps.'

Roehm nodded and slipped back into his thought while she fussed with the sheet for a few moments, then turned to walk away.

Without looking up, he asked, 'You don't happen to have a map of Poland, do you?'

'Not on the ward, Sir,' the nurse said, 'but if my memory serves me correctly, there's one on the wall in the hospital foyer.'

'Thanks!' he said with a false smile.

The officer had not shown any signs of waking, so Roehm thought he would investigate the map to pass the time. He attempted to stand without making any noise with his stool, but only managed to disturb the whole ward. Sadly, the unconscious soldier did not stir. Frustrated, Roehm picked up his cap and leather gloves, then walked briskly out through the wooden doors. The two sentries in the corridor saluted him, and he reciprocated without even slowing.

He hated these places. The smell of carbolic soap and the poor lighting unsettled him. There were so many wards and offices, he doubted the orderlies and porters would be able to find their way around. He hurried past the maternity unit and entered an impressive, rectangular foyer with a high-domed ceiling. Admiring the framed portraits of long-dead professors, he tried to locate the porter's office. A cheery face poked through a door and enquired if he could help. Two other porters sat inside the windowless room, smoking and playing cards. In the corner, a gramophone emitted a soft waltz.

'You were with the young officer they brought in earlier, weren't you?' the porter said.

'Yes,' replied Roehm, not interested in engaging in small talk.

'How's he doing?' said another of the porters, standing up to reduce the volume of the music. 'I hear he was in one hell of a mess. I do hope he pulls through, Sir.'

'It's a terrible shame,' the other added. That young lad can't be more than twenty.'

Roehm gave an absentminded grunt. 'Do you have a map of Poland around here somewhere?'

'Yes, of course, Sir. It is around this corner on the wall,' said the second porter, pointing in the general direction. 'Would you like me to show you?'

'No, I'll find it,' he said, walking away.

The large map was behind a glass screen, hanging on the wall in an alcove. It seemed incongruous in such a grand lobby. Roehm had come to Poland with the first wave of the Blitzkrieg, having never been to the country before. From what he had seen so far, it would not bother him if he never returned.

Studying the map, Roehm realised he was not familiar with the country's geography. It took him a while to find Danzig, then Warsaw and finally Krakow. The country was larger than he thought. He pulled out a small notebook from inside his jacket. Thumbing through the pages, he found the correct place. The fighter which had shot down the British plane had taken off from a makeshift airbase at Toruń. He drew a circle around it on the glass. The checkpoint where they had found the injured soldier was near Kwktzyń. Again, he circled the area.

Roehm studied the two regions carefully; they were quite close to each other. No other foreign combatants had been reported in Poland, so they must have been acting in isolation. What were they after? It was too far from any British settlement to be purely for reconnaissance. There were no major cities nearby, only dense forest stretching to East Prussia. A few small towns and villages littered the landscape, but nothing which should attract their attention. So why were the British interested in this part of Poland?

He stared absentmindedly when another thought struck him. The main geographical feature in this region was the Vistula River. It snaked through the various towns before it reached the Baltic Sea in the north. The river was to the west of where the enemy soldiers had been sighted. He moved his finger up the glass, tracing the course of the Vistula, stopping every few seconds to make notes of the places where roads crossed it. As they were travelling on foot, it meant the river would be an effective barrier to them.

Although his knowledge of the country was poor, Roehm was fully aware of the Vistula's notorious waters. Tens of people died every year from falling in or trying to swim across it. He realised he could use this to his advantage. If he increased the roadblocks on the river crossings, it would confine them to the eastern bank. With the Vistula in the west and the Prussian border to the east, they could not stray too far. If he was able to keep them hemmed in, finding them should be easy.

The area where the plane had been shot down was under the supervision of SS Regional Headquarters at Malbork. Tapping the glass with his pencil as his brain processed the information, he realised that maybe he should visit them. It would be easier to monitor developments from there compared with Danzig. Telecommunications had not been completely restored since the invasion, and any delay in a message getting through could hinder his chances of capturing the British soldiers.

Not wanting to waste any more time he hurried back to the ward, strode through the double doors, and marched up to the desk.

'Is there any sign of him waking soon?' Roehm asked the nurse in an impatient whisper.

'Not at the moment,' she said. 'It could be two hours, two days, or even longer. In fact, he may never wake up.'

'Thanks,' he said, wishing he had never asked.

He walked back down the corridor to the foyer. One of the porters looked out again. On seeing the hauptmann, he smiled and returned to his hand of cards. Roehm left the hospital, through a revolving door, then proceeded down some stone steps onto a driveway.

Dawn was starting to break, causing the edges of the sky to brighten. He opened the rear door of his squad car, waking the dozing driver. Swiftly taking his feet off the dashboard, the driver straightened his tie.

'How long will it take us to get to Malbork?' Roehm enquired, slamming the door.

Unfolding a map, the driver scanned the region before locating it.

'About an hour and a half,' he calculated.

'You have sixty minutes. Let's go.'

The journey was infuriatingly slow. In Poland, time

seemed to take twice as long to pass. The poor roads, military traffic, and even the weather slowed them down. There was currently a break in the rain, but a bitter chill made Roehm shiver. Various snapshot images from throughout the day whirled around in his head; Danzig, the checkpoint and the hospital. Soon they became intertwined and confused, way beyond reality. Within a few minutes, he had fallen asleep.

Roehm had slept for most of the trip, waking when the car went over a bump in the road. His head pounded, squeezing his forehead like a vice.

'How far to the castle?' he said, his tongue sticking to the roof of his mouth.

'Five minutes, Sir.'

'Excellent!' Roehm said, fidgeting to make himself comfortable on the back seat.

The squad car took a sweeping corner to the left, throwing Roehm across the seat, bringing in to view the magnificent medieval castle which towered over the Malbork skyline. Its red-brick construction and terracotta roof tiles rose above the River Nogat, making it stand out from the rest of the dreary town. The castle, built by the Teutonic Knights midway through the thirteenth century, had been taken over by the SS, becoming its Regional Headquarters. The medieval order had used the imposing building to strike fear into the hearts of the populace. How fitting.

They stopped at a checkpoint below the castle. A sentry peered menacingly through the open window, asking the driver about his business. When the guard saw an SS hauptmann in the back, his posture stiffened. He then raised his arm in a Nazi salute and waved them through.

The car trundled its way across a wooden bridge that traversed the slow-flowing river, then passed through an impressive, carved gateway. They followed the driveway around to the right before arriving in a giant courtyard at the heart of the castle complex. Having lost the sleepiness which had lingered, Roehm swung open the door and marched across the gravel. A very flustered SS officer hurried out to greet him.

'Heil Hitler,' exclaimed the red-faced man.

Roehm continued walking as if he was not listening.

'Sir, I am Lieutenant Stefan Kruse of the Malbork Regional Headquarters,' the dark-haired officer said, scurrying behind the hauptmann.

'I know who you are,' said Roehm tersely. 'I need to speak to you urgently.'

'Of course, Sir.'

'British soldiers have been spotted in your region during the last twenty-four hours,' Roehm said.

'British soldiers? We've not even heard rumours of any British forces in the area. Our patrols have not reported any sightings of them. Where were they seen?'

'One was captured yesterday by the Wehrmacht. Another was killed at a checkpoint near Kwktzyń.'

'Communications are understandably a little slow in getting through. I shall increase the number of patrols in the Kwktzyń area.'

Roehm made a mental note. It was clear, the Wehrmacht were not passing on regular patrol information to the SS. Clearly an attempt to gain favour with the Third Reich's high command. It came as no surprise to him. The friction between the two facets of the German military was well known. The Wehrmacht believed they were the real armed forces, but Hitler had created the SS as he did not trust their senior officers. Consequently, the SS was seen as over-privileged interlopers who abused their position of power and were given priority when it came to funding, training, and resources. Somehow Roehm needed to tap into any extra information the Wehrmacht had if he was going to catch the British soldiers.

'Is the general in his office?' the hauptmann asked, entering the great hall.

'No, Sir,' said Kruse. 'He left early this morning for a meeting in Danzig. I'm surprised you didn't see his car on the road.'

Roehm checked his pocketwatch, having stopped listening after the first words.

'I need to make a few phone calls. May I use your office?'

'Certainly, Sir.'

Kruse led Roehm down a magnificent corridor. The ceiling was twenty feet high and supported by ornate, hand-carved beams. He was surprised the cream-coloured walls were already covered with paintings of the Führer. These headquarters were more impressive than the Wehrmacht buildings in Danzig. The lieutenant strode up a grand staircase to the second floor where a series of narrow corridors spread out. Roehm could not help feeling the rooms on this level were much less ostentatious than those below, probably because fewer visitors saw these.

Kruse continued down a dark oak-panelled passageway, taking the last door on the left. They walked into the office, prompting a prim-looking woman to stand up from behind a neat desk.

'Hauptmann, may I introduce my secretary, Miss Agnes Trinke?'

'I am delighted to meet you, Miss Trinke,' he said.

'Agnes, this is Hauptmann Roehm. He's just arrived from Danzig.'

The aging, prim secretary smiled, shaking his hand politely. Kruse ushered the SS officer through a door into a private office.

'This is my office. Feel free to use it while you are here. How long do you plan to stay with us?'

'I haven't quite decided,' Roehm said, walking around the desk in the centre of the room.

'That's not a problem. I shall ask Agnes to organise a guest room for you. Is there anything else I can get you, Herr Hauptmann?'

'No, thank you,' he said. 'Now, if you don't mind, I wish to make a few phone calls in private.'

Kruse nodded before closing the door behind him. Roehm picked up the receiver, staring out of the window towards the river. After a few seconds, a female voice answered which he recognised as the secretary in the adjacent room.

'Miss Trinke, or may I call you Agnes?' he flirted.

'Of course, Sir. What may I do for you?'

'Well, Agnes, would you put me through to St. Catherine's Hospital in Danzig?'

14

The peculiar early morning light made the river shimmer. Dressed in his overcoat and a cloth cap he had found stowed in one of the cupboards, Alf looked every inch like a local bargeman. Below deck, O'Shea reviewed the status of their ammunition, while Travers slept in one of the bunks. With the map open across the table in front of him, Henry studied the map. With ten miles to go, it would soon be the time to ditch the barge and continue the rest of the journey on foot. He walked to the bottom of the steps and opened the door.

'What's the traffic like, Alf?' he said, remaining concealed.

'Not too bad at the moment, but I imagine it'll get heavier when the sun comes up.'

'Looking at the map, there's a bend in around five miles,' Henry said. 'Pull up on the left bank when we get there. We'll have to walk the rest.'

'Okay, Boss...' Alf's expression changing suddenly, his usually lighthearted demeanour becoming serious. 'Keep your head down and shut the door. Tell the others to keep quiet.'

'Why? What is it?'

'A German patrol boat.'

Henry closed the door and dashed back through the cabin. His sudden movement alerted O'Shea. Using hand gestures, he conveyed a warning, then knelt next to the bunk on which Travers was sleeping. He placed his hand over the teenager's mouth and woke him with the minimum of noise.

***

Still dozing beside him, Zofia wriggled. Trying hard not to disturb her, Viktor edged his way out of the bed. Across the landing, the two boys were still fast asleep on another mattress. He crept down the creaking staircase into the bar. The sun streamed through holes in the threadbare curtains, putting him in a good mood. Next, he grovelled around in the grate, attempting to light a fire. Fifteen minutes later, a copper kettle boiled away above the roaring flames. He made himself a mug of coffee, then wandered outside.

All traces of the dark rain clouds had gone. Miedziak, the only other member of the family who was awake, fed noisily on the long grass by the back door. Viktor patted the horse's neck, soaking up the early morning sun. How long he had stood there, he was not sure, but he jumped when a pair of arms crept around his chest and squeezed him. A warm, moist kiss on the back of his neck followed.

Zofia whispered 'I love you' and hugged him again.

Although she was not wearing makeup and her hair was uncombed, Viktor realised how much he loved her. He placed his arms around her waist and kissed her passionately on the lips.

'You haven't done that since we were teenagers,' she said, cuddling into him.

He smiled, stroking her long hair gently.

'I'm sorry to spoil this, but Peter and Niklos are awake. They'll be down soon, so I'd better prepare breakfast.'

'The kettle's already boiled,' he said helpfully, not wanting to let her go. 'Can we stay here for a few more minutes?'

Zofia began unpacking one of the boxes they had unloaded the previous night. Retrieving a small block of butter and some ham, she added them to the left-over bread and sausage from their meal the evening before. As she set the table, the boys made their way down the stairs, shattering the relative silence.

Sitting around one of the tables in the bar, the family ate their breakfast. The children sipped milk while struggling to eat chunks of bread too large for their mouths while their parents drank coffee and discussed the day ahead.

'Which route are we taking?' Zofia asked, removing the cup from her lips.

'I think we should take the back road towards Orneta,' Viktor said, trying to avoid meeting any more Germans troops.

'What a great idea!' she said excitedly. 'There is a beautiful waterfall there. My father used to take me there when I was a little girl. Will we have time to stop and have a look? I'd love to see it again.'

'Maybe,' he said, wanting to get to Olsztyn as soon as possible.

'That would be nice,' she smiled, remembering something from long ago. 'Now, come along, we have to leave.'

***

The grey, flat-bottomed patrol boat pulled up alongside them. A machine gun on its foredeck pointed straight at Alf. Not knowing what else to do, he waved as if he was a regular traveller on the river, his eyes scanning them as they approached. There were three crew members: a gunner, a pilot, and a guard standing against the side rail with a thick rope in his hand. In the wheelhouse, the pilot focussed on the front of his boat. Paying extra attention to the close proximity of the bow of the barge, Alf leant forward and surreptitiously knocked on the door which led below before the German crewman threw a rope towards him. With adrenaline surging through his veins, Alf clumsily secured the two boats together, then waited for him to come aboard. Before he even stepped onto the tiller platform, he began barking instructions and continued to shout, even when he stood toe to toe with the British soldier. The man spoke so fast, Alf struggled to understand, but it was clear he intended to go below deck.

Stalling for as long as possible, Alf led him down the steps into the living quarters.

He expected to see weapons and uniforms lying around, but instead, there was no trace of their equipment anywhere. Travers and O'Shea were sitting at the table in the far corner, where only moments before, Henry's map was spread open. The two British soldiers were dressed in civilian clothing, which they must have found in the overhead lockers. The medic sipped nervously from an enamel mug, while Travers smiled pleasantly at the crewman.

The soldier strode towards them, continuing shouting instructions in German.

'Hände hoch! Hände hoch!' he said firmly.

They remained sitting, as if oblivious to the soldier's request.

'Hände hoch! Hände hoch!' he said again, shouting

more aggressively.

Neither of them moved.

The German soldier reached inside his grey uniform jacket, producing a pistol, which he pointed at O'Shea. Pat's insides froze, giving him an ache deep in his belly. He and Travers stood with their arms raised. The guard continued to bellow at them, but no one responded. Coming to the end of his tether, the soldier drew back the firing pin on his pistol and forced the barrel against the medic's forehead. Pat closed his eyes, expecting to hear a gunshot at any minute, muttering a prayer under his breath.

Having watched events unfold through a crack in the door of the cramped lavatory cubicle, Henry crept out when O'Shea had been threatened. In one decisive movement, he sliced the man's neck from the midline at the front all the way round to the back. The soldier's body went rigid, collapsing backwards onto him. A look of surprise persisted on the stricken man's face, his chest contorting as he struggled to fill his deflated lungs with air. The deep wound in his neck bled profusely, his severed larynx making it impossible for him to cry out.

After a few seconds, Pat realised nothing had happened to him. Plucking up the courage to open his eyes, to his surprise, the German soldier lay on the floor with Henry standing over him.

'Now you've done it,' O'Shea said in a harsh whisper. 'What are we going to do now?'

'Have you forgotten there are more of them outside?' Travers panicked.

'Keep calm,' Henry scolded. 'We have to keep thinking straight.'

Without pausing, the sergeant set about undressing the dying soldier. First, he removed the grey uniform jacket and then his trousers. Apart from a blood-stained tidemark on the collar, it was acceptable. He explained his plan as he tried on the dead soldier's clothes.

Unfortunately, the sleeves were way too short, and it was a little tight across his chest. Even from a distance of several feet, he would have immediately been identified as an impostor. There was no way it was going to fit around the immense girth of Alf Morrison. Conversely, the uniform would bury the slight frame of O'Shea. As a last resort, Henry handed the jacket to Travers, who had a similar build to the crewman. Reluctantly, the youngster tried it on. The fit was not perfect, but they might get away with it. By default, the teenager had volunteered to go on deck to act as a decoy. He fastened the buttons, then placed the dying man's helmet on his head.

'Does everyone know what they're doing?' asked Henry.

His three companions nodded.

'Good Luck, Terry,' he said, patting Travers on the back. 'Just concentrate on what you have to do.'

'By the way, mate, grey really doesn't suit you,' Alf quipped, his attempt at humour failing to lighten the gravity of the situation.

With his helmet pulled down low and a machine pistol over his shoulder, Travers was visibly shaking as he started up the steps. On the tiller platform, the teenager stood with his back to the patrol boat.

Turning rapidly, the teenager squeezed the trigger. His main priority was the machine gunner. He sprayed the foredeck with bullets, causing the soldier's body to recoil as he took multiple hits, killing him instantly. The sound of gunfire prompted the three other British soldiers to commence firing through the small portholes in the side of the barge. Their target was the pilot. If he managed to escape, the entire German Army would descend on them.

The surprise of the attack had stunned the crew. With the machine gunner dead, the pilot was virtually defenceless. He opened up the throttle and attempted to speed away as Travers redirected his fire. The boat's engine fought against the rope, tethering it to the much heavier barge.

The wheelhouse windows shattered, throwing shards of glass into the air, the pilot's body slumping over the wheel.

'Cease firing!' cried Henry, prompting an immediate halt to the shooting.

The pilot was dead, but his hand remained on the throttle lever. With the engine revving wildly, the rope creaked under the strain before it snapped. As the force was released, the boat sped off.

The patrol boat hit the opposite riverbank hard, becoming airborne, before crashing into the woodland beyond. It eventually came to rest, hidden from view, deep in the undergrowth on the far side of the river. The engines still emitted a dreadful noise, likely to attract any nearby German patrols.

'Alf, take the barge over to the other side,' said Henry. 'Terry, keep your eyes peeled.'

Morrison leapt up to the tiller deck and restarted the barge's engine. He deftly guided them across the river, bringing the vessel alongside the other bank.

'Alf, keep a lookout,' he said, looking up the stairs to the platform. 'Pat and Terry, come with me.'

The three men jumped over the side rail, then hurried towards the noise. Hurdling several broken and uprooted trees, they were surprised by how far it had travelled. Henry and the medic climbed aboard cautiously, while Travers stayed hidden in case any unspotted crew members tried to make a getaway. Ducking underneath a low-hanging branch, the two of them edged around the gunwale of the boat. O'Shea nudged the machine gunner's body with his boot, causing the corpse to roll over, splaying its limbs awkwardly. He thumbed his weapon's safety catch anxiously as his sergeant ducked under the metal canopy into the small wheelhouse.

Broken glass crunched under Henry's boots as he shuffled into the narrow space. His stomach churned when he saw what remained of the pilot. The bullet-riddled body was slumped over the wheel, the back of his head missing, replaced by an oozing, stellate exit wound. The pilot's left hand was still gripping the throttle lever, causing his body to hang ghoulishly. Swallowing hard to fight back the revulsion, Henry grabbed the lever, pulling it into an upright position. The vibration underfoot reduced before he turned the key, bringing the engine to a stop.

In the eerie silence, he glanced again at the dead pilot before stepping onto the foredeck.

'It's a bit of a mess, isn't it?' Henry said.

O'Shea clutched a rosary in his one hand, while the middle finger on his other gripped the trigger guard of his weapon.

'Have a good look round and make sure no one else is on board.'

Henry signalled for Travers to join them.

'Right, Terry, what I need you to do is search every nook and cranny of the boat. I want as much rope as you can get your hands on.'

The teenager nodded, wondering what Henry was planning.

'Alf, can you tie all these together?' said Henry as his two colleagues dumped coils of rope onto the tiller platform.

'Sure thing, Sarge,' said Morrison.

'Pat, come below and gather up all our belongings,' Henry said. 'I don't want there to be any traces of us being here.'

Henry followed him. Dragging the body to the foot of the steps, while the others set about their work.

'Alf, can I come up?' he asked.

'Hold it,' he said, knotting two ends of rope together. Two barges are coming around the bend.'

'Let me know when it's clear.'

He waited impatiently until they had passed out of view.

'Okay, you're safe to come up now,' Alf said.

Henry dragged the body onto the platform, then heaved it over the side. He jumped down and lugged the corpse deep into the bushes. Morrison quickly checked the river was clear before waving him back aboard.

'I've finished the rope,' Alf announced. 'What do you want it for anyway?'

'We have to put the Germans off our scent,' he said, trying to catch his breath. 'They need to think we're on this side of the river.'

None the wiser, Morrison smiled.

'That's not going to be long enough,' said Henry frankly, studying Alf's handiwork. 'We need more.'

Alf prowled around the flat roof of the barge, but found nothing. Henry poked his head out of the doorway and checked that the coast was clear before dashing again to the patrol boat.

O'Shea had obviously been quite thorough with his search. After frantically scouring the vessel, Henry found nothing. As he was climbing back over the rail, a thought struck him. Due to the ghoulish appearance of the pilot's corpse, he suspected the medic may have avoided searching the wheelhouse. Henry trotted back across the foredeck to the pilot's body.

Coiled up on a hook at the back of the cabin was a length of cable used for towing. He threw it over his shoulder, then struggled with the heavy cable back through the undergrowth to the riverbank.

'This is what we needed,' he said jubilantly.

He gave one end to Alf to incorporate into the knotted rope he had been making.

'That's better. It's plenty long enough now,' said Henry.

'I don't understand,' Morrison said. 'What's it for?'

'All will become clear,' he said mysteriously. 'Take us over to the other bank.'

The barge's engine choked to life, and Alf

manoeuvred the boat accordingly.

'Are you two ready to go?'

'Yes,' came the reply as two faces appeared from at the foot of the steps.

Travers was wearing his British uniform again, and the medic was slipping on his jacket.

'I want you to unload all our kit,' Henry said. 'Dump it on the riverbank.'

O'Shea appeared with his medical bag and his own pack. He was about to climb over the rail when Henry stopped him. Taking the two bags from him, Henry dropped them over the side onto the ground.

'Go below and boil the kettle,' he said to the medic.

'Oh! Okay, Chief,' O'Shea said, somewhat bewildered.

Travers continued unloading their belongings while Alf sat on the tiller platform, watching the river. After five minutes, O'Shea's face appeared in the doorway. 'The water's boiling.'

Henry turned to Travers and Morrison. 'You two, take all our kit and hide in the treeline.'

'Okay,' they replied, confused as to what Henry was up to.

Henry disappeared below decks.

From where they stood, Alf and Travers could hear raised voices.

'I'm not doing it!' the medic refused.

'But you're the lightest,' Henry reasoned.

The shouting died down, and Henry appeared with a steaming kettle in one hand and a bath towel in the other. Alf looked quizzically at Travers, who shrugged. He jumped onto the riverbank and placed them on the ground.

'Alf, can you hand me one end of the rope?' Henry requested.

Morrison handed it to Henry, who struggled across the boggy, leaf-covered surface with the cumbersome length of knotted rope. He tied it around the trunk of a sizeable tree before returning to the barge.

'Are you ready, Pat?' asked Henry.

'Yep, is it safe to come up?'

To Terry and Alf's surprise, O'Shea appeared on the tiller platform wearing only his underpants. 'Tie this around your waist. Make sure it's secure,' Henry said, giving it to him. 'We wouldn't want to lose you.'

The medic fastened the rope as instructed, glaring at his sergeant. Meanwhile, Henry smiled back reassuringly, gathering O'Shea's clothes and boots in his arm.

'Take the barge over to the other side of the river and moor up,' Henry said. 'Do what you have to do, then let us know when you're ready.'

Pat nodded.

Rubbing his arms to stay warm, O'Shea started the engine and followed Henry's instructions. He disappeared from sight for a few moments, before climbing onto the footplate to face his colleagues. This was not going to be pleasant.

'Take the strain!' Henry said to his two colleagues.

Morrison and Travers picked up the rope and drew in the slack. Checking it was tied securely around his waist, Pat O'Shea gave a wave before diving into the river.

'Pull as hard as you can,' said Henry. 'We have to get him out of the water as quickly as possible.'

'One, two, three, pull!' he yelled. 'One, two, three, pull!'

The force of the fast-flowing waters made O'Shea more cumbersome. Alf and Travers struggled as the soggy rope became hard to grip. Henry joined in and started heaving the medic towards the riverbank.

'Keep going!' he ordered, as the strength of consecutive pulls weakened.

Every so often, O'Shea's body broke the surface, each stroke bringing him nearer to the bank.

Finally, O'Shea collapsed in the shallow waters. His

dripping body was blue, shivering continually. Henry ran into the water and dragged O'Shea back to the cover of the trees. Laying his colleague's quivering body on the ground, Alf swiftly wrapped him in the towel.

'Cover him up,' Henry said. 'We can't let him develop hypothermia.'

Morrison dried the medic briskly with the rough towel. At the same time, Travers stayed in the treeline, watching for signs of anyone approaching. They dressed O'Shea in his uniform, then placed Alf's overcoat around his shoulders.

Using the hot water from the kettle to heat a ration pack, Henry shovelled it into the frozen man's mouth. The medic slowly began to warm up, but it was many minutes before he was able to speak again.

'Don't ever make me do that again,' O'Shea said, his teeth chattering.

'How are you feeling?' he asked.

'I don't think you have any idea how cold that water was,' he shuddered, struggling to talk.

'You did a great job. It's over now. Just get yourself warm. Okay, everybody, listen up. We're leaving in five minutes,' said Henry. 'Alf, untie the rope from the tree. We're going to have to carry it for a while before we ditch it.'

'Why? It weighs a ton,' stated Travers.

'If they find it on the riverbank directly opposite the barge, it won't be long before the Germans put two and two together and conclude we're on this side of the river. That would mean Pat would have gone through all that for nothing. Not to mention, we would have wasted a lot of time. Time we can ill afford.'

'Do you think you're able to walk?' Henry asked the cold medic.

O'Shea nodded. 'Yeah, I'll be all right.'

'We've been in one place far too long,' he said. 'They're going to notice the patrol boat's missing soon.

When they do, they'll descend on this place in vast numbers. Hopefully, this little decoy will distract them for a while. So, grab your things. We have a long walk ahead of us.'

Alf helped O'Shea to his feet, offering to carry his backpack until he had recovered. After stuffing the damp towel into the top of his rucksack, Henry threw the half-full kettle into the fast-flowing waters of the Vistula. It floated at first, filling as it was dragged along by the current before sinking out of view.

15

Standing in Agnes Trinke's room, Lieutenant Kruse knocked sheepishly on the door of his own office.

'Come,' shouted the voice from inside.

'Hauptmann, may I have a word?' he asked nervously, closing the door behind him.

'What is it?' Roehm snapped from behind the desk.

'One of the Wehrmacht patrol boats has not reported in for nearly two hours. At first, we thought they had a problem with their radio. Now I'm wondering whether their disappearance has something to do with the British soldiers you mentioned,' he said, his voice falling to a barely audible mumble.

'When did you last hear from them?'

'A couple of hours ago. They were using one of our relay communications teams to update their Headquarters in Danzig.'

'What was their last message?'

'They were inspecting a barge travelling up the river.'

'Did they give any indication why they felt it warranted a closer inspection?'

'They said it was riding high in the water, but it was heading up the Vistula,' the lieutenant said, stumbling over his words.

Roehm did not understand.

'It suggests it had no cargo,' the lieutenant explained, unfolding a large map across the desk in front of him. 'Barges usually travel downstream to collect coal from the mines around Danzig. This barge appeared to be empty, but was travelling upstream, away from the city.'

Realisation dawned on the hauptmann's face.

'It doesn't sound important, but apparently it's really unusual,' Kruse added.

'I don't understand why you didn't tell me about this earlier,' Roehm said, his demeanour thawing slightly. 'We could've been out looking for them for the last couple of hours.'

'Sir, since the invasion started, we've been having serious problems with our radios. When you arrived, we had lost contact with twelve units. I didn't want to concern you unnecessarily if it turned out to be purely a communications problem. The network is now working, Sir, and we have reconnected with the others,' Kruse said, 'but not this one.

Roehm nodded, appreciating Kruse's predicament. 'Do you have their last coordinates?'

'Yes, Sir,' the lieutenant said, removing a piece of paper from his pocket. 'It's about an hour away by road.'

Kruse handed a transcript of the patrol boat's final message to the hauptmann.

'Okay, we need to double the number of patrols on this section of the river and make sure they all report in every thirty minutes. If they're even a minute late, I want to know about it, understood?'

'Very good, Sir.'

'Now, load up fifty of your men. We're going to find that boat.'

Roehm studied the map sprawled across the desk. He located the Wehrmacht boat's last known position and surveyed the surrounding area. All his instincts told him this was the work of the British soldiers. Where were they heading? To the east and west were forests and farmland. He could think of no reason why they would be interested in those. His finger followed the Vistula as it wound its way through the countryside. Suddenly, a shiver ran down his spine. Twelve miles to the south was the Pomeroze region. He did not know much about Poland, but he knew it was the industrial hub for the north of the country. The armament factories and the hydroelectric dam would make perfect targets for a small team of saboteurs.

One of the reasons for the invasion had been the region's industrial installations. These would boost Germany's manufacturing capabilities and bolster their war effort. The repercussions of losing them so soon did not bear thinking about. Alarmingly, the British soldiers were now moving with relative ease.

Grabbing the phone, he contacted the police and made them aware of the situation. Roehm then asked Agnes to connect him to the Wehrmacht garrison at the dam.

'I wish to speak to the officer in charge,' he asked politely.

'May I ask who is calling?' replied an officious-sounding secretary.

'Hauptmann Roehm of the SS,' he answered.

'I'm afraid Captain Miro is not in the office currently, Sir,' she said.

'Is there nobody I can talk to?'

'No Sir, the men are out on patrol at the moment. You could always call back later,' the receptionist said.

He presumed she must be a civilian due to the tone in which she spoke to someone of his rank. 'No, tell him to ring me at the SS headquarters in Malbork as soon as he returns.'

Roehm fidgeted with his collar while he waited impatiently for Kruse to organise his men, becoming more agitated as time ticked by. When the lieutenant was finally ready, he climbed into the cab of the lead truck while Kruse sat in the second vehicle. Unfolding a map across his thighs, the hauptmann showed the driver the position of the patrol boat's last known location.

A combination of tiredness and anxiety was causing Roehm's head to swim. He had to catch these British soldiers. Otherwise, things would become increasingly difficult for him in Berlin. The Roehm family name had been unpopular with the higher echelons of the Nazi Party ever since Hitler and his uncle, Ernst, had fallen out. The stigma was apparent whenever he met anyone of substantial rank. In private, everyone talked fondly of his father's late brother, but as soon as someone else was in earshot, their comments became much more acerbic.

After thirty minutes in the truck, the small convoy arrived on the eastern bank of the Vistula. Before the vehicle had stopped, Roehm had opened the door and was climbing out. The water flowed tranquilly in front of him. A cold breeze ruffled the hair sticking out from under his cap. A couple of hundred yards up the riverbank, a coal barge was tethered to the opposite bank. He thought nothing of it at first, but an unexplainable sixth sense made him curious.

'Damn, we're on the wrong side of the river,' he muttered to himself. 'Get back in the trucks!'

Hauling himself back into the cab, he instructed the driver to take them over to the other side. The throaty engine started. The driver crunched into first gear before driving slowly over the uneven riverbank. They lurched over the bumpy ground before rejoining the tarmac, gathering speed as they travelled along the leafy country lanes.

The driver slowed as they approached a stone bridge. A barrier, obviously erected hastily, spanned the road on the other side. The taller of two SS guards whispered something to his colleague before walking towards the driver. Roehm beckoned the sentry over as he wound down the window.

'Have you seen anything out of the ordinary?' the hauptmann asked.

'No, Sir,' the squad leader said after saluting. 'You're the first people we've seen since we arrived a few hours ago.'

'If you see anything suspicious, please contact the SS headquarters at Malbork immediately,' Roehm said, before adding, 'Keep up the good work.'

He closed the window and waited for the barrier to rise.

They made their way down to the river again, stopping a few yards from the barge. The hauptmann ran along the riverbank, scrutinising its external appearance. Nothing looked out of place, but he knew this had something to do with the British soldiers. Kruse and the other infantrymen jogged to catch up with him.

'Search the barge!' ordered the lieutenant, drawing level with Roehm.

Three SS soldiers stepped forward and climbed over the side onto the tiller deck. They removed the safety catches from their weapons and readied themselves. The lead soldier looked at the hauptmann, who nodded his confirmation. He forcibly kicked open the wooden door which led down to the barge's interior. As soon as his foot made contact with the door, a massive explosion rocked the barge, blowing off the soldier's lower leg. Letting out a sickening scream, he fell backwards onto the deck. The other two soldiers were killed instantly in the blast, one thrown into the river, the other slumped lifelessly against the deck rail.

'You,' Roehm bellowed at the soldiers nearest to him who had witnessed the grim scene. 'Get them onto the bank.'

A couple of soldiers waded into the water, then dragged their dead comrade back to the shore while the screaming, injured soldier was lowered carefully into the arms of a group of men. The lieutenant rushed to the wounded man, administering firm pressure to the blood vessels in his groin, attempting to stop the bleeding from his mutilated leg until a tourniquet could be applied.

A young, fair-headed man, wearing a Red Cross armband, sprinted along the bank, commenced bandaging the soldier's lower limb and giving him some morphine from an ampoule.

'Don't just stand there,' Roehm shouted to anyone who was listening. 'Search the area!'

The soldiers scattered as the hauptmann marched over to Kruse.

'Well, that leaves us in no doubt. The British are responsible for the disappearance of the patrol boat,' he commented, flexing his leather-gloved fingers.

After twenty minutes, a private came running. 'Lieutenant, Lieutenant,' he called.

Roehm and Kruse hurried towards him.

'I think you should see this,' said another ashen-faced squaddie standing at the water's edge.

They ducked under some low trees, then scrambled through to where some of the others had gathered. Pushing his way to the front, Roehm struggled to interpret what he was looking at. Embedded in the undergrowth was the missing Wehrmacht boat. Its propeller had gouged a deep scar into the forest floor, coming to rest at an angle up against a copse of trees.

The vessel was heavily pock-marked with bullet holes, the deck stained with dried blood.

'Is there any sign of the crewmen?' Roehm asked an unteroffizier who had climbed onto the beleaguered craft.

'They're all dead, Sir,' he replied reluctantly.

'Bag them up and load them onto the truck,' Kruse said, heading back out to the water's edge. 'Keep an eye out for any more booby traps.'

The two officers emerged from the undergrowth, deep in conversation.

'I'll instruct Berlin to inform their families,' Kruse said gravely.

Roehm nodded, staring out across the water. Two soldiers walked past, carrying one of the dead bodies covered with a sheet. He asked the men to stop. Pulling back the cover, he revealed the corpse of the pilot of the boat with the back of his head missing. From their position, they could see right into the vault of his skull. Kruse doubled up and vomited uncontrollably. Roehm replaced the sheet, letting the two stretcher-bearers continue their grim duty.

'We need to find them and make them pay for this,' Roehm said.

'I'll further increase the security on this side of the river,' the lieutenant mumbled, trying to collect himself.

Roehm paused before speaking, 'I want foot patrols up and down the riverbanks as far as the Pomeroze Industrial Area. Also, I think we should ask our friends the Luftwaffe to fly continually up and down the river to see if they can spot them from the air.'

Kruse nodded.

***

After several hours of trudging through the dense forest, the small group of British soldiers could see the dam. The light had begun to fade at around four o'clock. By five, the daylight had all but vanished, replaced by the dim glow of the moon. They had made their way up to higher ground so they could keep track of the comings and goings from the industrial complex in the valley below. The relative silence was shattered by a plane appearing overhead. Its spotlights raked the forest, causing them to press themselves against the surrounding trees.

Once it had passed, the four of them sat down, all

eyes focussing on Henry.

'If you find yourself separated from the rest of us, you must be back here by zero three hundred hours,' he said. 'Whatever happens, we'll be leaving at three. So, if you're not here, I'll assume you've been captured or killed, and we shall leave without you.'

'If we're late, what should we do?' Travers asked.

'If you are late, you'll have to make your own way to the pickup,' Henry said. 'Our rendezvous is at midnight tomorrow at the lake to the north of the town of Prebensz, about twenty-five miles west of here.'

'What if we miss it?' O'Shea asked.

'Trust me, you don't want to do that,' Henry said. 'If you miss the pickup, you basically have two options. You can either make your own way back to Britain or alternatively, you can hand yourselves over to the Germans. Hopefully, you'll spend the rest of the war as a POW.'

O'Shea fidgeted uncomfortably.

'My advice to you is, if you're stuck here on your own, make your way to one of the big cities. Then, make contact with the Polish resistance. They should be able to help you out of the country. But be careful you are not sold down the river by someone posing as a friend. If we succeed tonight, the entire Fourth Army will be out looking for us.'

Henry looked around the group. They were listening intently.

'Be under no illusions,' he continued. 'They'll want to make an example of us for the German propaganda machine.'

No one spoke for several minutes as they mulled over the grim possibilities.

Henry broke the awkward silence. 'Alf, what's the state of play with the explosives?'

'Remember these?' he said, unclipping one from his backpack. 'They're new, the Army has never used them,

141

but don't let that bother you. The two key things are: they're waterproof and weighted. They sink to the riverbed, so they are perfect for blowing up dams. All you have to do is set the clock, prime them, then drop them in the water next to something you want to blow up. Make sure you don't throw them too far from the dam because all they'll do is cause a big splash. Just remember, they need to be right next to the wall.

'I don't like it,' O'Shea said bitterly. 'I mean, we've not even practised with these explosives, and now we're expected to use them for real. What if they don't work?'

'These have been specifically designed for this mission,' Henry butted in before O'Shea's negativity gripped the whole group. 'They only arrived the day before we flew out. There was no time for us to practise, but I'm assured by the major they'll work fine. We have to ensure they land in the water close to the dam—right, Alf?'

'That's right,' Morrison said with a nod. 'They function in the same way to what we used back in Aldershot, the only difference is they're waterproof.'

'It feels like years since we were in England,' said Travers. 'I can't remember what we had to do with them.'

'Don't panic, mate. The explosives are fairly simple to use,' Morrison reassured him. 'Think of the timer as a small alarm clock. The difference being, you don't want to be lying next to it when it rings.'

No one laughed at Alf's feeble attempt at humour.

'What time are we setting the clocks for?' Morrison asked.

'Four o'clock,' Henry said. 'That'll give us an hour to get as far away as possible before they go off. Once they go off, things are likely to heat up.'

'Surely they'll know we're here by then?' asked Travers.

'No!' Henry replied. 'We can't go in guns blazing. We have to sneak in, plant the devices, and leave unnoticed. Remember, there are only four of us. We can't draw too much attention to ourselves, or we'll never get out of here alive.'

Sitting on the ground, everyone listened to the rest of Henry's briefing.

***

It was ten o'clock in the evening, and Captain Miro had not returned Roehm's call. He paced back and forth, irritated, while a tired and hassled Agnes tried to contact the garrison at the Industrial Area again. The secretary shrugged as it continued to be unanswered.

'Do I have to do everything myself?' he muttered to himself.

Miss Trinke kept quiet, placing the earpiece of the telephone back onto its cradle, avoiding making eye contact with the hauptmann. Roehm grabbed his overcoat from the hat stand in the corner of the office and stormed out. Barging past Kruse in the corridor, he hurried down the main staircase and out into the cold night air. The hauptmann tried to open the rear door of the squad car, but there was no sign of his driver. This was the final straw. He started ranting at the top of his voice, mostly expletives, at anyone or anything.

After a few minutes, Roehm's driver ran out, struggling to put on his jacket, while, simultaneously, trying to eat a chicken leg.

'Sorry, Sir,' he mumbled with his mouth full.

Roehm scowled as the flustered man fumbled with his keys.

'Take me to the Pomeroze Industrial Area as fast as you can,' he demanded.

'Yes, Sir,' replied the driver. 'I'll need to take a brief look at the map.'

The hauptmann fidgeted irritably in the back of the car as the driver worked out the route by torchlight.

'It'll take us several hours, Sir. The roads over that way look appalling.'

'Just get me there as quickly as possible.'

16

The four British soldiers were making their final preparations when searchlights illuminated the sky. Unperturbed by the interruption, Henry returned to the task of ensuring none of his kit squeaked or rattled. It would be disastrous if their position was revealed by a loose piece of equipment not appropriately secured.

Morrison screwed the lid onto the camouflage paint before returning the small, shallow tin to the side pocket of his rucksack. Next, he opened the body of the backpack and pulled out his 'waterproof bomb.' He turned it over in his hand, examining it. The device was quite weighty, and he looked forward to a time when he did not have to lug it around.

'Be honest with me,' O'Shea said, handing his explosives to Alf. 'Are these safe?'

'We've carried them this far without them going off,' he said, assuming Pat wanted him to carry it for him.'

'I mean, won't all the running around set them off?'

'No, it'll be fine. You could play football with it, providing it's not primed.'

'I'm not convinced. You know I'm not meant to have one of these, being a medic and all.'

'The mission is more important than the individual,' Henry interjected. 'You'll have to carry your own.'

Alf smiled, placing the device forcibly back into O'Shea's hands.

The four men descended the hillside nimbly, stopping on the outskirts of the industrial estate. The night sky was dominated by the silhouette of the tall furnace towers looming over the rows of warehouses and workshops.

Crouching behind a stone wall, he checked the compass bearing. As they were about to set off, torchlight appeared at the far end of the road. The British soldiers pressed their bellies against the cold earth, staying as low as possible to the ground. Travers flicked off his weapon's safety catch in preparation, but Alf placed a hand on the young man's shoulder and shook his head, prompting him to put it back on.

Watching the two men approach, Henry removed his combat knife from the scabbard on his leg. The guards were so close he could hear them talking. Deep in conversation, the two Wehrmacht infantrymen walked past their position, unaware they were being watched. They proceeded along the tarmac before disappearing from view down a side street. Feeling his comrades relax around him, Henry re-sheathed his knife.

The four men crept down a narrow alley, running parallel with the main road. Morrison stopped on the L-shaped path between rows of workshops and peered around the corner. Thirty yards ahead stood three German soldiers, with two Alsatians sitting obediently next to them. Alf turned back, relieved the dogs had given no sign of picking up his scent.

'We're going to have to find another way round' he whispered. 'More guards!'

Raising his eyebrows, Henry waved Travers back down the alley.

Silently, they retraced their steps until the teenager, now at the front of the group, raised his right arm, bringing them to a halt. The sergeant wormed his way forward, his eyes following the young lad's outstretched hand to a window in a building which was slightly ajar. He nodded approvingly.

Travers slowly eased it open, reaching inside and removing items from the internal sill. With Henry and O'Shea's help, the soldier clambered through into the workshop. His backpack and weapon were passed through to him, which he dumped on the floor. Crouching on a counter, Travers attempted to pull his sergeant through. Suddenly, at the other end of the vast room, he heard somebody rattling a key in the lock. Panicking, he let go of Henry, waving him away. With no time to think, the teenager gathered his equipment and crawled under a workbench.

The door opened as he struggled out of sight. From the oily grime, he observed a man carrying a torch amble down one side of the room. From his untidy appearance, Travers assumed the man was a caretaker rather than a soldier.

The man mumbled as he walked to the open window and slammed it down. Trembling with fear, Travers realised he was urinating uncontrollably. Oblivious to the teenager's presence, the caretaker locked the window using a key he wore on a chain hanging from his belt. Continuing to talk to himself, he completed his circuit of the room before locking the door behind him.

Embarrassed and petrified, Travers lay under the workbench, his trousers damp and cold against his skin. After his anxiety had dissipated, he summoned enough courage to slide out and approached the window.

He forced the frame, but the lock would not budge. It had been replaced recently and was too strong for him to open with his bare hands.

By the exit, he found a small office. Closing the door, he grappled around for a few seconds before locating a cord dangling next to the entrance. A bulb in the ceiling emitted a fierce light in the windowless room. A desk occupied the majority of the small room, and his eyes adjusted to the brightness. To Travers' disappointment, there was nothing except a pile of receipts and a pen holder. Next, he opened the drawers underneath, but inside was only a couple of ledger books and unimportant papers. Disappointed, he swore under his breath.

Mounted on the wall in front of him was a steel box secured with a padlock. Travers' first instinct was to wallop it with his rifle, but the risk of alerting the caretaker, or even the guards outside, stopped him. Looking around, he noticed the receipts on the desk were held together with a paperclip. He unwound it, then started jiggling it inside the padlock.

Frustratingly, Travers failed to move the tumblers within the lock. Beads of sweat were forming on his forehead as he continued to wiggle the piece of wire without success. Just as he was about to give up, the bar popped open with a satisfying click. He clawed the door back only to find two long door keys hanging on hooks inside; neither looked as if it would unlock the window.

Downhearted, he switched off the light and ventured back into the workshop. At the far end of the room, he could see a curious face looking in. Relieved it was his sergeant peering in, Travers scurried towards the window.

'The caretaker locked it,' the teenager mouthed exaggeratedly.

Henry could not figure out what the young lad was trying to say, so the young soldier tried again, but he was no wiser. Next, he performed an exaggerated charade, before Henry finally understood.

'A key,' he said, gesturing with his hands.

'I can't find one,' Travers replied, shaking his head.

Trying not to cry, the teenager looked away. A pair of pliers lay on the counter near to his knee; he must have moved them when he crawled in. He was surprised he had missed them when looking earlier. Not wasting any time, he picked them up and gripped the bar of the lock. Squeezing with all his might, it offered surprisingly little resistance before snapping.

Travers pulled the broken stub out of the way, then gently slid open the window. Henry crawled through, followed promptly by Morrison and O'Shea. When everyone was inside, Travers closed it before joining the rest of them on the floor.

'That was a bit scary,' he apologised, thankful the darkness concealed his damp clothing.

'Yeah, I bet it was,' Alf said. 'I didn't expect there to be anyone in here.'

'No, me neither,' said Henry. 'Anyway, we'd better move out before he comes back. How are we going to get out of here?'

'There are two keys in the office down there,' Travers said. 'One of them might open the workshop door. Hopefully, the other will unlock an outside door.'

'Come on,' Henry said. 'We're on a tight schedule.'

The four of them made their way to the other end of the cavernous room. The teenager crept in and fumbled around until he retrieved the keys, then scuttled back to the others waiting at the door. The first key fitted, but would not turn, but the second unlocked the door. After Henry was satisfied the coast was clear, they moved out into a dark corridor, illuminated periodically by the transient glare of the distant searchlights. They advanced sequentially through the ground floor of the building, occasionally hearing someone walking around upstairs.

In the centre of the property, a flight of stairs led up to the next level, and a wooden door provided a route outside. Henry was about to proceed down the corridor opposite when a door slammed at the top of the steps, followed by the sound of footsteps descending. He took up a position behind the foot of the staircase, waving the other three men down the far corridor.

Carrying his torch, the caretaker came down the last

few steps. The man paused at a row of coats and overalls which hung on hooks next to the entrance door. Holding his knife, Henry waited impatiently as the old man struggled into an old overcoat, unlocked the wooden doors, and left.

As soon as the door locked again, he crept to where the others were waiting.

'Sarge, Travers has found a way out,' the medic said softly, spotting the sergeant approaching.

'Good,' he said, re-sheathing his blade. 'The caretaker seems to have gone home for the night. That's one less thing to worry about.'

O'Shea and Alf crouched in the corridor with guns drawn while Travers and Henry made their way towards the door at the far end.

'I don't know what's on the other side of this, Sarge,' the teenager said. 'But the key fits the lock.'

'Right, remove the safety catch from your weapon,' said Henry. 'But don't fire unless we're fired upon. Understand?'

'Yep,' smiled Travers.

'If we get into a firefight, we're going to have to retrace our steps back to the workshop, out through the window, and fight our way back up into the hills. We don't want to become trapped in this building.'

Travers nodded grimly.

The young soldier eased the door open a few inches. Henry peered around the edge before creeping outside. They were in a delivery yard; a couple of civilian trucks were parked up ready for loading the next day. Once Alf and O'Shea were through the door, Travers went to lock it, but Henry stopped him, in case they had to flee through the building.

On the other side of the yard, an eight-foot-high, chain-link fence, topped with barbed wire, separated them from the dam complex. One by one, the four men dashed to the cover of a small group of trees.

'We'll climb over one at a time,' Henry said. 'Make sure you put your safety catches back on. We don't want anyone's weapons discharging as we're going over.

Everyone nodded.

'Once you're over, take cover behind those gorse bushes,' he instructed. 'Clear? Right, Pat, you go first!'

O'Shea agreed grudgingly.

As soon as the searchlights had passed, the medic launched himself onto the wire fence. He scaled it adeptly, dropping to the ground on the far side. Henry threw his items over. O'Shea gathered his things and headed for the gorse.

The lights came around once more. When the darkness returned, he signalled for Travers to set off. He too climbed over without difficulty and picked up his belongings. Henry went next. Once across, he slung his weapon over his shoulder, then dragged his pack to where the other two were hiding.

Alf waited nervously for light to complete their cycle. Once it had disappeared, he threw his MP-38 over the fence, then launched his backpack. It skimmed the barbed wire and fell back down onto the same side. He tried a second time, but it happened again. It was only on the third attempt that the pack successfully made it over. Realising there was not enough time for him to climb over before the probing beam returned, he took cover in the yard.

He prayed the guards operating the searchlights would not see the backpack. Expecting a siren to blare at any moment, he waited anxiously among the trees.

The bright light came and went, but thankfully there were no sirens. Sighing, he scaled the fence to be met by Travers, who grabbed his pack and led him to the others.

'That was lucky,' the young soldier said. 'They didn't see it.'

'Yeah, I think we got away with it,' Morrison said.

'Okay,' said Henry, refocusing them. 'We can't hang

around. So, we go in, plant the explosives along the whole length of the dam, then leave just as quickly. Now we're this close, there's going to be enemy everywhere. We'll coordinate our movements with both the searchlights and the guards. We're going to work in pairs. Alf and O'Shea, any problems?'

The two men shook their heads.

'Good,' he said. 'Terry, you're with me. Okay?'

Travers nodded.

They navigated the open land, before stopping at a boulder to look down onto the dam and the vast expanse of water. Henry studied the patterns of the guards and searchlights.

'Travers, you and I will disable the sentries. Keep the noise to a minimum, so use your blade. Remember, we can't leave bodies lying around as they'll be seen by the lights.'

The teenager smiled uncomfortably.

Speaking to the entire group, the sergeant said, 'I suggest we go back the same way we came in, back through the workshop. Once your team has placed their bombs, leave. Don't wait for the others. We'll all meet up again in the forest, okay? Let's go and good luck.'

The four men sneaked through a succession of trees and bushes until they stood next to a large, whitewashed building. The searchlights moved around again, causing them to press their bodies against the wall.

In the momentary, bright light, they could see a solitary guard walking along the single-lane road which crossed the dam.

'The daft buggers have only one soldier patrolling it,' Alf said under his breath. 'This should be easy enough.'

The Wehrmacht guard turned, then started to walk back towards them.

'Right, Terry, get ready,' he said to the nervous-looking teenager.

Travers unclipped his pack and handed it to his

sergeant. Blade in hand, he waited uneasily as the enemy soldier approached. The lights passed again. The guard, who was no more than a few feet away from their position, turned through one hundred and eighty degrees and set off back across the dam. Travers sneaked out from the shadows and stealthily pursued him.

From behind, he slammed his left hand over the guard's mouth and plunged the knife into the poor soldier's throat in one flowing movement. The blade severed the windpipe above the sternum, rendering the soldier incapable of making any noise. He twisted the knife before pulling it out, causing blood to spurt from wound. The solider tried to cry out but could only produce harsh, rasping breaths as air escaped from the hole in his neck. Grappling with the ailing soldier, he bundled the wounded man into the water. Now, he had to find somewhere to hide, but there was nowhere.

'Come on, Travers,' Henry whispered to himself.

With only seconds left, the young soldier climbed over the side and hung onto the wall by his fingertips. The searchlights illuminated the empty road temporarily. Henry breathed a sigh of relief.

Travers' arms and shoulders burned as his entire body was supported by his fingers. His feet dangled a few inches above the lake as he clung to the rough stone. After what seemed like an eternity, the lights moved on. The teenager scrambled back over, just as Morrison and O'Shea ran past.

His sergeant greeted him. 'Great work,' Henry said, handing the pack and weapon back to him. 'Let's get out of here.'

They sprinted as fast as they could, before hunkering down in their predetermined positions next to the stone wall. Travers unclipped his explosives from his backpack and set the timer for four o'clock. He dropped the bomb into the water near the middle of the dam just as Alf had taught him. Henry did the same, about a quarter of the distance from the bank. Once deployed, the two men raced to the cover of the whitewashed building.

17

Below, the searchlight continued to illuminate the valley periodically.

'They must have been captured,' Travers said restlessly. 'We should go.'

'No! We said we would leave at three,' snapped Henry. 'If there is still no sign of them then, we'll go.'

There were only ten minutes to go, and O'Shea and Morrison had still not returned to the forest clearing. He could not understand it. They had been right behind him when they left the dam. His stomach knotted. Where were they? When they flew out of England, he had been the leader of a group of seven. Now, possibly, only two remained.

From his vantage point, Henry looked down at the complex. It struck him that nothing had changed. The area was in total darkness, except for the probing swathe of light. If they had been detained, he expected there to be much more activity, sirens, lights, or something, but there was nothing. Where were they?

'It's three o'clock, Sarge,' Travers announced cautiously. 'They're still not here. We have to leave before those explosives go off.'

Sadly, his watch confirmed what the teenager had said. After one last look down into the valley, he nodded reluctantly before slipping on his backpack.

'C'mon then,' he said, the two of them setting off over the ridge towards Prebensz.

***

Roehm was exhausted. The day had been tough, and the journey in the squad car had left him drained. It was a little before three. He wound down the window, relieved to find everything was peaceful. They followed the river as it snaked across the flood plain towards the Pomeroze Industrial Estate. The vehicle stopped briefly at a checkpoint before continuing along a narrow road which climbed above the water. He was grateful when they pulled up outside a whitewashed building next to the dam. Stepping out, he stretched his weary body. The feel of the cold night air on his skin gave him a little extra energy, but he knew he needed to sleep soon.

It was the only place large enough to house the number of men garrisoned there, so he proceeded briskly up the stone steps, which led to some impressive doors. When he reached the top, he could not believe his eyes. In front of him, two Wehrmacht guards slept on a flagstone platform. One leaned back in his chair, neck fully extended with his mouth gaping. The other curled up beside him. Next to them, an automated searchlight revolved relentlessly, illuminating the night sky in arcs of light. Roehm's blood boiled.

'Incompetent fools,' he muttered tersely to himself.

Drawing his pistol out of its holster, he held the tip of the barrel against the nearest soldier's forehead. The cold metal against his skin made him jump.

'Where is your commanding officer?' Roehm

demanded.

The soldier sat bolt upright with his eyes wide open, the severity of the situation giving him instant clarity of mind.

'Don't make me ask you again,' he taunted, pulling back the hammer on his handgun.

'The captain is in the barracks, Sir,' said the terrified soldier.

'Take me to him, NOW!'

The quaking soldier struggled to his feet, nudging his colleague with his foot. Roehm re-holstered his gun as the young soldier's hand unlocked the wooden doors with a key from his pocket. Once inside, they continued down a dimly lit corridor before stopping at a room at the far end. The anxious man tentatively knocked on the door.

There was no reply, so Roehm banged impatiently with his gloved fist.

After a few seconds, a sleepy voice asked, 'What is it?'

'Sir, the SS are here to see you,' the nervous soldier said.

A wave of satisfaction washed over the hauptmann as he listened to the frantic movement inside. Moments later, a bespectacled captain appeared through a crack in the door. Roehm barged in, almost knocking over the man.

'I am SS Hauptmann Andreas Roehm. What kind of unit do you run here?'

'Sorry?' yawned Captain Miro, slightly perplexed.

'Am I speaking a foreign language, or do I have to ask everything twice around here? What kind of unit do you run here?'

'We're tasked with defending the dam and the surrounding area,' the captain replied. 'As interesting as these questions are, hauptmann, I am sure they could wait until the morning?'

'No! They can not,' Roehm shouted, clearly irritated by this officer's lackadaisical attitude. 'I found two of your men fast asleep at their post.'

Without thinking, Miro said, 'But the barges don't travel on the river at night.'

Not able to believe what he was hearing, Roehm's face reddened further. 'Are you saying it is acceptable for men to sleep while on duty?'

'No! No, I am not. Anyway, what is your business here, Herr Hauptmann? I'm sure the SS has better things to do than drive around the countryside in the middle of the night enquiring about the professionalism of the Wehrmacht.'

'I rang your office yesterday, but you did not return my call,' Roehm said with a supercilious air. 'Why?'

'Ah, yes! I received your message. I planned on calling you first thing in the morning.'

Roehm rolled his eyes.

'If you are told something is urgent, that tends to suggest it can't wait until the next morning,' he said. 'For your information, British soldiers have been seen in this area. I suspect this dam complex may be their target.'

The captain was suddenly awake and listening.

'Drag your men out of their grubby beds and get them out on patrol,' he said forcibly. 'Mark my words, if anything happens, I shall let the Führer know you are personally responsible. Do I make myself clear?'

Miro nodded, grabbing his uniform jacket from a hook on the back of the door. Once dressed, he turned to the soldier standing in the doorway and ordered him to wake Unteroffizier Klein.

The soldiers lined up outside the barracks; most were confused as to what was going on—specifically, why an SS hauptmann had woken them in the early hours of the morning. Miro walked back and forth in front of those assembled, explaining this was not a drill. He tried to explain they believed the dam was a likely target for a band of British saboteurs while Roehm stood menacingly behind him. With the aid of Klein, the men were divided into groups and ordered to search every inch of the complex.

Once the men had dispersed, Klein came over to where Miro and Roehm were talking.

'Sir, one of my men is unaccounted for,' the unteroffizier said, addressing the captain.

Miro went to speak, but Roehm beat him to it. 'Who is he?'

'Private Faulks, Sir,' the young officer replied. 'He's meant to be on foot patrol, but there's no sign of him.'

'Faulks,' exclaimed the captain. 'He's one of our most diligent soldiers.

The hauptmann looked at Miro despairingly before saying, 'Let me know when he turns up.'

Roehm sat on the stone steps leading up to the barracks. The landscape was speckled with torchlight from the soldiers searching the complex. Letting out an exhausted sigh, he stared out across the lake behind the dam. His body ached, but he had a horrid feeling of uneasiness. The missing soldier confirmed the British were nearby. He was sure of it.

An object drifted into Roehm's peripheral vision, distracting him. Something was in the water. He squinted hard, trying to work out what it was. Strangely, it did not reflect the moonlight as the rest of the lake did. Realisation dawned on him; it was a man's lifeless body. The mystery of Private Faulks was over. Roehm sprang to his feet and headed for the water's edge, but an explosion threw him back onto the steps. From where he lay, he could see a pillar of water rising into the air. It seemed to hang for several seconds before cascading into the valley. Several other explosions followed in quick succession, visibly shaking the dam.

Despite being a hundred yards from the water's edge, pieces of masonry peppered the ground around him. A small fragment stung his cheek as it whizzed past him. He watched helplessly as a trickle of water seeped through cracks which had developed. Ominously, the structure let out a sickening groan as the rate of flow increased.

Miro ran from the barracks in time to witness the spectacular failure of the dam, releasing a roaring torrent. Roehm smashed his fist angrily on the step next to him.

'The Führer will hear about this, Captain,' he said, his voice livid.

Miro said nothing.

'Gather your men. The British can't be too far away. I hope for your sake we find them.'

Roehm made his way inside, marching along the corridor to Miro's office. Picking up the telephone, he attempted to call Kruse in Malbork, but the line was dead. He rattled the receiver's cradle, but it made no difference. His driver had joined Miro on the steps. They were watching the final demise of the dam as Roehm emerged from the building.

'Take this letter to Lieutenant Kruse,' he ordered. 'I need him to send us reinforcements as soon as possible. Give it to him, and no one else. I don't care how you get there, drive across fields if you have to. Just get it to him as soon as you can, okay?'

The driver nodded, then started the engine.

18

Unable to sleep, Viktor crept from the cart and made breakfast for the rest of the family. He woke Zofia and the children and then hurried them during breakfast. By five o'clock, everything had been cleared away, and they were back on the road. He had hoped their early start would have allowed them to make better progress, but as with most of this trip, their plans had not come to fruition. Frustratingly, they had come to a complete standstill. A queue of traffic wound into the distance.

'Can anything else possibly go wrong? he muttered to himself.

Sensing his frustration, Zofia placed her hand on his knee, but it did little to ease his agitation. He jumped from the cart and walked along the queue, talking to the various tradesmen and other refugees; all victims of the traffic.

'Apparently, the bridge has been washed away,' a grizzled farmer said, sitting high up on a hay cart.

'What? It hasn't rained that hard!'

'Oh, no! They say there has been a problem with the dam at Pomoroze. The whole valley is flooded. Hundreds of people have been killed.'

'How awful.' Viktor's face saddened. 'When do you

think they'll reopen the road?'

'A soldier came by about half an hour ago. He said we're going to be here for at least a couple of hours. They're waiting for some engineers from Danzig to repair the damage.'

'I'm trying to get to Olsztyn. Is there any other way through?'

'I don't fancy your chances. They say all the bridges around here have been knocked out by the flood. So, wherever you go, I suspect you'll find the same problem.'

'Thanks,' he said despondently, trudging back to his cart.

Viktor walked back with his hands in his pockets, the weight of the world on his shoulders.

'What is it?' Zofia asked.

'There's been a flood. We're going to be here for a few hours.'

She shook her head in disbelief. 'What are we going to do now?'

'Just wait, I suppose. There's not much else we can do, is there?'

After an hour of waiting, the two boys were becoming restless and whined continually. To prevent the usual squabbles, Zofia suggested they should all go for a walk. Viktor declined immediately, saying he should stay with the cart. So, taking the two children by the hand, she headed into the trees at the side of the road.

Their shoes frequently disappeared as they struggled down the soft, muddy hill. Zofia held them tightly, stabilizing herself as they descended the slippery bank. Peter was the first to stumble, but she managed to pull him to his feet before he touched the ground. A couple of steps later, she caught her foot awkwardly and went over on her ankle, landing on her knees.

An expanse of fast-flowing water prevented them from going further. Standing at the water's edge, Zofia took in the unusual scenery. The river was clearly much deeper than usual. Water submerged some of the trees and someone's boot lay at her feet next to an unhinged cupboard door. Her thoughts turned to the bakery in Danzig. What state would it be in now? Would it even be standing?

Peter attempted to show Niklos how to skim stones on the river. The boy was unable to copy his older brother and was beginning to sulk. Peter tried to show him again, but the younger child's pebble sank as soon as it made contact with the water. Niklos started to cry, so Zofia intervened.

'Choose a long, flat one,' she whispered.

The young boy scrambled around, trying to find a suitable stone.

'No, that one's too round.'

Niklos showed her another.

'No. That one will be too heavy. What about this one?' she said, pointing to a stone about the right size and shape.

He held it in his hand, about to lob it.

'Hang on,' she said. 'The secret is to throw underarm, like this, so the stone just touches the surface and bounces.'

Zofia bent down, picking up another. Having not done this since she was a little girl, her recollections brought a smile to her face. She went through the motions of swinging her arm so Niklos could observe how to do it.

'You try,' she said encouragingly.

Concentration was etched over the little boy's face. His tongue stuck out of the side of his mouth, firmly held between his teeth. Every sinew was focused on making this stone bounce. He planted his feet, then swung his arm as he had been shown. The stone hit the water, bounced once, before plopping under the surface. Niklos jumped up and down, cheering. The enthusiastic celebration was infectious. Soon the three of them were hugging each other joyfully.

'Well done,' said Zofia. 'Now let's see how many times you can make it jump.'

The boys scoured the ground for appropriate pebbles, while she sat on a rock, staring out across the river. More debris floated by—pieces of wood from a doorframe and, to Zofia's surprise, an armchair bobbed past in the surging current.

'Those poor people,' she thought.

Niklos and Peter continued to skim stones on the water, unable to understand that the items floating down the river had belonged to someone.

After an hour, she decided it was time to head back. The road might be open.

'C'mon you two, it's time to go,' she said.

'Can't we stay a few more minutes?' asked Peter.

'One more throw each and then we're going.'

The two boys took their remaining turns before obediently taking their mother's hands.

She took one last look at the river as the bloated body of an old woman floated past. The old lady was obviously dead, her body swollen and purple. The corpse had weed around its face, her leg grossly deformed. Zofia quickly looked at her children, but they were concentrating on climbing the hill and had not seen what was behind them. Silently holding their hands, she climbed back up to the road.

As they emerged through the trees, a large truck, emblazoned with Nazi insignia, headed for the front of the queue at speed. This was shortly followed by two troop transporters full of SS soldiers.

After the vehicles had passed, Zofia led the children towards the cart.

'What have you been up to?' Viktor asked the boys as they approached.

'I've learnt how to skim stones,' Niklos said proudly.

'Well done,' he said.

'Mine skipped six times,' bragged Peter.

'Six?' their father said with mock astonishment in his voice. 'That really is clever.'

Viktor turned to Zofia, who was pale and shaken.

'It looks as if they're here to repair the bridge. Hopefully, we'll be able to set off soon.'

She did not reply.

'What's the matter?' he asked, noticing his wife's demeanour.

'I don't want to talk about it,' she said tearfully.

'Is it the boys?'

'No. I'll tell you later when they're asleep.'

He put his arm around her waist and kissed her on the forehead.

They sat in silence as the soldiers constructed a temporary bridge over the river. Every time Viktor tried to speak, she would close down the conversation, refusing to make eye contact. After two long, painfully quiet hours, the road reopened.

19

Daylight had begun to fade as the cart neared Olsztyn. Ahead, Viktor caught sight of the fields of his parents' farm on the other side of the city. The boys lay in the back, hiding from the early-evening chill under a threadbare blanket. Famous for its surrounding lakes and forest, Olsztyn had been part of many different empires, but since 1932, it had been ruled by the regional Nazi Party. The Germans preferred to call it Allenstein, whereas the native Polish minority called it Olsztyn. There had always been cultural tensions, but he knew his family would be safer here.

To be honest, he had never understood why his parents had come here, leaving behind their family and lifelong friends. In his eyes, Danzig offered everything they could wish for. He could not comprehend why anyone would choose to leave. For one thing, Danzig was much more cosmopolitan, probably due to the port and the many foreign travellers it attracted. In comparison, Olsztyn somehow seemed sleepy and lethargic, a place for visiting rather than inhabiting.

'Nearly there,' he said to Zofia, who snuggled into his side as they plodded along.

'I can't wait. All I want to do is curl up in bed,' she said, stifling a tired yawn.

'I know what you mean,' he smiled, stretching his aching shoulders. 'But, it's going to be a while before we can turn in for the night. The cart will need unloading, the horse will want feeding, then my parents will want to talk.'

'I hope we're not expected to stay up too long making polite conversation,' she said. 'I'm struggling to keep my eyes open as it is.'

'You know what they're like. We haven't seen them in months, so they'll want all the gossip, not to mention news of what's happening in Danzig.'

Zofia rolled her eyes in frustration.

'I'll tell you what,' he said. 'You can sit with them while I get the boys settled for the night. That way we'll get to sleep much quicker.'

'Don't you leave me on my own with them. They're your parents. You talk to them, and I'll put the kids to bed.'

Passing through the impressive high gate in the medieval wall of the city, they trundled along the cobbled streets. He could not help noticing the vast number of pro-Nazi flags decorating the houses and shop fronts. These were new; never before had he seen such strong expressions of German nationalism here.

As they lumbered along, Viktor gazed absentmindedly at the goods on display in the stores. First, there was a jeweller, next door to a greengrocer. At the end of the row stood a bakery, half the size of his premises back in Danzig. From its external appearance, it was making a kingly profit. He smiled to himself. When all this was over, if they had no house to return to, then maybe they could open up shop here in Olsztyn.

'Viktor, look out!' Zofia screamed.

A young woman wearing a bright red headscarf stepped into the path of the horse, pushing a pram in front of her. Pulling back hard on the reins, he caused Miedziak to veer to the left, making the cart mount the pavement. The woman continued across the street, blissfully unaware of the danger.

Viktor struggled to gain control, his forearms aching as he prevented them from fishtailing along the road.

'Whoa, boy!' he said, trying to calm the startled animal.

After a few nervous moments, he finally brought them to a halt. Leaving his seat, he started to pat the frightened horse.

'You're okay,' he said, stroking the anxious horse's neck. 'Not long now, then you can have a well-deserved rest, eh?'

He stroked Miedziak for several minutes until he looked less agitated before starting the final leg of their journey.

'I don't believe it,' Zofia said in hushed tones. 'They didn't wake up.'

Viktor checked over his left shoulder. The two young boys were cuddled together under a blanket, still soundly asleep.

'They'll soon be in warm beds, and then we can relax,' he said.

She smiled, hugging his arm as they set off once more.

They passed the castle with its elaborate, round tower and continued through the inner heart of the city. The trees growing beside the road swayed in the gentle breeze, causing Viktor to instinctively turn up the collar of his overcoat. Half a mile on, the cart rounded a bend, bringing the impressive sight of St. Jacob's cathedral into view, the last landmark before their destination. It gave him a tremendous feeling of relief.

With a jolt, they turned onto the driveway. Viktor's parents appeared at the front door of the black and white farmhouse. His father was a tall, gaunt man who had been quite handsome in his youth. In contrast, his mother, a short, squat lady, wore many layers of clothing which exaggerated her rotund figure.

'Hello, Mama,' he shouted.

Zofia waved halfheartedly.

Woken by the voices, the two boys started calling out to their grandparents. Viktor brought the cart to a standstill next to the house. Instantly, the children jumped down and ran towards them. Niklos grabbed hold of his grandmother's waist as Peter was hoisted aloft by his namesake grandfather.

'Come inside,' said Viktor's mother, embracing her daughter-in-law. 'Supper won't be long.'

Zofia and the boys went into the house as Viktor and his father set about unloading the cart and settling the horse for the night.

'How was the journey, son?' the older man asked, carrying some of their belongings under his arms.

'Awful,' he said. 'I can't see us going back for a long time. We were lucky to get out alive.'

'Were things really that bad? The newspapers said Danzig fell with little resistance.'

'Don't believe the propaganda you're spoonfed by the press. The reason for the 'little resistance' was they bombed the city from the air,' he said.

'Thank God, you all escaped. It sounds terrible.'

'It was truly awful,' said Viktor, unhitching the horse.

The old man frowned as his son recited the horror of the last few days.

'Zofia and I are worried about the boys. I mean, seeing all that, it's bound to affect them, isn't it?'

'They seem okay to me,' the old man said, not knowing what to say.

'It was terrifying. Planes were swooping down and opening fire. I'm hoping they think it's a bad dream.'

Viktor's father placed his arm around his son's shoulders and gave him an awkward hug before they unloaded the rest of the cart in silence.

Zofia popped her head around the door, leading to the kitchen.

'Are you two ready to eat?' she said, more of an instruction than a question.

'Yes, we will,' the older man said, waving to acknowledge her.

Viktor led the weary horse into one of the stalls in the stable block, making sure there was plenty of water and fresh hay before bolting the door.

Heavily laden with boxes, he staggered into the dimly lit kitchen and immediately felt at home. The fire burning in the range, the aroma of freshly baked bread, and his mother ladling steaming stew into bowls comforted him. He placed the items on the floor, taking a chair at the table next to Niklos.

'Not before you've rinsed your hands,' his mother said sternly.

The young boy sniggered as his father, pretending to be a naughty schoolboy, sheepishly walking over to the sink. After washing his hands ostentatiously, Viktor returned to his seat and caught Zofia's eye. She smirked back. It was apparent who ruled the roost in this household. Once everyone was seated, the old lady tore a chunk from a flat, round loaf and then passed it to Zofia. This was an unofficial signal for the family to start eating without fear of reprimand.

The boys wolfed down their food, fighting over second helpings, while Zofia was less than halfway through hers. Despite the pleasant surroundings and a hot meal, all she wanted was to go to bed.

'You look tired, my dear,' Viktor's father said.

'You want to take better care of yourself in your condition,' Viktor's mother said before she could reply.

'I'm fine,' she said. 'Nothing a good night's sleep won't solve.'

'Well, your beds are ready,' his mother said. 'I put hot water bottles in them about an hour ago. They'll be just right by now.'

'Sounds heavenly,' Zofia said.

'Viktor, I'll need some help in the morning,' his father said, changing the subject. 'I need to butcher one of the pigs.'

'It's been a while since I've done it, but I'm sure between us we can do it,' he said, placing a large piece of soup-soaked bread into his mouth.

They washed up while his parents put the children to bed. His father told the story of three brothers—Lech, Czech, and Rus—and their encounter with an eagle. Peter and Niklos' heads started nodding quickly before they drifted off to sleep.

'I think we'll go up now,' he said, hanging a tea towel over the fire guard.

'Of course, you know where everything is, don't you?' his mother said.

'Thanks, Mama.' Zofia kissed her on the cheek.

Viktor walked upstairs, carrying a solitary candle on a wax-encrusted stand. They popped their heads into the boys' bedroom, relieved to find them fast asleep, then walked across the landing to their own room.

After changing into her nightclothes, Zofia washed in the bowl on top of a chest of drawers. She pulled back the bed covers, removed the hot water bottle, and wriggled under the eiderdown.

'Night, my love,' she said, as Viktor unfastened his shirt buttons. 'How nice is it to have a roof over our heads again.'

'It certainly is,' he said, stepping out of his trousers.

He leaned down and kissed her on the lips, but she was already asleep.

'Sweet dreams,' he whispered.

20

The flooding hampered everything. Roads were rendered impassable, and most of the telephone lines were down. Thankfully, the line connecting Pomeroze with Malbork had been restored. Roehm had made it a priority. There had been no further sightings of the British soldiers. It was as if they had disappeared from the face of the earth. He kept replaying the events of the last few days in his head, attempting to recall any clue to where they could be hiding. A thought hit him: Maybe they had linked up with a Polish militia group? Perhaps they were going to be smuggled out of the country? The more he thought about it, the more it made sense. They must be getting help from someone locally; it would explain why they had vanished.

Reaching for the phone, he waited patiently for his call to be connected. He had appointed Kruse to lead the search. Having pulled strings with Wehrmacht High Command, Miro had been given the job repairing the damage caused by the flood.

'Kruse, it's Roehm. Has there been any more contact with the British soldiers?'

'Unfortunately not, Sir,' the familiar voice answered.

'Do you think some of the locals could be shielding

them?'

'I guess so. We should start door-to-door searches in the villages around here.'

'I want every house, factory, and outbuilding searched,' he said. 'It might be worth having a chat with the local police too. They'll be able to tell you who the sympathisers are. I think you should pay them a visit.'

'Okay,' Kruse said, hesitating before speaking again. 'I don't want to appear rude, Sir, but is there a chance of more troops? A door-to-door search is going to be relatively ineffective with the numbers we have.'

'I know, I called Danzig. They're sending a hundred more men to you as we speak. They should be with you within the next couple of hours.'

'SS or Wehrmacht, Sir?' Kruse asked delicately.

'Wehrmacht,' the hauptmann said. 'But, don't worry, they'll report to you temporarily.'

'I can't imagine High Command being happy with an SS officer commanding Wehrmacht troops.'

'They're not, but I told them they had no choice since it was their negligence which led to the loss of the Pomeroze dam.'

Kruse paused, not knowing how to respond. 'Excellent, Sir. I shall keep you informed.'

The line went dead.

Impressed with the young officer, Roehm hung up the receiver. His attention turned to the map in front of him. He located Malbork, then the Pomoroze industrial region. Realistically, how far could they have travelled since the explosion? Surely no more than fifteen or twenty kilometres? He took a pen from a desk drawer and drew a circle around the dam, scrutinising the area within the red line. *Where were they hiding?*

***

Having run throughout the night and most of the subsequent day, every inspiration was burnt and his legs were leaden. Unable to continue, Henry pulled up, gasping hard. Thankful for the opportunity to rest, Travers dropped into the long grass, breathing heavily. Neither of them were capable of speaking. Struggling to his feet, Henry staggered away from the teenager. The world continued to swirl around him, causing him to vomit. He slumped under a tree. It took ten minutes before he was able to crawl over to Travers, who was wincing with every breath.

'How are you doing?' he asked, his head pounding.

'Badly,' Travers said after a few moments.

Henry unclipped his canteen and unscrewed the top, pouring water into his mouth without touching the sides. Having rinsed out the taste of vomit, he spat onto the ground.

'Do you want some?' he said, offering the container to his companion.

'Thanks, Sarge,' Travers panted, wiping it with his sleeve.

'There are only a couple of hours of daylight left. We should try and make it to Prebensz before sundown,' he said.

The teenager nodded, unable to string a sentence together.

By Henry's reckoning, they were only five miles from the outskirts of the town. Travers was still struggling, but Henry helped him to his feet nonetheless. After a swift check of the map and compass, the two men set off again, but at a slower pace.

Every so often, they could see the buildings through the trees.

'Let's find somewhere warm and dry to spend the next few hours,' Henry suggested.

'That would be nice,' Travers smiled. 'Perhaps a place with room service?'

Scanning the skyline, the young soldier nudged Henry, pointing to a steeple peeping over the top of a distant row of shops. Without speaking, they proceeded down a paved lane and across the main road.

The bell tower was high in the middle of the red brick church's facade. At its base were two intricately carved doors that opened straight onto the pavement. Henry stayed hidden as Travers tried the door. The gold handle turned easily, opening the door enough for them to slip inside.

Groping around in near blackness, they explored their surroundings. Slowly, their eyes became accustomed to the poor light. They were in a small entrance vestibule. Ahead of them was a windowed wall with two panelled doors, beyond which were rows of wooden pews. Travers went to lean against a wall but stumbled backwards onto a flight of stone steps which led upwards. Grateful his sergeant had not seen, he leapt to his feet, whispering, 'I wonder where these lead?'

Reaching into the inside pocket of his jacket, Henry pulled out a box of matches, fumbling around before striking one. Waving for the teenager to follow him, he slowly climbed the stone staircase. They arrived on a square landing with a door, similar to the one downstairs, leading to a balcony. In the fading light of the match, it appeared repair work was underway. A decorator's ladder led up to a decorative ceiling, the cloying smell of fresh paint hanging in the air. Climbing up a couple of rungs, he lifted a hatch above him. Inside was a dark, dusty tower occupied predominantly by the bells on their wooden carriages and a maintenance platform. The flame started to burn his hand, instinctively sucking his index finger to soothe the pain. He replaced the cover and slid back down.

Travers opened the door and then stepped onto the

creaking balcony with its many pews. Below, at the front of the church, the altar draped in purple velvet was festooned with candles. Slipping off his backpack, he slumped into one of the pews. A noise came from behind him. It was a simple click, but it was enough to send a shiver down the spine of any soldier. It was the sound of a safety catch being removed from a weapon. He recognised it instantly.

'Halt!' a voice shouted.

Both Henry and Travers froze, reluctantly lifting their arms in unison. Henry's eyes frantically scanned the shadows but could see no one.

After a few seconds the voice spoke again. 'Sarge, is that you?'

Henry breathed a sigh of relief, 'Yes, Alf. Please put the gun down.'

'We thought you'd been captured,' said O'Shea, standing behind them, his weapon pointing at Travers.

'We thought the same about you,' Henry replied, grinning broadly.

'Is it okay to put my hands down?' the teenager asked awkwardly, causing Alf's face to wrinkle into a smile.

The four men sat together on the uncomfortable pews with their kit strewn around them.

'So, what happened to you guys?' asked Travers.

'We planted our explosives and had just made it back across the dam when a squad car stopped right in front of us,' Morrison answered.

'How they didn't see us I'll never know,' interrupted O' Shea.

'We couldn't move, could we?' Alf said, looking at O'Shea. 'So, we crouched behind this low wall.'

'We were there for the best part of an hour.'

'Who was in it?' Henry interjected.

'You will never guess,' the medic said excitedly. 'An SS hauptmann. He was angry about something, even before the bombs went off. He disappeared into the white building and brought out the whole bleeding garrison.'

'I thought we'd had it,' said Morrison.

'Why didn't you make a break for it when he went inside?' asked Travers.

'We couldn't go anywhere, his driver was leaning against the car, having a smoke,' said Alf.

'A bit worrying, isn't it?' Henry said. 'It sounds like this SS officer, whoever he was, knew exactly where we were going to be,'

'Did you see the explosives go off?' the teenager asked eagerly.

'Oh yes,' Morrison said proudly. 'They went off just as planned.'

'You should have seen them,' said O'Shea. 'They caused a massive plume of water which washed the dam clean away.'

'So, how did you manage to get away?' said Travers, continuing with his questions.

'When it blew, we just ran for it,' Alf said. 'We sneaked out when they were all staring at the water.'

'Oh! Sarge, there was water everywhere,' the medic said excitedly. 'They were running around like headless chickens.'

'But how did he know what our target was?' Henry mused.

O'Shea had assured him Mayberry would not have survived with such severe injuries. He knew Tommy would not have given anything away unless he had been tortured. The thought of this put him on edge. The mental image of Tommy being abused was distressing enough, but what if he had told them the details of the pickup? He felt helpless. They had to make the rendezvous. It was too late to relocate or reschedule it; the plane would have already left several hours ago. Whatever happened, they had to take their chances. They had no other option.

From the street came a screech of brakes followed by the sound of hob-nailed boots on cobbles. This jolted

Henry from his ponderings.

'Quick, get up into the bell tower,' he said. 'Don't leave anything behind.'

O'Shea and Morrison gathered their things while Travers and his sergeant climbed into the cramped space. Through the wooden, louvre window, Henry could see an SS troop carrier parked outside. Soldiers ran from house to house, kicking down doors and barking orders, accompanied by shrieks as families were herded into the streets. It was only a matter of time before they entered the church.

'Quickly,' he whispered through the hatch.

O'Shea threw his and Alf's backpack up for them to catch, then Alf clambered up, swiftly followed by the medic.

'Don't leave the ladder down there. Pull it up here,' Henry ordered.

The four men hoisted it into the confined space of the bell tower.

'Careful,' said Henry. 'Try not to hit the bells. We don't want everyone to know we're here.'

With it safely stowed, O'Shea replaced the cover.

They sat silently in the cramped space, unable to move. Through the slats, Henry watched the SS soldiers systematically searching each house, dragging the occupants out into the street. Anyone who put up resistance was beaten severely.

The cold, night air was filled with cries and shouting. Their pleas were ignored as the SS meticulously searched the street. Suddenly, the voices grew louder as the large external doors of the church were opened. From the tower, they could hear the chink of boots on the stone floor.

'Have your weapons ready,' Henry instructed in a barely audible whisper.

In the moonlight coming through the slatted window, he could see the anxious expressions on his colleagues' faces. His own breathing quickening as his finger hovered on the trigger of his machine pistol.

Below, there was much shouting, with the occasional rumble of tables being overturned, their contents clattering to the ground. Worryingly, the footsteps were coming upstairs. From the different voices, Henry estimated there were at least five of them on the balcony and probably a similar number on the lower floor. They would stand no chance if they were discovered.

After twenty minutes or so, the Wehrmacht soldiers begin to drift downstairs and out into the street. A couple of voices started chatting beneath them. Although not able to speak German, Henry discerned it was an officer talking to one of his subordinates. They listened nervously until the two soldiers descended the stairs and left. The group let out a collective sigh as doors scraped shut.

Bringing his index finger up to his lips, Henry looked around at his three comrades. The engine of the troop carrier started. The soldiers, dressed in their grey uniforms with distinctive black collars, climbed back into the vehicles as the engines idled. Finally, the truck drove away.

'Stay as you are,' he ordered in a firm whisper. 'Its nineteen hundred hours. Although it's cramped in here, we're safe for the time being. Let's not take any unnecessary chances. We're nearly home, lads.'

'I suggest O'Shea and Travers keep watch, while Alf and I get some sleep for ninety minutes. At twenty-thirty hours, we'll take over, and you guys can get some shut-eye. We'll aim to leave here at twenty-two hundred. Okay?'

No one spoke; only reluctant nods.

21

The minute hand had not moved since Henry last checked his watch. Images of Mayberry and Scotty, dead and dying, played on his mind. Their twisted bodies seemed to blame him for their predicament. He started to sweat, despite the cold breeze percolating through the louvre window. His thoughts drifted to memories of the secretary back in Aldershot, regretting the missed opportunity. When he returned to England, he would take her out for dinner.

O'Shea quietly removed the hatch cover, allowing Henry to pop his head through to check if it was safe. Thankfully, there was nothing except darkness on the landing below. With a confirmatory nod, Travers and O'Shea lowered the ladder and Henry descended first, closely followed by the others.

'We have two and a half hours to get to the pickup,' he whispered. 'So, we'd better leave now.'

They crouched in the vestibule on the ground floor while O'Shea opened the door, ensuring the coast was clear. The four heavily encumbered men jogged west into the damp, windswept night. As they navigated the back streets, they spotted a couple of uniformed soldiers walking in the town. The Wehrmacht guards appeared more interested in finding a bar than locating them.

After twenty minutes, Prebensz was far behind them. A chilly, easterly breeze laden with fine drizzle made the conditions unpleasant.

'How far is it?' Travers whined, trudging in a roadside ditch alongside a hedgerow.

'About another hour,' replied Henry. 'Now, no chatter. We don't want to be discovered.'

'Can't we walk on the tarmac, Sarge?' the teenager grumbled, stumbling on the uneven ground. 'My feet are killing me.'

'Shhh!' he said, becoming increasingly annoyed. 'We're walking here so if a vehicle comes along we'll have some cover. If you're standing in the middle of the road, you'll be caught in the headlights like a startled rabbit. Now keep quiet.'

Alf grabbed Travers' arm, persuading him not to protest any more.

At the top of a hill, they stared into the eddying mist in the valley. Every now and then, a gap would appear, revealing the reflective surface of a lake.

'That's the rendezvous point,' Henry said excitedly. 'Now, look for a white farmhouse with two outbuildings.'

The four men stood waiting for the fog to clear.

'Over there!' exclaimed O'Shea, pointing down to the far end.

'Okay! We'll take cover in one of the barns. Travers, lead the way.'

They walked in single file down the hillside towards the farmhouse. Their movements hindered by waist-high grass whipping against them in the frequent gusts of wind. Henry surveyed the house. Some of the windows were broken, and no lights shone within.

'Let's settle down in that building,' he said, pointing across a weed-strewn courtyard at the larger of the two barns.

The open-fronted barn contained the rusting hulk of

a tractor and a mound of old hay. They placed their backpacks on the straw-covered floor but continued to carry their weapons.

'Can't we stay in the house?' Travers asked after a few moments. 'The weather's awful, Sarge. I'm sure it'll be warmer in there.'

Henry glared at the young soldier, swallowing hard to avoid losing his temper.

'If we're indoors, we might not hear the plane, whereas if we're out in the barn, we won't miss it,' he said beginning to become irritated.

'Sarge, where will they land?' asked Alf. 'I mean, there's no runway around here, is there?'

'I don't know,' said Henry, having not given it any thought. 'I presume they'll send one of those flying boats.'

'Oh!' said Alf, a little surprised.

'Right! Listen out for it,' Henry said. 'We'll need to let the pilot know it's safe to land.

Sitting on a bale of hay, Henry fidgeted nervously. What if it does not arrive? How would they get out of Poland? What about Mayberry and Tommy Rogers?

After a further twenty minutes, a faint, distant hum began. The sound grew louder until the cyclical noise of propellers was directly above them. He ran outside, but the dense cloud cover obscured his view of the sky. Taking his torch from his pack, he turned it on and started waving it skywards.

A few moments later, the pitch of the engine changed, as the aircraft began its final approach.

'Collect your things,' announced Henry. 'We're going home.'

Travers was the first to see the peculiar-looking plane. It had floats instead of wheels, and four propellers suspended below a single broad wing which spanned the cockpit. They waited impatiently beside the barn as it came in to land. As it touched down on the water, the pilot slipped the engines into reverse before reducing the throttle.

The cold night air suddenly became illuminated by a red flare as German soldiers poured over the valley sides. The deafening machine gunfire opened up all around them.

'Return fire!' Henry cried, bullets throwing up clods of earth near him. 'Make every shot count.'

A grenade exploded at ground level about fifty yards from where they were lying. The explosion threw mud into the air, showering them with debris. Vastly outnumbered, the plane was their only realistic chance of survival. Henry squinted over his shoulder towards the aircraft. It was now nearing the end of the lake.

'O'Shea, Travers! Make for the plane,' he shouted, his voice faltering. 'Alf and I will cover you.'

They did not need to be asked twice. The two men scrambled for the water, as Morrison and Henry returned fire. Looking around, his heart sank. Despite Alf firing repeated bursts at the approaching troops, it was clear they would soon be overrun.

A mortar whistled overhead and exploded near the water's edge; an acrid smoke began to hang in the air.

'Alf, are you ready to go?' he said.

'Yep.'

Travers and O'Shea started to return fire from the plane while Morrison and Henry set off. Bullets whistled past them, as they sprinted across the uneven ground. One passing very close to Henry's left ear. Reaching the shore, he could not find Alf. He scoured the landscape, finally spotting the massive shape of Morrison lying face down about fifty yards away. Slipping off his backpack, Henry made his way towards his stricken colleague. Henry slid into the grassy tussock next to his comrade.

'Are you hit?'

'No, I went over on my ankle. I can't stand.'

Henry placed his left arm around the big man's shoulders and hauled him upright. The two of them moved awkwardly over the grass.

Over his shoulder, he could see the enemy were near. A bullet clipped Henry's helmet, causing him to stumble. His grip weakened, sending Alf to the ground. Henry struggled back to his feet, then began dragging Morrison towards the lake. As he got closer, bullets pinged off the plane. Travers and O'Shea continued to provide covering fire from inside the aircraft as Henry, with his boots in the water, bundled Alf onto the float. The plane lurched under his weight, and the sergeant gave him a forceful shove through the narrow hatch. Thinking everyone was aboard, the pilot increased the throttle.

Buffeted by the spray, Henry scrambled onto the float and edged along the fuselage, inching closer as the plane gained speed. O'Shea leant out of the hatch, his arm outstretched, trying to reach his sergeant. Henry felt something hot hit his right shoulder. A searing pain shot through his body, causing him to lose grip. Like a prize-fighter, disorientated by successive punches, Henry's legs buckled, and he fell backwards into the water.

In indescribable agony, he saw the aircraft rise from the surface and then disappear into the night sky, the soldiers at the water's edge continuing to fire at it.

A couple of men from the crowd waded out and dragged Henry's soaking body back to the shore. Expecting another bullet, he lay in the shallows, paralysed by pain, cold and exhausted. One of the soldiers kicked him repeatedly about the chest and abdomen, spurred on by the cheers of the onlookers. Each jarring blow exacerbated the ache in his shoulder, making him wince, but he was determined not to cry out. He tried to raise his hands to protect himself, but moving his arm hurt more than the actual blows, so he just lay there. An angry face stared into Henry's eyes; his uniform was different from the others. Henry presumed he must be an officer, but he could not see any insignia.

The officer cleared his throat, producing a droplet of

saliva which hung from his lips. Its slimy, pendulous attachment gradually narrowed, before the globule started to fall towards Henry. Instinctively, he turned his head, causing a searing pain in his shoulder. The baying crowd roared victoriously as the saliva splattered onto the corner of Henry's mouth.

Barking an order, the officer walked away, and another soldier moved into Henry's line of vision. Menacingly, the grim-faced infantryman held his rifle butt above Henry's head. It hung for a few tormenting seconds before it was rammed into his forehead. He heard a sickening crunch, accompanied by a brief explosion of colour before everything went black.

22

'Morning!' Viktor's mother said, entering the room. 'After all your travels, I thought you'd want breakfast in bed.'

'Thanks, Mama,' Viktor grunted without opening his eyes.

'Your father's up in the top field doing something to the fence,' she added, placing the tray on the bedside cabinet. 'Apparently, it was windy last night. Not that I heard anything, mind you. I slept like a log.'

They laid there with their eyes closed, hoping his mother would leave, but after several minutes of banal chatter, she showed no sign of going.

'What time is it?' Viktor asked eventually.

'Oh, it's just after six,' she said before returning to her ramblings. Six! Why had she woken them up so early? He did not have to go to work. After the events of the last few days, would it have been too much to ask to be allowed to wake up naturally?

'Are the boys awake?' he asked, now quite sure she was not going to go away.

'Not yet. I was about to get them up, so they could have breakfast with me.'

His mother pulled back the curtains, letting in streams

186

of early morning sunlight. He screwed up his eyes and Zofia wriggled down in the bed, pulling the bedding over her head.

'Your father's going to the market at nine. He wants a hand butchering the pig hanging in the barn,' his mother said.

'Okay, okay. Give me a few minutes, then I'll go and find him,' he said with an air of resignation.

Slowly, Viktor opened his eyes. He rolled over to kiss Zofia, but she was cocooned in the eiderdown with no visible part of her exposed. He interpreted this as 'Do not disturb,' so he staggered to his feet and stumbled his way over to the water bowl.

Through the yellowed, net curtain he could see a figure, presumably his father, working on a distant hill. Viktor dipped his hands in cold water from the previous night and splashed his face. His skin tightened, but he was not fully awake.

After drying himself with a rough towel, he slipped on a clean shirt, then put on his trousers, which were hanging untidily over the back of the chair. From the tray his mother had left next to the bed, he helped himself to a slice of toast, leaving behind the jam, butter, and coffee she had intended to accompany it.

Before climbing the hill, he poked his head through the door of the stable where Miedziak had spent the night. The horse was eating happily, making Viktor feel guilty because his father had not only risen early to repair the wind-damaged fence but had done some of his chores too.

He walked across the cobbled courtyard, then through a metal gate. He ascended the muddy path alongside a rugged, stone wall. Halfway up, his breathing became laboured. Three-quarters of the way to the top, his legs ached, and he was red-faced and blowing hard.

'Good morning,' the old man greeted him with a cheery smile.

'Morning, Dad,' he said between breaths.

'That's what happens when you're surrounded by flour dust every day. When we first moved here, I used to be like that.'

Viktor knew the old man was being kind.

'Is there anything I can do for you?' he asked, trying hard not to pant too loudly.

'Nah, I've nearly finished up here. The fence only wanted a few nails, but I'll need a hand to butcher the pig.'

As his father completed his work, Viktor sat on a grassy mound and admired the view of the city, having walked up the hill for nothing.

'Did you sleep okay?' his father asked as they strolled down the path.

'Fine, thanks. Until Mama woke us, that is.'

The old man smiled. 'She's so excited you're all here. I told her to let you rest, but her excitement obviously got the better of her. She probably couldn't wait any longer,' said the old man. 'You're her only son, Viktor. Give her a break.'

The two men entered one of the outhouses next to the stable block. Inside, the carcass of a pig hung from a hook in one of the roof beams. The animal dangled lifelessly, a small pool of blood collecting on the sawdust-covered floor.

'Do you remember how to do this, son?'

Viktor smiled, his mind racing back to the last time he had done this almost fifteen years ago.

'Yeah, what was it you always said? The most important thing is to sharpen the knives, otherwise...'

'There's no point in starting,' they said together.

'Well, I'm glad some of the things I taught you have stuck,' his father said, rolling up his sleeves and selecting a long, pointed butcher's knife from the table.

Making the first tentative incision along the midline of the pig's belly, his father spread the wound, letting the bowels spill out. Viktor looked away squeamishly.

'Living in the city has made you soft,' the old man

said with a wry smile.

'But you lived there for most of your life too,' Viktor replied, swallowing bile.

'Yes, but we always kept our own animals,' the old man said, looking at the pig. 'You're pampered, going to the local butcher. It's important you remember where your food comes from.'

Up to his elbows in the animal's abdomen, his father made three precise cuts, causing the entrails to fall to the floor. Viktor felt decidedly queasy, stepping outside to get some fresh air.

'You okay?' his father said.

'Yeah, I'll be fine. Just give me a few seconds.'

The old man smirked to himself and continued his work.

Moments later, having composed himself, he returned to find his father wrestling the pig's body to a workbench. Taking hold of the tail end, he helped heave it onto the rough wooden surface.

'Glad you could join me,' the old man said with a twinkle in his eye. 'Take one of those cleavers and divide the legs up.'

Viktor nodded.

'Remember, trotters, hocks, then hams,' said Viktor's father. 'Try and keep as much meat on the ham as possible. Looking at the size of the pig, we should get a fair price for those.'

As his father separated the joints from the carcass, Viktor chopped them with the cleaver, separating them effortlessly. He wrapped them individually in waxed paper, ready to sell later that day. Within the hour, the job was done. The various cuts of pork had been placed neatly in baskets to be transported with the other meat his father had prepared the previous day.

'Do you fancy a drink?' the older man asked.

'Yes.'

'I'll ask your mother to put the kettle on. After that,

we should head off for the market. Otherwise, all the best pitches will have gone.'

Viktor realised he had not spoken to Zofia this morning. He knew she would be less than impressed if he spent the whole day out with his father, leaving her and the boys with his mother.

The two men walked back through the courtyard into the warm kitchen, where Zofia and Viktor's mother were around the table chatting.

'Morning, darling,' Viktor said, kissing his wife on the forehead. 'Did you sleep okay?'

'Yes,' she said. 'What have you two been up to?'

'Oh. We've been sorting out the pig so we can take it to market later today. Where are the kids?'

'They've gone off to play in the bottom field. I can see them through the window—they're okay,' she said.

'I'm sure they'll be fine,' his mother said. 'It'll do them good to run around in the fresh air.'

'When are you going to the market?' Zofia asked.

'I guess we should leave in the next half hour,' his father butted in before Viktor had time to speak.

'When will you be back?' his mother asked. 'So, I know when to have dinner ready.'

'We'll try and be back for five,' the elder of the two men said. 'Is that okay?'

'Of course,' said Viktor's mother. 'What will you do for lunch?'

'We hoped you would make us some sandwiches. Have I told you how much I love you today?' the old man said playfully, putting his arms around her waist and giving her a kiss.

'Get off, you soppy old man,' the old lady laughed. 'Men!' she said in mock frustration. 'They're no different than little boys. Take my word for it; they never grow up, no matter how old they are.'

Viktor and his father looked sheepishly at each other.

'I thought you two would need something, so I made

you some earlier,' she said. 'I've put them in the larder. There are some apples and a few slices of cake to go with them.'

'Thanks, Mama,' he said.

'Right, we'd better be off if we're to get any work done,' Viktor's father said.

Viktor looked at Zofia. It was clear she was not impressed. He mouthed an apology, but she scowled back. He tried to give her a hug, but she did not reciprocate, so he pecked her on the cheek and then left.

The market nestled in the heart of the medieval city. Soon they were setting out their small stall opposite a haberdasher's. The two men placed the baskets containing different cuts of pork and beef on the wooden counter, with the two freshly butchered hams taking pride of place in the centre of their display.

While they stood behind the counter, waiting for their first customer, Viktor observed the people walking past and could not help being fascinated by what he saw. Young, old, fat, and short; every conceivable combination came to town on market day. He sniggered at the sight of a tall, attractive, dark-skinned woman walking with a short, plump blond man.

Clearly, opposites attract, he thought.

Seeing the thriving stalls helped him forget about the troubles in Danzig. It was refreshing seeing other people go about their everyday lives.

Suddenly, over to Viktor's left, there was a commotion. It drew his attention away from his thoughts. To his horror, three SS soldiers tipped over the stall of an elderly Jewish goldsmith. The guards hurled abuse at the old man, who was cowering on the floor, trying to protect his wares. Two of the soldiers laughed openly as the third set about kicking the powerless man.

By now, a sizeable crowd had gathered, hissing and jeering at the Jewish man. Viktor was appalled. Most of them had known this man for many years, so why should they turn on him now? He could not tell whether this was latent anti-Semitism or part of an elaborate pantomime to placate the German guards. Whichever it was, he was not going to stand by and let this old man be victimised. He turned to find his father, but the old man was no longer next to him. Looking through the crowd, he saw his father pushing through the throng.

Viktor fought his way through the mob in time to see his father step between the goldsmith and the soldiers. The intervention of his father provoked resentment from the gathering crowd. Infuriated by this old man's audacity, all three of the SS infantrymen raised their rifles towards him. Viktor's heart raced.

'Get out of the way, old man,' one of the guards said. 'This is nothing to do with you.'

'Leave him alone,' his father said boldly. 'What's he ever done to you?'

'Don't make me shoot you, old man.'

'Is Hitler afraid of elderly Jews?' his father asked defiantly.

'Move out of the way, or we'll kill both of you,' the other soldier said tersely.

'Answer me one thing,' his father said stubbornly. 'What kind of army has to fight defenceless old men to prove your manliness?'

Their frustration was becoming apparent. Viktor could not bear to watch as his father continued to antagonise them. The guard who had done most of the talking stepped forward, kicking his father in the leg, but the old man did not flinch. The SS guard starting shouting at Viktor's father. Another lifted his rifle, thrusting the butt into his father's abdomen, causing him to double over, but he stayed on his feet.

'Go down, you stubborn old fool,' Viktor muttered under his breath.

The angry guard struck the old man with his weapon again, catching him on the nose. It caused an eruption of blood which streamed down his face. The tone of the watching crowd changed. They were no longer hostile; instead, they appeared appalled. The soldiers sensed it, the uncertainty visible in their eyes.

From the back of the group of onlookers, an SS unteroffizier barked a one-word command, causing the guards to stand to attention, their faces now concerned. The officer shouted another order, and the three guardsmen marched solemnly out of the square.

'Broni, are you okay?' the frail Jewish man asked.

'I'm fine,' he said, rubbing his leg. 'If I'd been twenty years younger, I would've thrashed all three of them all the way back to Germany.'

'I am very grateful,' the Jew said. 'My family and I are forever in your debt.'

'Nonsense,' said Viktor's father. 'I wasn't going to let three young boys, barely out of nappies, take advantage of you.'

'Less of the old, if you don't mind,' he said with a pleasant smile. 'If my memory serves me correctly, you're the same age as I am.'

'I think you'll find I'm three months younger than you, and at our time of life, that makes all the difference!'

The two friends embraced, laughing together.

'Dad! Are you all right?' asked Viktor, breaking through the rapidly dispersing crowd.

'Yes, I'm fine, now don't fuss. They're mindless bullies, and this is their playground.'

'It's ridiculous. The people watching thought it's acceptable to beat old Jews, but not Poles. What kind of nonsense is this?'

'These are the times we live in,' the goldsmith said. 'To some people, being Jewish means we are lower than animals.'

'Ben, this is my son, Viktor,' his father said.

'Pleased to meet you. I'm Ben, Ben Feldman. In the few years I've known your father he's always been a little hot-headed, but this time I'm grateful.'

'Are you hurt?' he asked his father.

'No, only my pride has been damaged.'

23

Slowly, the lucid periods became more frequent; a nauseating throb developing deep within his head. In a moment of clarity, Henry realised he was blind. Panic overwhelmed him. Had the blow to his head taken his sight? Once he had regained control of his breathing again, he noticed a hessian sack had been secured over his head. Feeling claustrophobic, he tried to raise his arms to remove the blindfold, but his wrists were fastened behind his back, and his shoulder throbbed.

Unfamiliar noises startled him. Unsure what was happening, he rolled into the fetal position, trying to protect himself. The unmistakable creak of a door hinge preceded the sound of hob-nailed boots on a stone floor.

'So, you're awake!' a deep voice said in heavily accented English.

Henry did not reply.

'Stand up!'

He struggled to sit up but was not quick enough.

'I said, stand up!' the voice repeated, more aggressively.

A hand grabbed him and manhandled him to his feet. Rocking a little, he tried to find his balance. Another voice spoke, this time from further away, prompting his captors to shove him out of the room.

'Sit!' came a harsh voice.

He felt for a chair with his legs but failed to locate one.

'SIT!'

The chair was thrust into the back of his knees, causing them to buckle. He fell backwards onto the seat. A searing pain shot through his shoulder, making him whimper.

Henry sat silently, waiting for his guards to speak. After several minutes, someone loosened his hood before forcibly removing it. A bright light shone directly into his eyes, causing him to blink repeatedly. Someone behind him released the bonds which held his wrists.

'Let me introduce myself. I am Hauptmann Andreas Roehm of the SS. What is your name?' the accented voice said from behind the light.

He looked for the face of the person talking, but could only see shadows.

'Maybe the head injury has affected your memory. So, I'll ask you again, what is your name?'

He attempted to talk, but could only utter a faint whisper. 'Henry Taylor.'

'What?' the voice asked. 'I can't hear you.'

'Henry Taylor,' he said, slightly louder.

'What is your rank?'

'Sergeant.'

'Good! Now we are getting somewhere. What is your serial number?'

'Six four two three five,' he said, his voice growing stronger each time he spoke.

He looked down and saw heavy strapping had been placed on his right shoulder.

'What is your purpose in Poland?'

'Sorry, Sir. Under the Geneva Convention, I don't have to answer that.'

Someone kicked the back of Henry's chair.

'What is the name of your unit?'

'Again, Sir. I am unable to comment,' Henry said defiantly.

'Sergeant Taylor, you are a prisoner of the Third Reich. It is in your interest to cooperate with us. Do you understand?'

'I'm sorry, but I've given you all the information I can.'

After a long period of silence, the voice spoke again. 'Okay, take him back.'

Replacing the sack over his head and securing his hands, the guards cajoled Henry back into his cell.

That went better than I expected, he thought, hearing the door being locked.

He was thankful for the interrogation training he had received back in Aldershot. The well-rehearsed 'Geneva Convention' line seemed to have done the trick. Inside the hood, he smiled to himself.

Not sure how long he had been asleep, he was awoken by the click of the lock. From what he could tell, several men were in the room, shouting at him. The guards heaved him into a corner of the room, turning him to face the wall despite his hood. He felt a strange low-pitched rumble as his captors dragged something into the room.

After a few seconds, a gramophone started blaring out some Wagnerian operatic aria. Henry smirked. Was this the best they could do? He hummed along loudly with the familiar tune.

Several minutes later, the music stopped. Only the white noise of the needle grating on the revolving record remained. It caused an irritating, repetitive sound. Whoever operated the gramophone turned up the volume, so the noise became so loud it set Henry's teeth on edge. It was relentless. His brain screamed for the din to stop. Meanwhile, the guards yelled, taunting him about king and country, roast beef and all things quintessentially English.

Every time he moved, someone swiped him across the back of his legs with a cane. To start with, only his larger movements were punished, but the slightest readjustment of posture was enough to warrant a beating. Henry blinked back the tears.

The gramophone stopped abruptly.

'Why don't you make it easy on yourself?'

The voice belonged to the person who had identified himself as Roehm during his interrogation.

'Tell us what you are doing in Poland, and all this will stop.'

He strained to catch a glimpse of Roehm's face through the fabric, but his actions were greeted with a swipe across the legs.

'Sorry, under the Geneva Convention, I can't answer that.'

Another lash followed, making him yelp.

'Henry, you don't need to do this,' Roehm said softly. 'All this can stop if you just talk to us.'

'Sir. I cannot say any more.'

'Very well,' the hauptmann said. 'Carry on.'

The music started again. Henry stood to attention as best he could, almost statue-like, afraid of more beatings on his throbbing legs. Once the aria stopped, the white noise returned. He blocked out the sound by thinking about his brother, but he soon imagined David being captured. This disturbed him, and he quickly erased it from his mind. His mind went blank, and he found the disorientating sound seducing. He forced himself to think about something else. His thoughts turned to the mission. Apart from the casualties, it had been a relative success. They had successfully destroyed the target and, consequently, the industrial estate would be out of commission for quite some time.

He prayed for the noise and the beatings to stop. Surely, his captors knew Henry and his men were responsible for the destruction of the dam. So, why was

Roehm asking for him to confirm this? Maybe, if he told them what they wanted, they would leave him alone. Instinctively, his training kicked in. He had been taught to give nothing away. The smallest piece of information, even confirming what they already knew, could provide them with inroads for other, more pressing questions.

Eventually, it fell silent, but a high-pitched ringing sensation persisted in his ears. His head spun from the hours of white noise and the repeated beatings. Once again, Henry was pushed out of the room and then dumped unceremoniously onto the chair. Like last time, Roehm spoke from behind the light as his hood was removed.

'Sergeant Taylor, I hope you appreciate our hospitality. I can say that we are enjoying your company. So much so, our chef has prepared this magnificent meal for you.'

A plate containing a delicious-looking roast dinner was placed in front of him.

'You must be hungry. I'm sure you'll agree, this smells wonderful, and it can all be yours. All you have to do is tell us why you are in Poland and who your contacts are?'

The food smelled so good. Henry savoured the aroma before answering, fighting the temptation to give in. Despite extreme hunger, he shuffled back in the seat obstinately and stared straight ahead.

'Sorry, Sir. Under the Geneva Convention, I do not have to answer that question.'

'Are you sure? This meal does look good, doesn't it? There's roast beef with horseradish, cabbage, turnips, and potatoes. All covered in a deep, rich gravy. I'm becoming hungry just looking at it.'

Henry stared into the darkness rather than look at the plate. The aroma caused him to salivate and his empty stomach to rumble. He glanced fleetingly at the food. It looked good. Briefly, he considered telling them what they wanted to hear, just to be able to eat it, but he knew he had to resist.

'No, Sir, I am unable to tell you any more information.'

'So be it,' said the German officer. 'Take him back to the cell.'

Henry remained undisturbed for several hours. The bruises on his legs and the wound to his shoulder ached, but nonetheless, he slept soundly until the jangling of keys woke him. The routine was becoming familiar. He was dragged roughly from his bed before being pushed into the interrogation room.

'Hello, Sergeant Taylor,' Roehm said jovially. 'I trust you have rested.'

Henry kept silent, suspicious of what was going to happen.

'You've had enough time to consider your options. Let's call an end to this pretence. Tell us what your mission is, and who your contacts are, then all this silliness will stop,'

'Sir, I am sorry, but I have told you all I can,' he replied.

'Very well. Please let me introduce you to one of my colleagues, Herr Lehrer. He is keen to meet you.'

Without any further words, the sack was forced over his head again, and then he was dragged down the corridor. Henry fought against his captors, but their grip was too strong. They took him to a different room before his back was slammed against something cold and hard, the guards fastening his hands and feet again.

The hood was removed once again. Piles of junk lay untidily around what was presumably a storeroom. Alarmingly, his ankles and wrists had been fastened with thick leather straps to an upended metal bed frame.

A well-built, bald man appeared in front of him.

'My name is Lehrer. I have been asked to persuade you to talk.'

Henry shrugged, trying to appear nonchalant.

'I admire your arrogance. Let's see if you feel the same way in an hour.'

Lehrer unbuttoned his shirt, revealing a well-defined, muscular torso. A tattoo of an eagle perched on a swastika adorned his right pectoral region. Without warning, the interrogator kicked him hard in the abdomen, causing him to crease in the middle. The tattooed man beat him with a hammer-like blow.

'Do you want to remain silent?' Lehrer lifted Henry's head by his hair.

Henry stalled for as long as possible before nodding.

His interrogator slapped him across the face, rocking the whole frame. Rivulets of blood began to trickle from his nose. Henry tried to catch his breath as he received another kick. The blows fell relentlessly, one after another. Henry haemorrhaged profusely, spitting a large clot feebly onto the floor. As Lehrer continued, Henry focussed on the solitary lightbulb dangling from the ceiling. As every blow landed, he concentrated on the bulb, working hard to blank out the pain.

The interrogator turned his attention to Henry's injured shoulder. The muscular German took a bamboo cane from under a counter and started slashing the right side of his chest. Henry broke into a cold sweat and almost vomited.

After an hour, he was ready to talk, but to his surprise, Lehrer stopped. The interrogator walked away, perspiring and panting hard.

His head hung down, blood dripping from his nose. A smartly dressed SS officer entered the room, and immediately started speaking to Henry. 'Is there anything you'd like to tell us?'

This was Roehm, the man from behind the light.

Struggling to look up, he caught sight of the officer's angular face and black, curly hair. Henry spat at the hauptmann. The German officer walloped him across the face, sending a shower of sweat, blood, and saliva into the air.

'Your insolence will be your downfall.'

He turned and walked towards the door. 'Carry on,' he said coldly.

The interrogator smiled, walking to the desk on Henry's left. Out of the corner of his eye, he watched Lehrer adjusting dials and switches. Suddenly, electricity crackled through the metal bed frame which supported him. The current coursed through him, causing his muscles to contract. The pain was excruciating, causing him to scream uncontrollably before the power subsided.

After a few seconds, the surge returned, more agonising than before. His body deformed by another spasm; unable to catch his breath. As the electricity was turned off, his muscles relaxed. He slumped forward, his aching body supported only by his restraints. Panting, he waited for the next shock. When it came, it was unbearable, as if every one of his nerves was being torn from his body. The tendons in his limbs pulled wildly at his tired bones, hideously contorting his wrists and ankles. The last thing he remembered was his bladder emptying before he passed out.

24

'Oh my God,' Viktor's mother screamed as the two men walked up to the house. 'What happened?'

'Don't fuss, woman!' the old man said sternly.

'Look at you—you're plastered in blood,' she replied.

Zofia looked at Viktor who, up until now, had said nothing, but he only shrugged.

'It is nothing, just a bloodied nose. I'll be fine,' his father said.

'Will someone tell me what's going on?' the old lady said, becoming increasingly frustrated.

'I had a slight altercation with a German soldier,' he said, not making eye contact with his wife. 'There! Are you happy now?'

'It doesn't look slight to me!' she said. 'You're old enough to know better than to pick a fight.'

'Three young guards were up to no good. I swear they would've killed Ben Feldman if I hadn't stepped in.'

'Oh!' After a long pause, she said, 'Is Ben all right now?'

'Yes. Now, we shall say no more about it.'

With that, he went into the farmhouse and disappeared upstairs.

'Are you okay?' Zofia asked, giving Viktor a hug.

'I'm fine, thanks,' he said. 'Honestly, there was nothing I could do. I only turned my back for a second. When I turned around, Dad had waded in to protect his friend.'

'I don't understand. Why were they picking on an old man anyway?'

'You're not going to believe this; it was because he's Jewish.'

'What?' she exclaimed. 'You're kidding.'

'Awful, isn't it?'

'I knew there's been a lot of anti-Semitism recently, but are things really this bad?'

'There was a story in the paper last summer,' he said. 'I didn't pay much attention at the time, but looking back, I guess it was a sign of what was to come.'

Zofia looked at him blankly. Not one for politics, she had more important things in life to deal with, like bringing up the children and putting food on the table.

'You remember, some rabbi in Danzig sold the valuables from his synagogue to a museum in New York so he could pay for his congregation to leave the country. You must have noticed fewer Jews around?'

'Has it come to this?' she asked incredulously. 'I mean, these people have lived here as long as anyone can remember. Then, some idiot in Germany says the Israelites are evil, so the whole world turns against them. What's happened to friendship and loyalty?'

'You should have seen the people at the market, booing and jeering Mr. Feldman. Dad was the only one who tried to help him.'

Zofia stared at him, not believing what she was hearing.

'While we're on the subject, Mr. Feldman asked us over for dinner tonight. I suppose it is his way of saying thank you. You and Mama were invited, of course, but I said you'd be here looking after the children. Is that okay?'

Zofia nodded reluctantly. 'Make sure you and your father get home in one piece this time.'

Viktor and his father had dressed in their smartest clothes and said their goodbyes before setting off into the city. A strong easterly wind plagued them as they made their way down the open road. As they entered the built-up area, the breeze dropped, and the two men were able to walk more comfortably.

'Where does Mr. Feldman live?' Viktor asked, replacing his cap after flattening his hair.

'Down by the river. Not too far now. If you don't mind me asking, I couldn't help noticing Zofia didn't appear happy about you coming out tonight. Is everything okay?'

'She's not seen much of me since we've been here. Give it a couple of days, and she'll be fine.'

The old man said wisely, 'As long as everything is all right.'

After a further fifteen minutes, they reached the home of Mr. and Mrs. Feldman. It was not a grand place, but the house was spotless. Dinner was served within half an hour of their arrival, and both he and his father ate until they could eat no more.

Sitting in an armchair next to a roaring fire, Viktor chewed on his pipe while his father shared a hilarious anecdote of one of his many adventures. An enjoyable evening was topped off by Mrs. Feldman bringing in a tray of rich coffee with some sugary treats. Viktor savoured the warmth of the coffee and could have stayed next to the fireplace all night.

'How did it get this late?' his father said.

'It has been a pleasure spending the evening with you,' said Mr. Feldman. 'Once again, I cannot thank you enough for what happened earlier today.'

'What are friends for?' Viktor's father shrugged.

The streets were relatively empty, the city's inhabitants avoiding the fine rain which now fell. Despite the weather, they chatted about their night, the war, the Nazis, and the Jews. Through the window of a noisy bar, Viktor saw a group of German soldiers standing around a piano, swinging huge steins of frothy beer and singing loudly. They had not gone more than fifty yards when several drunken men spilt out onto the street.

'Dad, I think it's those fools from earlier,' he whispered, quickening his pace.

'Damn! Keep moving—act as if you haven't seen them.'

'Okay. Where can we lose them?'

'C'mon. I know just the place.'

Father and son walked swiftly.

'In here,' said his father, darting through a rusting gate.

'Where are we?' Viktor asked, glancing uneasily over his shoulder.

'The old Jewish cemetery. Down at the bottom is a row of trees,' he pointed. 'On the other side of them is the lower field of our farm. Let's split up and we'll meet up at home.'

'Shouldn't we stick together?'

'They're bullies, but on their own they're nothing,' his father said. 'They won't follow both of us.'

'Will you be all right?'

'Of course,' his father smiled. 'You don't think I've done this before?'

Away from the streetlights, it was as black as pitch. The two men separated, running in opposite directions. Behind him, German voices shouted angrily. He hoped his father was safely away.

Viktor took a deep breath, then ran across several rows of graves. Crouching behind a large stone memorial, he watched their silhouettes moving amongst the gravestones. Panting hard, his eyes darted around. There was no trace of his father.

As he ran as fast as he could, the ground changed

from gravel to mud. His ankle went from under him, but he regained his balance without breaking his stride. Out of nowhere, something hit him square between the eye. It took him a few seconds to recover. Of all the stupid things, he had run into a tree. He instinctively rubbed his forehead and struggled to his feet. As he rose, he felt a hand on his shoulder. He turned, expecting to see his father, but a forceful punch greeted him, knocking him onto his back.

Gaps in his memory plagued him, some spanning several hours. In front of him, iron bars reached from the ceiling to the floor. The other three walls were made from unfinished bricks lined with benches occupied by around twenty other inmates. A narrow corridor ran on the other side of the bars, but his captors were nowhere to be seen.

Sitting cross-legged on the concrete floor, Viktor studied the others who were locked up with him. Some of them were dirty with torn clothes; others looked well-dressed and not accustomed to captivity. All of them were battered and bruised. Thankfully, his father was not one of them. The old man must have escaped.

25

Over time, the periods of isolation became more frequent, the beatings fewer. After a couple of weeks, the violence had stopped altogether. Occasional episodes of roughness continued, but nothing matching Henry's first few days in captivity. His daily routine had become almost predictable; breakfast, solitary confinement, lunch, more solitary, dinner, then bed. He had resigned himself to the fact this was how he was going to spend the rest of the war.

Henry lay absentmindedly, staring at the ceiling, listening to the sound of the rain outside. His shoulder felt back to normal, but his wrists remained heavily bruised from being restrained repeatedly. The hood had been discarded a week after his capture.

Two guards burst into his cell, dragging him down the corridor without a word. Iron shackles were forcibly placed around his ankles, then tightly fastened. The soldiers ushered him through a wooden door into a vast entrance hall, the cold metal digging into his legs as he walked.

Ten other prisoners stood in the hall, closely scrutinised by the four SS guards standing against the walls. Henry kept his head down and followed the instructions. A fifth guard worked his way along the line, passing a thick chain through the bonds around the men's ankles. Last in the queue, Henry was unable to go anywhere unless the others went with him. Unlike him, they wore dirty and torn civilian clothing.

Two of the guards swung open the double doors which occupied the far wall. Outside, a troop carrier waited with its engine running.

A German unteroffizier bullied the prisoners into climbing into the back of the truck, and reluctantly, the queue started moving towards the truck, the chains around their ankles clanking as they walked. The onlooking guards sniggered as the line of men struggled onto the vehicle. Henry stumbled as he tried to keep in step with the man in front of him.

Henry was determined not to make a fool of himself. The chain restricted his movements, and the only way he could get aboard was to hold his right leg at an awkward angle and then hop. He managed to clamber aboard in an undignified manner, then took his place at the end of one of the benches.

The soldiers climbed up, sitting opposite the prisoners. A guard banged on the back wall of the cab, and shortly afterwards the truck's engine started. The guards chatted but had their rifles lying ominously across their knees. They talked loudly, sharing cigarettes amongst themselves, occasionally blowing smoke over their captives. The grey canvas roof had a small pinhole in it directly above Henry's head. Drops of rain landed on his head, trickling down his neck, causing him to shiver.

After twenty minutes, the bumpy journey ended. The soldiers leapt out, followed by Henry, who gingerly lowered himself onto the grass. He took the opportunity to enjoy the feeling of being outdoors for the first time in several months. To his surprise, they were not in the town, but somewhere in the countryside.

Fields spread as far as he could see. Out of keeping

with the relatively peaceful surroundings, a massive bomb crater, containing the twisted remains of a railway track, occupied the valley floor. Once the prisoners had been unloaded, a guard removed the chain connecting them. The prisoners were split into two groups. One was sent to repair the track, while the other had to erect telegraph poles to run alongside it, presumably to reconnect Poland with Berlin.

Many men worked on this section of railway line—like him, their legs in shackles. He assumed they had come from other prisons in the area, their German overseers prowling among them.

Henry was given a pickaxe and paired with one of the Polish prisoners to dig holes. With his ankles secured, he limped off to the site of the first pole. The ground appeared grey, still frozen from the overnight frost, and the first swing of his pick made little impression. It took them forty minutes to finish their first hole.

Stopping to mop his brow, he watched other troop carriers arrive. Yet more prisoners were unloaded. A passing German guard walking a large dog noticed Henry's inactivity. The soldier strode over and started bawling at him to return to work. He was defiant at first but quickly obeyed when the animal fought against its leash and bared its teeth in a ferocious grimace.

As he worked, Henry glanced around periodically. The prisoners looked similar—torn clothes, grey-skinned, and dirty. Each had the same expression of resignation. As an enemy combatant, there was a reason for him to be detained, but why were they here? Perhaps they were common criminals, or maybe their only crime had been to be in the wrong place at the wrong time. Kidnapping seemed to provide a cheap, virtually limitless workforce.

'Do you speak English?' Henry whispered to his companion.

'A little,' said the Pole. 'I understand, but my speaking no good.'

'What's your name?'

'Viktor,' said the tall man with a swarthy complexion. 'And you?'

'Henry. Henry Taylor.'

'You're British, no?'

He nodded.

'How you end here?'

'That is a long story, old chap. I'm beginning to wonder why myself. What about you? How have you ended up here?'

He did not reply immediately as a guard walked past, eyeing them suspiciously.

'For being friends with a Jew,' he said once the coast was clear.

'You're kidding? That's madness! I mean...'

He froze suddenly, his gaze fixed over Viktor's shoulder. On the other side of the plot, he could see a blond man wearing a British Army uniform. Henry peered carefully through the crowd of workers; his heart raced. He thought he recognised him, but he could not be sure.

Having seen Henry's work rate drop, the guard levelled his rifle and started shouting. The prisoners nearby turned to look at the commotion, before working harder to avoid the same fate. Henry and Viktor returned to their digging, hoping the soldier would lose interest in them.

Henry continued to watch while he worked. The man across the track smiled at one of his workmates. Even at this distance, he would recognise that smile anywhere. It was Tommy Rogers, the corporal, who had disappeared when they first landed in this God-forsaken country. Part of him wanted to shout out and wave, but he knew his punishment would probably be a beating or worse.

Spurred on, Henry set about digging the next hole with a newly found vigour. His mood lifted dramatically over the hours that followed, and his mind raced with ideas and plans. Thoughts of escape raced around his head. The more he thought about it, the more the idea propagated itself. First, though, he had to speak to Tommy.

Henry and Viktor completed their row of holes. Exhausted, they called over their guard, who examined their handiwork. Their reward was a cup of coffee from the supervisor's cabin. The two men joined the queue of prisoners waiting outside the timber hut with its corrugated steel roof.

The line of men moved slowly. The soldier supervising them had lost interest and wandered off for a smoke. From where he stood, Henry had an excellent view of the uniformed man on the other side of the damaged track. He was sure it was his corporal.

After a few moments, the blond British soldier spoke to one of the guards, who waved him towards the cabin. This was Henry's chance.

'Tommy!' he said, sneaking along the line.

'Sarge! Is that you?'

'How've you been? What happened to you?'

'I'm all right, Sarge. I came down in the middle of an enemy unit. I'd lost my rifle when we jumped, so I gave myself up. It was a little hairy, though. I thought they were going kill me for sure. Where are the others?'

'Scotty's dead. His parachute became tangled in a tree on the way down. They shot him as he hung there. Mayberry took a nasty wound to the chest. O'Shea said he wouldn't survive, so we left him to be picked up by a patrol. The others got away after we blew the dam.'

'Sad news about Scotty and Mayberry,' said Tommy sincerely. 'But to be honest, I thought I was the only survivor. It's great you got the dam, though—good on you,' he said, punching Henry quite hard. 'How come they escaped, and you didn't?'

'The pilot got a little jumpy at the pickup. He set off before we were all aboard. Unfortunately, I took a round in the shoulder and was left behind.'

'Sounds awful.'

'Yeah, it was for a while, but things have eased off now. How long have they been bringing you here?'

'The last couple of days. Before that, it was a different location. This is my sixth site.'

'What do they have you doing?'

'It has been the same thing every day for the last three months, railways and telegraph poles.'

'Who are the other prisoners?'

'Locals, from across this part of Poland. Every time they move, it's a new group of men.'

'I guess it stops you from getting too friendly with each other.'

'The Germans are paranoid there is going to be a prisoner uprising. That's why they're so harsh if anyone steps out of line.'

'What are they like—you know, the prisoners?'

'Some are nice, but be careful. Some of 'em would sell their own mother if they thought they would receive payment.'

An officer appeared from inside the supervisor's cabin. Tommy stayed in the queue, looking straight ahead, as Henry remained crouched next to him, hidden by the other prisoner's legs. As the line moved, so did he. Thankfully the soldier passed without suspicion.

'We shouldn't be seen together too often. In these uniforms, we're so conspicuous. If they see us talking they'll become suspicious,' said Tommy.

'What's security like? Could we escape?'

'The main problem is these chains. We're not going very far wearing these.' Tommy gestured to the shackles around his ankles.

'Okay, let me think about it. I'll catch you later.'

After checking that the coast was clear, Henry stood and walked away.

He found Viktor sitting on the floor against a low dry-stone wall, cradling an empty, enamel mug in his hands. Henry joined him after a cursory look to ensure no one was listening.

'How you doing?' Henry asked, but the Pole seemed confused, unable to understand Henry's colloquialism.

'Are you okay?' he tried again.

'Yes.'

'I've been meaning to ask, where in Poland are you from?'

'Danzig.'

Henry nodded, looking around once more. 'That's excellent. You're just the man we're after. The other British soldier and I are thinking of escaping. We need someone to come with us; somebody who knows the area. Are you up for it?'

At first, Viktor looked shocked, 'Where would we go?'

'To Danzig,' Henry said with a wry smile.

He shook his head. That was the Wehrmacht's operational headquarters. Certainly not the kind of place one would expect escapees to return to.

'Would you be able to help us find a ship out across the Baltic?' Henry asked.

Viktor listened thoughtfully. This man had to be genuine. No one trying to trick him would ever suggest returning to Danzig. It was occupied by the most significant military presence outside of Germany.

'How far do you reckon we are from Danzig?' Henry persisted.

'Fifty to sixty kilometers.'

'That's about forty miles,' he said, quickly doing a calculation in his head. 'Do you think we could make it?'

'You really want to go there?'

'Yes, I know the place is crawling with Germans, but Danzig's the only place where we're likely to sail from.'

'Yes, Viktor will find you a ship. First, get us out of here,' the Pole said.

'Leave that to me. Are you interested in helping us?'

Viktor thought for a few moments. 'Yes!' he

answered finally. 'But only to Danzig. My family now in Olsztyn.'

'Hang on! You said you were from Danzig.'

'I am. We stay with my parents to miss the war. Don't worry, I take you to Danzig.'

'Fair enough! You're a good man, Viktor.' Henry smiled.

'So, when leaving?'

'Today.'

26

A meagre lunch was held in a draughty, canvas marquee. Trestle tables had been placed on the cold earth, flanked by benches running the whole length of the makeshift room. Henry had orchestrated for Viktor to sit next to Tommy. While the other prisoners tucked into their food with relish, Henry smiled as the Polish man made his introductions.

A particularly gruff-looking corporal patrolled among the chairs, passing close to Henry's colleagues. He could tell from Tommy's puzzled expression that Viktor had switched to speaking his native language to avoid drawing attention to them when the guard came into earshot. It was clear, the Pole could be trusted.

In heavily accented English, Viktor set about explaining Henry's plan. The blond soldier kept looking across, searching for confirmation. A confirmatory wink from the other side of the marquee provided all the reassurance he needed. Happy the conversation was achieving its desired result, he took some of the remaining cold sausage from a serving plate in the middle of the table. Rolling it in a slice of dark, brown bread, he popped it into his mouth. Tough to chew, the mouthful sat heavily in his stomach.

While the prisoners around him babbled in their foreign tongue, Henry's eyes flitted between Tommy's face and the prowling guards. Things appeared to be progressing well. Pleased with himself, he ate one last piece of bread, putting several slices discreetly into his jacket pocket for later.

When the two men finished their conversation, Henry left his table, weaving in and out of the crowd until he was directly behind them.

'Tommy!' he whispered. 'What do you think?'

'Do you honestly think we can do it?' the blond soldier asked quietly without turning around.

'I've been watching the guards for most of the morning. I'm sure we can.'

'Shouldn't we hang on for a few days and work the plan through? To make sure it won't fail.'

'You said it yourself, we don't have that luxury. They might move us to a different site tomorrow. We can't be certain we'll both be in the same place again, so it has to be today.'

'Okay, but one other thing. That Polish chap, can we trust him?'

'He seems on the level. From chatting to him, he appears to hate the Krauts as much as we do.'

'He could be leading us into a trap,' Tommy said anxiously. 'If we're caught escaping they'll shoot first and ask questions later.'

'I guess if the German's wanted an excuse to get rid of us, they would've done it by now. They wouldn't need to orchestrate such an elaborate plan to bump us off.'

'Fair point,' said Tommy. 'Oh, what the hell, count me in. I can't eat much more of this horrid food anyway.'

'I know what you mean. It is somewhat indigestible.'

'Okay, we go at the next break. Get to the vehicle compound, but make sure no one sees you.'

With that, the blond soldier disappeared into the

crowd.

The watery, winter sun had taken most of the chill out of the air. All around them the rhythmical thud of metal against rock rang out, as they returned to digging post holes. Henry found it difficult to make himself heard above the din, so they only spoke when needed. Possibilities and pitfalls of their escape plan tumbled through his head, providing him with a new motivation to work.

The afternoon flew by. The warmer earth meant they completed their task quickly. After inspection, the guard sent them back to the queue for another drink. Henry nodded at Tommy, who was watching them like a hawk. This was it.

As the majority of men continued to work busily working around them, Henry hoped it would be easy to slip away without being seen. He walked calmly past the line of prisoners outside the cabin. Surprisingly, the chatting guards were oblivious to the fact he had strayed out of bounds. Even though his heart was pounding, he did not adjust his pace until he had disappeared through the trees.

Henry crouched behind a grassy bank, peering back from where he had come. Things seemed to be continuing as they had, and no one was pursuing him. Slumping as low as possible, he caught his breath.

Carrying his pickaxe, Viktor strode purposely across the open ground. The chains around his ankles clanked as he moved, but the soldiers paid little attention. He dropped into the trench which Tommy and his colleague were digging. He swapped his axe for Tommy's spade. Out of sight, he jumped on the spade's handle until it snapped. The British soldier's work partner appeared somewhat bemused as the stranger took the pieces to the nearest guard.

'I'm afraid it's broken, Sir,' Viktor said in German.

'You'd better go and find the quartermaster,' said the

soldier uninterestedly.

He thanked him and then headed towards the temporary building, near the site's entrance.

The quartermaster's office was much bigger than the supervisor's cabin. Viktor walked up to the desk. The clerk was busy checking balance sheets laid out on the counter in front of him.

'I have been sent for a replacement,' Viktor said, holding up the broken implement for the man to see.

'Put it in that box with the others,' the bespectacled clerk said without looking up from his paperwork. 'Take another from one of the stacks.'

Without hesitation, he threw the remains of the spade into the crate of muddy, damaged tools. Surveying his options, Viktor selected some bulk croppers from one of the piles of equipment before leaving. Outside, he turned the opposite direction from which he had come and headed for the vehicle park.

On hearing footsteps approaching, Henry dropped to the floor, rolling under the nearest truck. A pair of feet appeared in his restricted field of view. Thankfully, they were not the feet of a German soldier.

'Henry?' a familiar voice whispered.

'Viktor, under here,' he replied, crawling out. Were you followed?'

'No.'

After a few moments, Tommy joined them from the supervisor's cabin. He looked around nervously, but their absence did not appear to have been noticed.

'That was easier than I thought,' he said. 'They didn't seem to be interested.'

'Don't be lulled into a false sense of security. It won't be long before they notice we're missing. Let's remove these,' Henry said, gesturing to the manacles around his ankles.

The metal shackles around Henry's ankle yielded with a satisfying click as Viktor crushed them with the heavy tool. Within a couple of minutes, all three men were free of their bonds.

'Which way are we heading?' asked Tommy.

'Once out, we need to head north,' said Viktor

'Good, so let's get ready,' Henry said eagerly.

They crept through the trucks. Peering around the cab of one of the troop transporters, Henry halted the group with his hand. Up ahead, three chatting guards stood at the site entrance, unaware they were being watched. This was the only way in and out, and there was no obvious way past them. The forest on the far side of the road might as well be a hundred miles away.

'How are we going to get out?' Tommy asked.

'I don't know,' Henry said. 'If we dash for it, we're bound to be seen. Any ideas?'

His companions shook their heads.

He leant back against the truck and started to think, annoyed by falling at the first hurdle. Meanwhile, Viktor dropped to his hands and knees and disappeared under the vehicle.

'Are you all right?' Henry asked.

'I am okay,' he said in his heavy accent. 'I think I have something. Come under.'

The two British soldiers looked at each other quizzically, before joining the Pole beneath the truck.

'We stay here. We can hang on until outside,' Viktor said, gesticulating, unsure of the English words.

Henry nodded with a smile.

'Hold here and feet like this,' Viktor demonstrated, grabbing the chassis.

'I see. Once we're beyond the compound gates, the trucks will turn one way or the other,' said Henry, continuing with Viktor's idea. 'As they are turning, their speed will reduce, so we can drop off and roll into the undergrowth on the far side of the road.

'Great,' said Tommy. 'What about the guards at the site entrance. Won't they be able to see us?'

220

'We'll go the moment the truck starts its turn. That way we'll be hidden from view,' Henry said.

'Can't fit,' said Viktor, pointing at them. 'Not enough holding places.'

'No,' Henry said, following what the tall Pole was saying. 'And there wouldn't be enough time for all of us to roll away in the time it would take for one vehicle to turn. It'll need to be one man per truck, I guess.'

The other two nodded.

'Our timing will need to be perfect,' Henry said with a smile, 'but I'm sure we can do it.'

After lengthy discussions, the finer details were ironed out. The three men hid under their own vehicles and waited. Suddenly, a siren started to wail, sending guards running in all directions. From where he lay, Henry could hear raised voices shouting angrily in German.

The communal chain was replaced between the prisoners' ankles before they were forced back onto the vehicles. Controlling his breathing, Henry waited as one by one the trucks pulled away.

The truck he was underneath rattled to life. He grabbed the chassis, preparing for it to set off. The vibrations from the idling engine and the dense smell of diesel were nauseating. Henry gripped the frame tightly as the vehicle lurched forward, his back barely clearing the ground.

After a few yards, they stopped abruptly. Inches from his face were the boots of two sentries standing beside the cab. As the soldiers talked to the driver, he clung on in silent agony.

They passed through the entrance gates before the truck began to turn right. Henry let go, falling backwards onto the hard tarmac. Rolling between the moving wheels on the far side, he tumbled into a ditch which ran parallel with the road. Viktor was already waiting for him.

More trucks passed, but there was no sign of Tommy. Henry became anxious. Where was he? He moved along

221

the ditch, not taking his eyes off the compound. Several German guards had stayed within the fence, those who remained searching for the missing prisoners. It would not be long before they began looking beyond the perimeter. *Come on, Tommy! Where are you?*

***

There was a knock at the door.

'Come in!' said Roehm without looking up from his papers.

'Sir, I'm afraid I have more bad news,' said Lieutenant Kruse after he saluted.

'What?' asked the hauptmann, his eyes now fixed on his subordinate.

'Three prisoners have escaped from one of our railway repair working parties,' said the nervous lieutenant. 'We've returned all the others to their cells. The Wehrmacht are doubling the number of men searching the area. I'm assured it will only be a matter of time before they are back in custody.'

'Which prisoners?' he asked, suspecting he knew the answer.

There was a pause before Kruse spoke again, 'The two British soldiers and a civilian captured in the East Prussia.'

Roehm banged his fist hard on the desk, glaring at the lieutenant. Before speaking, he calmed himself. 'What kind of idiot puts soldiers from the same unit in the same workcamp?'

'It was an administrative error, Sir,' Kruse said. 'The Wehrmacht coordinate the deployment of slave labour. Apparently, they didn't think it would be an issue.'

'Didn't think it was an issue?' Roehm ranted. 'They're the only two in all of Poland. Of course it's an issue.'

Kruse stood awkwardly in silence.

'We are where we are,' the hauptmann said, trying to regain his focus. 'We have to play the hand we're dealt. What do we know about the Polish escapee?'

'He was a political prisoner from Olsztyn. According to the report filed by the arresting Wehrmacht officer, he was responsible for a demonstration against the Führer.'

'Do you think he was the British soldiers' contact in Poland?'

'Up until now, we had no reason to suspect he was. I mean, he was arrested in a different part of the country. There's no record of him being a member of any of the resistance movements.'

'Okay, so he may be an opportunistic connection. Now, we have a game of cat and mouse, but we are the cat.'

Kruse looked confused, 'How, Sir?'

'This time we know they are trying to leave Poland,' Roehm said. 'First, I want you to do some digging into the background of the Polish prisoner. Find out if he has any influential friends. I suspect the British soldiers are going to use his knowledge to escape. I want you to increase the military presence on all borders. I will need to ask Berlin for more troops. This Godforsaken country needs to be watertight.'

'Excellent, Sir!' Kruse said, clicking his heels as he saluted before leaving the room.

27

Leaves rustled behind them. Henry turned, relieved to see Tommy's mop of hair through the bushes.

'Sarge?' Tommy whispered.

Cautiously, they slithered on their bellies to the soldier's position.

'We can't hang about,' Henry said. 'Let's get going. You can tell us about your vacation on the way.'

Using mud as a primitive camouflage, they crept nervously through the undergrowth. Once out of sight of the road, they scurried across the fields towards Danzig, taking cover in the hedgerows. They crossed streams wherever possible, hoping to confuse any dogs tracking their scent.

Being in the open air was exhilarating. Even though Henry had to keep looking over his shoulder, it really felt fantastic to be free again. An angry dog barked, bringing him back to reality. Worryingly, it sounded near.

'We have to speed up,' he said, looking around.

Viktor, already exhausted, nodded and pushed on

silently.

Within the hour, they were in almost darkness, the last vestiges of daylight dwindling. Nighttime brought relief, allowing them to move more freely with less risk of being seen.

A main road lay beyond a hawthorn bush. Henry was about to dash across when he heard the unmistakable noise of trucks approaching.

'Keep down,' he said, motioning with his hand.

Tommy looked back, but thankfully the field behind them remained empty.

Taking cover against the hedge, they peeped through the sparse, springtime leaves. The sound continued to increase until four sets of headlamps hurtled around the bend. The three men watched from their concealed position as open-topped troop carriers drove past at speed. In the back were dozens of Wehrmacht soldiers wearing full-length, grey overcoats, preparing for a cold night out of doors. Much to Henry's relief, the trucks passed without slowing.

'They look like they mean business,' Henry said.

'Look!' said Viktor, grabbing Henry's arm. In the distance, arcs of torchlight swept the ground only a couple of fields behind them.

'That's only about a mile away,' Tommy observed.

'They've pulled out all the stops to find us,' said Henry. 'We'd better get a move on before we're spotted.'

They ran across the tarmac, then vaulted a wooden fence on the other side before racing across a recently planted wheat field.

'I've been wondering,' Henry said, as they jogged side by side. 'What did happen to you?'

'When?' Tommy asked, without breaking stride.

'When we escaped. You disappeared for ages.'

'The driver sped out of the gates so quickly I would have been killed if I had let go.'

'So, what did you do?'

'As the truck accelerated, I hung on for dear life,' Tommy continued. 'Eventually, we caught up with a couple of vehicles which had stopped to give way at a narrow bridge. As soon as it was safe, I snuck out and hid behind a hedge. Once the road was clear, I made my way back to you two.'

'You have a bad habit of disappearing, haven't you?' Henry joked.

The three of them ran through the night, putting distance between them and the torches. As day broke, they returned to creeping through hedges and behind walls.

'How far do you think we are from Danzig?' Tommy asked.

'About four miles,' the Pole said.

'Viktor, how are you feeling?' Henry asked, handing out the pieces of bread he had pilfered from the marquee the previous day.

'I'm okay,' he replied, looking weary.

'If we stop, they'll catch us for sure,' Tommy said. 'We should keep moving.'

'I agree,' said Henry. 'Tommy, you take the lead.'

As the day progressed, the light inevitably began to fade. Like the evening before, the temperature dropped rapidly, the cold biting hard. Nonetheless, Henry was reassured, their pursuers would not be so enthusiastic in their chase.

A coastal breeze greeted them as they came over the

hills; the lights of Danzig twinkled below them. In the distance, Henry could see the black, amorphous mass of the Baltic Sea. The last time he had seen it was when they had flown into Poland several months earlier. Standing in silence, the three men took in the view.

'Is that a fire?' Henry said, looking at a large, orange glow in the centre of the city.'

The others followed his gaze.

'Looks like it,' Tommy said. 'I wonder whether it's left over from the bombing.'

'I'm not sure. That was some time ago,' Henry said. 'I would have thought any fires should be out by now. What do you think?'

'It is Długi Targ,' the Pole said after studying the scene below. 'The main street.'

'Why would it be on fire?' Tommy asked.

Viktor shrugged before setting off down the hill.

'Germans looking for three men. Your clothes bad,' Viktor said, pointing at their uniforms. 'I find better. Back in one hour.'

'But we can't wait here,' said Tommy. 'There's nowhere to hide.'

'Come,' Viktor said reassuringly.

He led them down the valley towards a stream, flanked by trees.

'I meet you here,' he said.

They shook his hand before Viktor disappeared down the hillside into the darkness.

28

Surprisingly, the streets were empty. Nobody walked on the pavements, and the trams were not running. It all seemed a little odd. Nonetheless, the familiar surroundings of Danzig were a welcome relief from the chaos of the last few months.

As he rounded the corner, he heard excited shouting. Curious, he crept to the edge of a building and peered around. In the main street, long shadows danced on the walls of the buildings, cast by the flickering glow of a massive bonfire. A crowd of people listened intently to a dignitary high on a podium, standing against a backdrop of a swastika fluttering in the night breeze. Even this far away, the heat from the fire caused him to perspire.

Facing the audience, a row of closely cropped teenagers stood to attention, while a party official gave his animated oratory. The youths in their khaki shirts and armbands watched eagerly as an SS officers threw books onto the giant fire. As they applauded the poisonous anti-Semitic rhetoric being spewed from the rostrum, Viktor recognised many of the faces around the flames. The crowd, including the soldiers around the periphery, were transfixed by the speaker, allowing him to creep past.

Parts of the town were in ruins, while other areas appeared unharmed. Near the port, the destruction was worst. Large craters dotted the roads, and some of the houses bore the signs of battle. Worrying about the state of his own home, Viktor quickened his pace.

He rounded the corner of Drzewny Road onto Hucisko Street, stopping in front of his small shop. Home! It was wonderful to be back. Despite the crack in the shopfront window, everything else appeared to be intact. He walked down the alley at the side of the building, navigating the fence which now littered the floor. All the contents of his pockets had been taken from him when he was captured in Olsztyn. He rattled the backdoor hard, but it would not give. Sitting on the step, he wearily put his head into his hands. To come this far and to be defeated by a locked door on his own house infuriated him.

The yard reminded him of their awful journey to Olsztyn. He missed Zofia and the boys desperately. Frustratingly, his horse was probably warmer and better fed than he was right now. The horse, of course! He headed across the courtyard, avoiding the rubble which littered the ground. Entering the empty stable with its familiar damp smell, he groped his way into the dark, far corner. High on a shelf, which no one else would ever know was there, he located a rusty, green and white tobacco tin. Flicking it open with his thumb, he retrieved the spare key wrapped in a small, brown paper bag which he kept for emergencies. Viktor hurried back towards the house, unlocked the house door, and slipped inside.

Greeted by the familiar yeasty aroma of the bakery, he instantly felt at home, but there was a striking hollowness too. Overcome with emotion, he slumped to his knees and sobbed uncontrollably. As the adrenaline wore off, Viktor began to shiver. Having been unoccupied for several months, the house was bitterly cold.

He scrabbled around, relying on his memory to locate things. On the windowsill, he found an oil lamp, then stumbled his way across the room. Next, Viktor fumbled in the cash register until he found the matches he kept in the money tray. It was a strange place to keep them, but they were out of the reach of their two small boys, who seemed to have a natural curiosity for all things dangerous.

Striking a match on the side of the box, Viktor lit the wick and lowered the lamp's glass wind sleeve. He was thankful the shop had been untouched by the chaos. With the light, he moved easily from room to room. He grabbed his delivery bag, hanging on the back of the door, before proceeding upstairs.

In his and Zofia's bedroom, he opened a chest of drawers and started stuffing clothes into the holdall like a man possessed. With the bag near to bursting, he returned to the kitchen. Catching sight of himself in the mirror by the back door, he realised he had forgotten about the mud on his face. Swilling himself with the cold water which remained in the bowl, he removed all traces of his makeshift camouflage.

With his bag thrown over his shoulder, he kept his head down and hurried back through the streets. Walking through these familiar surroundings reminded him of his family. They must be worried sick. If only he could send a message to them. There would be little point in trying to post a letter, as the county's infrastructure was likely to be in a dreadful state, not to mention the fact he was an escaped convict. Every fibre of him wanted to set off for Olsztyn, but he knew he owed the British soldiers for helping him escape.

'You, stop!' a stern voice shouted in German,' A Danzig police officer in his dark green overcoat strode towards him.

His heart sank.

'Where are you going in such a hurry?'

'I'm on my way home from work,' he said, noticing another policeman on the other side of the street watching on.

'It's a bit late to be finishing, isn't it?'

'No, I drive the cranes at the docks,' Viktor lied, trying hard to force a smile. 'There have been several large ships in today. They had to be unloaded before this morning's high tide.'

'What's in the bag?' the policeman asked, removing it from Viktor's shoulder and opening its drawstring.

'They're only work clothes. I'm taking them home for my wife to wash.'

'I see,' said the officer, pulling out a shirt collar. 'Well, you can't keep the little woman waiting, can you?'

'Heil Hitler,' Viktor said awkwardly.

The soldier reciprocated.

***

The two British soldiers had found the trees by the stream as the Pole had described. Tommy had fallen asleep on a mound of grass while Henry kept watch. It was just before dawn, and soon the sun would begin to peep over the horizon. Tiredness and anxiety toyed with Henry's mind. *We need to be in the city before daylight. Otherwise, we'll be spotted. What if Viktor was going to shop them to the Germans or leave them out in the open to fend for themselves? Where was he?*

The longer he waited, the more these thoughts played on his mind. Out of habit, Henry kept looking at his wrist where his watch used to be. Maybe Viktor has no intention of returning.

'Do you think he's been caught?' Tommy whispered, catching him by surprise.

'I don't know,' he said. 'But he is taking his time, isn't he?'

Finally, a lone figure appeared on the path at the foot of the hill and headed towards them.

'Is that him?' Tommy nudged Henry.

231

'I think so, but let's stay hidden until we're sure he doesn't have company.'

The two British soldiers scrutinised the man as he approached. At about a hundred yards, they recognised him. Once satisfied the man was alone, Henry stood up from behind the bush and waved the tall Pole over.

'The city is full of Germans,' he said. 'We haven't got long. Put these on.'

He threw the bag on the floor and looked around nervously as the two men grabbed at it like vultures at a dead animal's carcass. They pulled out the items of clothing and stripped off their torn and dirty uniforms. The clothes did not fit them perfectly, but they were much less conspicuous. Stuffing their belongings into the holdall, they looked to Viktor for guidance as to what to do next.

'Wash your face,' he said, pointing at the stream.

As they splashed ice-cold water over themselves, he continued to talk. 'Big gathering. Nazis. Come, we'd better go quick.'

He slung the bag over his shoulder, then set off back down. The two British soldiers hurried after him.

'We can't walk together,' said Henry. 'We'll arouse too much suspicion. Viktor. You go first. I will be twenty seconds behind you and Tommy, I want you walking on the other side of the street, okay?'

They nodded.

'Whatever happens, we can't lose sight of Viktor,' he said.

'What do we do if we become separated?' Tommy asked.

'Go bakery on Hucisko Street,' the Pole said.

'Good,' said Henry. 'But what if we can't find it? We can't ask anyone, can we?'

'Big church on Piwna Street. You can see it from docks. No miss it, too big.'

'Excellent!' the blond soldier replied. 'Let's get moving.'

The two British soldiers followed, some distance behind the tall Pole. As he entered the city, Viktor noticed the atmosphere had changed. The streets had been empty, but now the pavements were packed. Everyone was talking enthusiastically as they walked along. Many wore Nazi emblems on armbands; others carried flags and banners. It felt like returning from a football match on a Saturday afternoon. People chatted excitedly as if there had been a home win. Henry pulled down the peak of his cap, his eyes never leaving Viktor's back.

It was difficult to follow him in the crowd. Occasionally, he would catch a glimpse of the bag Viktor carried, reassuring him they were heading in the right direction. Similarly, Tommy battled his way through the people on the opposite pavement. For Viktor, it was even harder. People recognised him. He would smile and nod politely but walked on relentlessly.

An old customer spotted him, grabbing him by the arm. He started asking about his family. Frustrated, Viktor made polite conversation as Henry continued past.

'When did you get back?' the old man asked.

'A few days ago. Zofia and the kids are with my parents in Olsztyn.'

'What did you think of the rally? The speaker was excellent, wasn't he?'

'It was good,' Viktor said. 'I'm really sorry, I have to hurry back to light the ovens in the bakery, so they are ready for today.'

'Oh! Don't let me keep you. It's been lovely bumping into you. Maybe I'll pop round to see you tomorrow. It would be good to catch up.'

Viktor thanked him and then set off once more.

Breaking into a sweat every time he passed someone in uniform, Viktor tried to locate his friends. To make matters worse, a company of German guards marched down the street back towards their barracks.

Eventually, he spotted Henry and Tommy up ahead.

'Hello again,' said the voice from behind him.

Viktor turned and saw the police officer who had stopped him in the street earlier.

'Did you get your washing done?' he asked, nodding towards the bag.

Viktor's heart sank. This was all he needed, a friendly policeman.

'No, my wife was at the rally,' he said as the British soldiers walked past. 'I'm afraid I have to rush off. I need some sleep before I have to be back at work,' said Viktor, praying the officer would not look in the holdall again. 'We have to start loading again in a couple of hours.'

'No rest for the wicked. Sleep well.'

Where had the other two gone? He negotiated the crowd, frantically searching for his two friends. Thankfully, he found them standing in a doorway, a few hundred yards from where the policeman had stopped him. He smiled apologetically.

Viktor reached the bakery first. Letting himself in, he relit the lamp on the kitchen windowsill. Henry was next to arrive, closely followed by Tommy. Once everyone was inside, breathing a huge sigh of relief, he locked the door.

'Welcome,' Viktor announced with a warm smile.

29

Henry's slumber was finally disturbed by the gnawing ache of a full bladder. He tried to ignore it, but the discomfort became unbearable. Flinching as his feet made contact with the ice-cold linoleum, he yawned. He rubbed his eyes as they contended with the sunlight streaming through the threadbare curtains.

The room was relatively spartan. A brightly coloured, cross-stitched picture hung on the wall at the foot of the bed. On top of a rickety table in the corner rested a ceramic washbowl next to a well-loved teddy bear. A snore emanated from Tommy, who remained fast asleep in a single bed adjacent to his. Henry smiled, content in the knowledge he was no longer a prisoner, even if he was now on the run.

Viktor knocked on the door, making Henry jump.

'Breakfast soon,' he said, placing down two steaming jugs of water on the table. 'I've got razor blades and soap.'

Tommy put his hand to his mouth and yawned while nodding his appreciation.

'Thanks, Viktor. But I think we'll keep our beards, so we're not so easy to recognise.'

'I suppose you're right,' said the blond corporal. 'Any

Nazi sympathiser between here and Berlin will be looking for us.'

'I hate having a beard,' Henry confessed. 'It's so itchy, but we have to change our appearance. The entire German Army will be looking for us.'

Viktor disappeared downstairs, leaving Henry to stagger over to the table and pour some water into the bowl. He washed his hands and face before letting out another yawn. Next, he took one of the razor blades and tidied the edges of his already shaggy face. Once finished, he admired his neat, rudimentary beard in the mirror. Sadly, it would be a few weeks before his facial hair would provide an adequate disguise. Slipping on the clothes from the previous night, he set off in search of a lavatory.

In the kitchen, their host removed some freshly baked bread from the oven, while a kettle boiled on the stove.

'You must have woken early,' Henry said, taking a seat at the table.

'Not really. Missing my wife.'

'What time is it?'

'Just after midday.'

'Gosh, I didn't realise it was that late.'

'You needed the sleep,' he said, sounding like a parent talking to a child.

'I wanted to say thank you for helping us escape and letting us stay here. We appreciate everything you've done.'

Viktor smiled uncomfortably, not used to receiving compliments.

The two men stood in awkward silence, Henry realising he hardly knew this man.

'Viktor, something's been bothering me,' he said tentatively.

'What?' he asked, turning out the bread onto a wire rack.

'Surely the Germans know your address from when they captured you in Olsztyn. Won't they come straight here?'

'I used wrong name. All fine, all fine.'

'That was quick thinking, but why?'

'Protecting my family. The soldiers hurt my father,' said Viktor. 'I wanted everyone safe.'

Tommy bounced into the room and interrupted the conversation inadvertently.

'For the first time in a long while, I feel human. So, what've we got to eat, Viktor?' he asked.

'Only bread and coffee. I'm sorry.'

Without invitation, Henry cut the loaf and tore a slice in two. Smothering each piece with butter, he waited for it to partially melt. The flavour was terrific, far better than anything he had eaten in the last few months. The three men ate hungrily, savouring every morsel.

'This beats that awful brown bread they served in the work camp,' said Tommy.

'Sure does,' Henry said. 'What's the plan for today?'

'You two must hide,' Viktor replied, spreading jam. 'I'm going out.'

'Where are you going?' asked Henry, still worrying their host would return with some Germans.

'Must go bank then buying a few things.'

'Great. I'm sorry we can't contribute financially,' Tommy said sincerely.

'Have you any thoughts on how we can get home?' Henry asked.

'My cousin,' Viktor said.

'Can he be trusted?' Tommy asked anxiously.

Henry kicked him for asking such an ungracious question.

'Of course,' said Viktor with warm reassurance. 'He very good man.'

Tommy rolled up the last piece of bread and ate it before finishing the remnants of the coffee.

The two soldiers cleared the table and began washing up at the large kitchen sink.

'Tell us about your cousin,' Henry said while Viktor straightened his tie in front of the mirror.

'Gregori,' he said. He's fisherman in Gdynia.'

'Where's Gdynia?' asked Tommy.

'Eighteen miles west.'

'Aren't there fishermen in Danzig you could ask? Wouldn't it be easier to use one of them?'

'Danzig was German until the last war,' he said politely. 'Can't trust here. Gregori is good Polish. Good Polish.'

The two British soldiers listened intently as Viktor continued.

'So, you're saying the population around here are mostly German sympathisers,' Henry said. 'That explains the attendance at last night's meeting in the city square.'

Viktor nodded.

'I see,' said Tommy. 'But won't this Gdynia place have been captured during the invasion too?'

'Yes,' said Viktor, 'but Polish, not German.'

'It seems to make sense,' Henry reflected. 'We'll trust your judgement.'

'So, when do we meet your cousin?' Tommy asked eagerly.

'I go on my own. I ask him. Too risky for you.'

Reluctantly, the British soldiers agreed.

'You two stay here. I'll be back before dark.'

'Fine, we understand,' said Henry, looking for a nod of approval from Tommy. 'How is your cousin going to help?'

'He crosses the Baltic often,' Viktor said. 'He goes to Sweden. They have better fish prices. He take a letter to the English in Stockholm.'

'You mean to the British Consulate,' Henry said, trying to follow what Viktor was saying.

'Yes,' said Viktor. 'They arrange boat to take you home.'

'Why don't we go with him?' Tommy asked.

'Too risky for him if caught,' Viktor said. 'This best way.'

Henry agreed. Tommy nodded grimly.

'Gregori usually come home on Wednesday for Thursday's market,' he said. 'You write letter now.'

After discussing what they should write, the two British soldiers set about composing their letter. Henry wanted to keep the text suitably vague, in case the letter fell into the wrong hands, but it had to contain enough detail to explain their situation adequately. It might raise some awkward questions, particularly around how they ended up in Poland, but that didn't matter right now. They decided it was better to avoid writing their names. Instead, they included their service numbers, so if the letter arrived in London, Major Fosdyke would be informed. Tommy had the idea of describing themselves as 'Escaped Prisoners of War,' hoping it would encourage the British government to repatriate them quickly. Henry was not sure.

When they were both happy with the content, Henry neatly folded the sheet of paper before placing it into a small, brown envelope which Viktor had provided.

'Hang on! Today's Wednesday, isn't it?' Tommy said in realisation.

'Yes,' said Viktor. 'Must go now,' he said, pocketing the letter and putting on his overcoat and cap before locking the two men in the house.

Tommy made more coffee on the stove, while, through the yellowed net curtains, Henry watched Viktor disappear down the alleyway.

'Do you think we're safe here?' Tommy asked.

'As safe as we can be,' he said nervously. 'Remember, Viktor's neck is on the line too.'

'But waiting here is torture.'

'I know it's frustrating, but all we can do is lie low and hope Viktor and his cousin come through for us.'

'I swear I'll go crazy being locked up in here.'

Be patient. Being here is much better than being in a cell. Anyway, I think we need an escape strategy.'

'Isn't that what Viktor is trying to organise?'

'No, I mean a plan, just in case the Germans come looking for us here.'

'Oh! What do you have in mind?'

30

Viktor hurried down the high street, becoming increasingly self-consciousness. A constant pang of nausea gripped him, causing perspiration to run down his chest. He knew he had to do this, so he kept his head down, avoiding eye contact with anyone.

After twenty minutes, he was still only third in the queue at the bank, stuck behind a rotund lady carrying a wicker basket and a frustrated-looking businessman in a dark suit. The red second hand on the clock ahead of him moved slowly. Behind him stood a middle-aged man dressed in an overcoat and a fur hat. Viktor did not recognise him, but the man continually glared at him.

A cashier rang a bell. Viktor looked up and realised he was at the front of the line. Beckoning him to the desk, she smiled politely. He tried his best to act naturally, smiling back as genuinely as he could. Handing over his bank book, he requested a modest withdrawal from his account. The cashier selected several banknotes from a hidden drawer. She counted the notes methodically before stamping his paperwork and placing the money inside the front cover. Thanking her, he stuffed the book into his jacket pocket. On his way out, he passed the people waiting in the line. The man in the fur hat was still staring at him.

Unsettled, he walked the short distance to the grocers where he bought some odds and ends, beads of sweat collecting on his forehead as he paid. As he left the shop, the man in the hat came out of the bank. Viktor smiled lamely, but the man scowled back. Feeling besieged, he crossed the road.

The man was walking parallel with him on the other side of the street. He was certain the Germans were onto him. After a few yards, he glanced across. It took him several seconds to locate the man in the hat—now some distance behind, heading in the opposite direction. Breathing a massive sigh of relief, he proceeded down a side road, entering a familiar yard.

The warehouse seemed to have remained undamaged by the recent conflict.

'Hello, Viktor,' said a voice, startling him.

'Hi, Kasper,' he replied, recognising him instantly.

'I haven't seen you for a while. How are you?' asked Mr Kosinski, the local flour merchant. 'I thought you and your family headed east to stay with your parents.'

'We did. Zofia and the kids are still there, but I'm back now. I thought I'd drop in and say hello. You seem unscathed despite everything that's gone on.'

'We were fortunate,' said Kasper, one of Viktor's oldest friends. 'It was a terrible business. I think you made the right choice. You know, leaving when you did.'

'Are Ioana and the children all right?'

'Yes, the wife's okay. But the little ones were a bit shaken by the invasion. Things have settled down now. Well mostly,' he said, lowering his voice. 'We're worried about our eldest, though. He's volunteered for the Wehrmacht.'

'No!' Viktor said in disbelief. 'How did Ioana take that?'

'She cried for days. But there wasn't anything we

could do—he's old enough to make his own decisions. We're just praying he'll be okay.'

'I'm sure he will be. Does he buy into this Nazi stuff?'

'Not really. They were recruiting in the centre of Danzig, and those who didn't 'volunteer' tended to disappear. Anyway, enough about my woes. How's your family?'

'They're well. I'd thought they'd be safer staying in Olsztyn.'

'Very wise, as always. Are you opening up the bakery again?'

'I'm not sure yet. There's a little bit of damage which needs repairing first.'

'I can come and give you a hand if you'd like.'

'No, it'll be fine.'

'Why don't you have a drink before you leave?'

'I don't mind if I do,' he said, hoping to lose the man with the hat for good.

The two men sat in Kasper's cramped office. Pouring two cups of coffee from a flask, the flour merchant handed one to him. 'Things have changed. Shortly after the invasion, a German officer came here demanding I supply the Wehrmacht. To be honest, I wasn't given much of a choice. They pay well enough, mind you, but I barely have enough to supply my customers.'

'I can't imagine your regulars are happy about that.'

'You soon find out which of your friends are German sympathisers,' Kasper said, sipping from his cup. 'They think I'm a hero for supporting the war effort. The Poles, on the other hand, have stopped talking to me completely.'

'That's so unfair. It's not your fault,' Viktor said. 'As you say, you weren't given an option.'

'My customers don't see it like that,' said Kasper, glancing at his watch. 'You're going to have to excuse me, I'm expecting a Wehrmacht truck any minute. You can stay here while they're here if you want. It would be good to catch up some more.'

'No, I'd better be going,' he said, draining the remnants of his coffee. 'As you can imagine, I've much to do.'

'I understand,' said Kasper, shaking his hand vigorously. 'It's so good to see you.'

'You too. I'll drop by in a few days when I have resolved a couple of issues.'

Carrying his groceries under his arm, Viktor headed towards the port. A robust, icy breeze blew in from the sea. Thankfully, the man with the hat was now nowhere to be seen. To his frustration, new security barriers had been erected since he was last here, sealing off the entrance to the harbour. Mounted on the wall, next to the barrier, were four brass clocks showing the tide times for the day. The next high tide was at five-thirty that afternoon. Perfect.

He returned to find the two British soldiers sitting at the kitchen table, playing noughts and crosses.

'Welcome back,' said Tommy after Viktor had locked the door.

'How is it out there?' Henry asked.

'Awful. I'm not cut out for this kind of business.'

'You're doing a great job,' he said reassuringly. 'Come, sit down and have something to drink. Tommy's just made some.'

'I'd never made it before,' said the blond soldier. 'We only really have tea back home. I'm afraid my coffee making has been somewhat experimental.'

'His last few attempts were way too strong. It was totally undrinkable.'

'I think I have it sussed now,' said Tommy proudly.

The two British soldiers listened carefully as Viktor described the heavy Wehrmacht presence in the city and the new security at the port.

'Sounds like we can't take too many chances,' said Henry.

'No, you must stay hidden.'

'We do appreciate everything you are doing for us,'

Tommy said.

Viktor smiled before describing his plans for making contact with his cousin.

After a light lunch, he prepared for his meeting with Gregori. It was clear his anxiety was returning.

'Take a book to read,' Henry said helpfully. 'You might be waiting for your cousin's ship to come in, and it'll help you take your mind off everything.'

'Good idea,' said Viktor, disappearing upstairs for a few minutes.

'I think I'm ready,' he said when he returned.

'Not quite,' said Tommy, handing him the letter for the British Consulate.

'Ah, yes. Mustn't forget that,' Viktor said before departing.

'What are we going to do now?' Tommy said, closing the door. 'I'm bored with playing games. All the books are in Polish, and so is the radio.'

'We're just going to have to sit it out,' said Henry.

'I'm worried about Viktor. He seems very jumpy.'

'Yeah, it can't be easy for him. I'm sure he'll be okay.'

'I do hope so.'

With the envelope safely tucked into his inside jacket pocket, Viktor walked down the alleyway towards Hucisko Street. He rejoined the everyday hustle and bustle of the city's pavements, strolling to the tram terminal where he would begin his two-stop journey.

Under the shelter, trying to remain inconspicuous, he waited until the number twenty-nine to Sopot appeared. Climbing aboard the burgundy and cream tram, he paid the conductor for his ticket and then settled into a seat two-thirds of the way towards the back, opposite the side door.

Through the window, he watched the queue of passengers on the platform boarding the tram. Worryingly, an SS soldier took his place on the front row, behind the driver. A stocky middle-aged lady made her way down the aisle, taking the seat next to Viktor. This was perfect. Everyone, including the guard, would think they were married. Hopefully, a couple would draw less attention than a single man would.

The sight of the station of Sopot brought him great relief. As the noisy tram slowed into the seaside town, the lady stood in preparation for leaving. Viktor exited via the side door and ambled along the platform, trying not to draw attention to himself. A group of Wehrmacht soldiers came towards him, chatting among themselves. Wherever he looked, there were Germans. Unperturbed, he searched for his next tram to Gdynia.

After showing his ticket to the conductor, Viktor took a seat. Within a few seconds of boarding, they began the slow, noisy trundle out of the station. This time, there were no soldiers on board, so he relaxed, staring out at the scenery.

After several hours of travelling, the tram pulled into Gdynia. He left the terminus building and commenced the short walk to the quay where he hoped to find his cousin. As he got nearer, he saw a similar level of security to the docks back in Danzig. Suddenly, he felt a hand on his shoulder. His heart sank, his legs turning to jelly, as he turned around.

'Viktor, I thought it was you,' said Gregori, giving him a firm hug. 'What brings you all the way out here?'

'Hello,' he said softly. 'I need to speak with you in private.'

'Of course. It sounds serious. Are your Zofia and the kids okay?'

'They're fine, I think. I've left them in Olsztyn. It's a long story. I need a favour from you, but we can't talk about it here.'

'Okay, Come with me.'

They walked up to the barrier, which led to the quayside. A Wehrmacht guard looked at them menacingly, enquiring about their business. Gregori explained he was the captain of a trawler and Viktor had applied to be a member of his crew. The guards looked the two men up and down, checked their identity papers, then let them both pass.

Gregori's boat, *Powodzenie*, was moored about a hundred yards along the barnacle-covered quay. The fisherman jumped nimbly onto the deck, helping his less agile cousin aboard. The ship lurched, causing Viktor to grab desperately to the side rail. They went below to a simple cabin with a bunk in the corner.

'We can talk here,' he said, closing the door.

'I don't even know where to start,' Viktor said.

'It must be important if you have travelled all this way to see me,' Gregori said, pouring two small shots of vodka into two battered mugs.

Viktor told his cousin about the events of the last few months. The fisherman laughed at the thought of him being a fugitive, but Viktor did not think it was funny.

'I can't think of a less likely criminal,' Gregori said with a smirk. 'But where do I fit into all this? Please don't ask me to help them escape. If I am caught, they'll shoot me.'

'No, I wouldn't ask you to do that, but I have a letter I'd like you to take to Sweden. I want you to deliver it to the British Embassy in Stockholm. It tells them about the soldiers and asks their government to arrange their rescue.'

'I see. So, you want me to be the messenger?'

Viktor nodded, sipping at the vodka.

Gregori sat in silence, thinking for a few moments before agreeing.

'It's going to be tricky,' he said. 'The Germans are like hawks at the moment. They're watching the ports and meticulously checking documents. So, if I have the slightest notion the Germans have gotten wind of this, the letter goes into the water in a weighted bag, okay?'

'I understand. When do you next go to sea?'

'If this weather holds, and with the tides being what

they are, we should be good for tomorrow night. The crew don't need to know about our agreement. The fewer people who do, the better. We often stop over in Stockholm anyhow, so they shouldn't suspect anything.'

Viktor thanked him, handing over the envelope. 'When will you return?'

'We are usually at sea for six days,' Gregori answered, walking across the room and placing the letter in a safe concealed behind a wall panel. 'If we come back any sooner, the Germans will ask too many questions. I want to keep everything as normal as possible.'

'I do understand, but it's going to be a long wait.'

'I know, but I can't do anything out of the ordinary. It's too risky.'

'Where shall I meet you?'

'I'll aim for us to be unloading our catch on Tuesday evening, ready for Wednesday's fish auctions. The good thing is when a fishing boat returns there are so many people on the quayside, you know, harbour staff and fisheries personnel. The Germans probably won't notice you.'

'Tuesday it is then. I'll look for you at the barrier.'

31

The two British soldiers were extremely bored while Viktor prowled around the house, always on edge. After endless hours of prowling back and forth, anxiety got the better of him.

'Why don't we open the shop?' he asked.

The other two stared at him incredulously.

'If you work the ovens, I could serve,' Viktor added.

'But we know nothing about baking,' said Tommy.

'No, I teach you. It's easy,' he replied. 'I make mixture, and you put in oven.'

'If you think we can do it, then let's have a go,' Henry said positively. 'It would sure liven up this place.'

He showed them around the cramped kitchens behind the bakery before spending several hours making dough. Tommy chalked notes on a blackboard, recording how long each type of bread took in the oven. After sampling their handiwork over lunch, they made multiple batches of tarts and biscuits.

By the evening, trays of loaves, cakes, doughnuts, and cookies were stacked on the worktops, more than enough for the next day. For the first time since arriving in Danzig, they went to their respective rooms laughing. Viktor kissed

Zofia's pillow before quickly falling asleep with a smile on his face.

After a hearty breakfast, Henry and Tommy started work in the kitchen, while Viktor prepared for the reopening. Once satisfied with the appearance of the shop's interior, he turned the sign around on the back of the door, then lugged a steel advertisement onto the pavement outside. It was two hours before the first customer came in. However, by midday, a steady stream had returned as word circulated about the Cwiklinskis being back in business.

Occasionally, a bell would ring, summoning Viktor to the kitchen to resolve a problem, but otherwise, it felt good to return to normality. With something to take their minds off their incarceration, the atmosphere had improved, and the two British soldiers appeared to be thriving. At the end of the day, the till was full of money, and the house echoed with laughter.

The little bakery on the corner of Hucisko Street and Drzewny Road became increasingly busy over the next few days. Alarmingly, they even received a regular order from the Wehrmacht headquarters.

On Tuesday morning, he opened as usual, but Viktor placed a handwritten notice in the window saying today would be half-day closing. Mrs. Dabrowski, one of his most loyal customers, was waiting outside when he unlocked the door.

'Morning, Mr. Cwiklinski,' she said.

'Good morning, Magda. What can I do for you this morning?'

'I would like a rye loaf and half a dozen lemon tarts,' she said. 'Some of the ladies are coming for afternoon tea.'

'That sounds lovely,' said Viktor, placing the bread in a white paper bag and the pastries in two cardboard boxes.

'How are the family?'

'Oh, they're very well. They're staying with my family at the moment.'

He rang the items through the cash register, counting out the coins she had given him as he placed them into the drawer of the till.

'Enjoy your afternoon with your friends,' he said, handing her the correct change.

'Thank you,' she called back over her shoulder as she left the shop.

Midway through another busy morning, the quartermaster from the Wehrmacht garrison joined the back of the small queue of customers. Viktor's anxiety levels rose as the soldier moved along the line. The officer collected his regular order of five trays of croissants, and Viktor gave him an additional couple of cakes for free. Thankfully, Tommy and Henry were out of sight in the kitchen.

Standing behind the counter, Viktor rested on his elbow, daydreaming. The bell on the door rang, dragging him back from his thoughts. He looked up to greet the next customer as an SS hauptmann entered the bakery.

Viktor swallowed hard and greeted the officer warmly, his pulse racing. Had his cousin been captured? Had the Germans found the letter?'

'Good morning.'

'Hello. How can I help you?'

'You look familiar. Have we met before? the hauptmann said.

Viktor recognised the man too but was unable to place him.

'I don't think so,' he said, trying to appear casual. 'Is it bread or cakes you're after?'

'I'm afraid I am not here to buy anything. I'm making some enquiries.'

It dawned on him, this was the officer who had virtually strangled him in front of Zofia and the children all those weeks ago.

'How can I help?' Viktor asked, hiding his quaking legs.

'We're investigating some British soldiers who may be sheltering in Danzig.'

'British soldiers?' he said, shaking his head. 'No, why would they be here?'

'Escaped prisoners. We don't know for certain they're in the city, but if you encounter anything suspicious, please report it straight away?'

'Of course, Sir. I will keep a lookout, but I must lock up now. Today is my half-day, but if I come across anything, I will inform the police immediately.'

'Thank you.'

'Would you like these for later?' Viktor said, showing two cherry buns before placing them in a paper bag.

'That's very kind,' he said, taking the gift.

With that, the hauptmann left and proceeded next door to continue his enquiries. As soon as the officer had gone, he locked the door and then rushed into the kitchen.

'What is it?' asked Henry. 'You look like you've seen a ghost.'

'Worse,' he said. 'SS hauptmann been in shop.'

His words caused both of them to freeze.

'Can you describe him?' Tommy asked.

'I've met him before,' he said, having described the dark-haired hauptmann. 'A few months ago, when my wife and I were travelling. He's searching for you two. I forget his name.'

'Roehm!' said the two soldiers in unison.

'Damn!' Henry said. 'We can't stay here.'

'I have to leave now. I go see Gregori. Don't light lamp and keep away from windows.'

Viktor put on his coat, grabbing his hat, scarf, and gloves before leaving.

***

Roehm walked along the seafront, lost in his thoughts. Where were the British soldiers? He stared out into the bay, watching the turbulent, grey water breaking onto the pebbly beach. His leather-clad hands gripped the railings while he continued to stare straight out to sea. Something was bothering him. He knew the baker from somewhere, and there was a connection with the British soldiers, but how?

The salty breeze caused a tear to run down his cheek. Suddenly, he remembered; the checkpoint where they had first been spotted. He reconstructed the events of the last several months. Could the baker have been their contact in the country? Where did he say he was going? Come on, Andreas, think! Where was he going that day? Was it Olsztyn?

Roehm could not be sure, but Olsztyn was where the Polish political activist, who had escaped with the British soldiers, had been arrested. In his world, coincidences never happened. This was too important to ignore. He scurried back down the promenade where his squad car was waiting. As the hauptmann approached, the driver straightened his tie and then started the engine. Climbing onto the back seat, Roehm shouted, 'Take me to the Fourth Army's headquarters now!'

From the tone of his superior's voice, he knew not to ask any further questions and sped away.

Roehm beat his fist in anger as they became stuck behind a slow-moving delivery van. They moved infuriatingly slowly until the vehicle turned down a side road, allowing the driver to floor the accelerator. With wheels screeching, they careened through the city.

The car snaked through the narrow streets, nearly colliding with a market stall. Eventually they pulled up outside the Civic Hall. A giant Nazi flag flapped in the bitter breeze as he barged his way into the building, towering over a corporal who sat behind the reception desk.

'I need to speak to the duty officer.'

'May I ask who you are?'

'I'm Hauptmann Roehm of the SS. Now please don't waste my time. This is urgent.'

'He's in a meeting.'

'Well, go and get him.'

The corporal thought about challenging him, but thought better of it. 'Yes, Sir.'

Agitated, Roehm paced back and forth in the dark foyer, fidgeting endlessly with his pocketwatch.

'The duty officer will see you now,' the soldier said.

He grunted his recognition, following the young man upstairs to the first floor. Striding past the corporal, he addressed the officer directly.

'My name's Roehm, SS hauptmann for the Eastern Section.'

The squat Wehrmacht officer shook Roehm's hand without standing and gestured to a seat opposite him.

'What can I do for you, Hauptmann?'

'I'm investigating the escape of two British prisoners and a Polish national from a work camp south of here. I believe they are hiding in the city.'

'Ah, yes! Do you mean these?' The officer handed Roehm a printed sheet containing photographs of the fugitives. The images were not good likenesses, but it was clearly the baker and the two escapees.

'Yes,' he said excitedly.

'Copies of this poster will be delivered to every military installation, railway station, and port in Poland. They will not be able to get far without someone recognising them. Do you have an idea where they could be?'

'I believe they're in a bakery on Hucisko Street, near the harbour.'

'If you know where they are, Hauptmann, why do you need my help?'

'I need some of your men and a few vehicles to

ensure they don't escape.'

The officer thought for a while. He wanted to say 'no,' because the SS were asking, but he was an ambitious man. If he was part of the successful capture of the three prisoners, his name would be talked about, perhaps even in Berlin.

'I see,' he said, pressing both of his index fingers to his lips, pretending to think, before picking up the phone.

'I can let you have twenty infantry and a couple of troop carriers. Will that be enough?' he asked, holding the telephone's handset away from his mouth.

Roehm nodded impatiently.

Terminating the call, the duty officer looked straight at him.

'There is one condition,' he said. 'My men will not take orders from the SS. I shall come with you.'

32

Roehm and his borrowed army headed for Hucisko Street in the cramped truck. After a short drive through the town, the vehicles drove up the broad thoroughfare, stopping outside the bakery. The noise of the engines startled Henry as he rested in the bedroom. He peered bravely around the curtains, but what he saw struck terror into his heart.

'Tommy, get out the back door now!' he shouted.

A metal tray clattered to the floor, as Henry jumped down the stairs, three at a time. Tommy was already outside, wearing their 'emergency' bag across his chest as Henry grabbed his coat from the hook behind the door. They vaulted the remains of the fence and sprinted onto the cobbles of Drzewny Road. As he ran, Tommy took off his blue and white striped apron, dumping it on the ground.

As the two British soldiers turned onto Hucisko Street, a crowd began to gather as the German infantrymen carried out their raid. Everyone was looking the other way, allowing the two men to walk past unnoticed on the other side of the road.

'Your hands are covered in flour,' Henry whispered.

'Put them in your pockets.'

Roehm stood with his back to them, deep in conversation with the Wehrmacht officer standing beside him. Other soldiers ran in and out, shouting instructions while Henry and Tommy kept walking with their heads down.

After fifteen minutes of searching, an unteroffizier came out, bypassed the SS hauptmann, and spoke directly to his superior.

'Sir, the building is empty. But, it would appear someone's been here recently. The kettle is still hot, and three of the beds have been slept in.'

Roehm slammed through the door, uttering a stream of expletives. An upturned tray lay scattered on the floor, and the ovens were still lit.

'Someone left in a hurry,' he said to the duty officer who struggled to keep up.

Opening the heavy, fire door between the shop and the rest of the house, he walked around the property. In the pokey kitchen, the water in the kettle on the stove was indeed warm, but so far there was no conclusive evidence the British soldiers had ever been here.

The lounge was dark and dingy, the chairs and sofa looked quite uncomfortable. Roehm prowled from room to room, stopping in the children's bedroom. The bed clothes were scattered untidily, but nothing out of the ordinary. Frustrated, he turned to leave when a wardrobe in the corner caught his eye. He opened the door, revealing clothes on hangers suspended from a rail. At the back was a red suitcase standing on its end. Pulling it onto the worn carpet, he popped the clasps and lifted the lid. Inside, screwed up and dirty, were two British Army uniforms.

'I knew it,' he yelled.

***

Viktor watched as Gregori's boat pulled into the harbour; one of the many ships which had docked while he had been waiting. As soon as it had moored, the crew began hauling wooden crates packed with ice and fish onto the quayside, eager to head home after several days at sea. Wholesalers and tradesmen moved through the crowds of fishermen, inspecting the catch while gulls on the harbour wall squabbled over a tasty morsel, thrown by one of the crew members. Gregori chatted to a couple of the other captains as he strolled toward the barrier where Viktor waited nervously.

Deep in conversation, the Wehrmacht guards paid little attention to the two cousins as they greeted each other. Saying very little, Gregori handed over an indistinct envelope which Viktor placed carefully into his inside pocket.

All the way home, he kept checking he had not lost the letter. As the sliding doors opened, he hurried onto the bustling platform and headed for home. Near the exit, he noticed a large poster on a noticeboard on the station wall. It had not been there when he had left for Gdynia. Curious, he pushed through the commuters who were boarding the tram to get a better look. Rather than an advertisement, the crude poster contained photographs of him and the two soldiers accompanied by the headline 'Chciał!' ('Wanted!') Alarmed, Viktor pulled the brim of his cap down a little lower and adjusted his scarf in an attempt to reduce the likelihood of anyone recognising him.

Thankfully, the light had begun to fade; the darkness would help him remain unnoticed. Tired, and with his nerves in tatters, Viktor joined the mass of people walking home at the end of their working day.

Near the city square, he was jolted from his anxious thoughts when a pedestrian bumped into him.

'Act normal and follow me,' the familiar voice

whispered.

He looked up and caught sight of Tommy, who continued past him.

With his heart fit to explode, Viktor pretended to check the time before changing direction, following the British soldier who was now on the opposite pavement. After a hundred yards, he crossed the street, only a few steps behind Tommy.

The soldier turned down one of Danzig's many anonymous alleyways. Viktor followed, slowing his pace to avoid being associated with the blond man.

'Over here,' Tommy waved from the backyard of a seemingly unoccupied terrace house.

'What's happened?' he asked, spotting Henry lurking in the shadows.

'Roehm came back with reinforcements.'

'We fled out the back door,' the sergeant added. 'We were lucky to get away.'

'Well, we can't go back,' Viktor said desperately. 'What do we do?'

'Let's not panic,' Henry said calmly. 'First, we need somewhere warm and dry to spend the night. Can you think of anywhere we can go? Some place where we can talk without being overheard,' said Tommy.

Viktor thought for a while. 'There's a church on Piwna Street. We go there.'

'It sounds perfect,' said Henry. 'We can't walk through the town in a group. Not now - every corner has a poster with our ugly faces on them. We'll have to split up.'

'That's not a problem. The streets are busy,' Tommy said. 'We won't have to spread out too much.'

'Viktor, if you lead the way, the two of us will follow on behind.'

'Oh! I nearly forgot,' Henry interrupted. 'How did you get on with Gregori?'

'Good. I have a letter from the British Government,' he replied, reaching inside his jacket.

'Hang onto it until we get to the church.'

33

The Basilica of Saint Mary, a massive fifteenth-century brick church, dominated the skyline of the northern part of the city. Inside, the high-vaulted ceilings swept down to enormous stone pillars. Giant candles burnt continually, illuminating numerous ancient icons residing in dingy alcoves. From the hard, wooden pew, Henry stared absentmindedly at the two lines of chandeliers, mesmerised by their flickering candlelight.

Despite being late, a steady stream of worshippers continued to come into the church. Tommy and Viktor sat elsewhere in the building to avoid drawing attention to themselves. Henry took out the letter once again, studying every word in case he had missed a vital detail. The following morning, a Norwegian trawler called *Margarite* would dock in the harbour. The ship would be their passage home, but the Germans had the city in lockdown.

A lady in a shabby, brown housecoat sat on Henry's pew, disturbing his thoughts. He greeted her with a smile before lowering his head, pretending to pray. With his eyes shut, he soon realised he was actually praying. First, he prayed for his own safety and for their success. He thanked God for Viktor before saying a prayer for his brother.

'Just keep him safe,' he muttered in an inaudible whisper. 'Just keep him safe.'

Henry's legs felt stiff, so he sauntered to the back of the church towards an insignificant side door. His curiosity got the better of him. He turned the handle and snuck into what appeared to be a classroom containing an upright piano, presumably to accompany choristers while they practised. At the far end of the room, an archway led to a flight of stone stairs.

After a tiring climb, Henry found himself at the top of a tower. The paint peeled from the walls, and there was an overwhelming smell of bird droppings. Clearly, this part of the church was rarely used. He stood with his arms on a windowsill, staring through the glassless hole, taking in the nighttime view of the city. In the distance, he could see many lights, shining brightly in the harbour with the black void of the Baltic beyond them.

When morning came, the sun streamed through the stained-glass windows, disturbing Henry after an uncomfortable night's sleep. Looking around, Viktor and Tommy were spaced out among the pews, clearly asleep. His stomach groaned. The supplies in their emergency bag had not lasted the night. Someone passed his pew—he assumed it was another member of the public—paying little attention. A wave of nausea rose up inside him as a young man wearing a Wehrmacht uniform crept respectfully down the aisle. He fought the temptation to run, cursing the tiredness numbing his senses.

Taking a seat, a couple of rows in front of him, the soldier began to pray. After ten minutes, the man left without paying much attention to him or his companions. The fact an enemy soldier had walked into the church without them noticing caused Henry concern. How could they have been so sloppy?

He rose from his seat, pretending to admire an icon in the alcove near Tommy.

'I'm going up into the tower again,' Henry said. 'Come with me.'

Tommy's eyes flickered open. He yawned and then nodded.

The two men climbed to the top of the stairs, standing in silence as they admired the view.

'We need to be more careful. If that soldier had been looking for us, we would not have stood a chance,'

'Sorry, boss,' Tommy said. 'I fell asleep.'

'It is noon,' a soft voice said from behind them. They turned to see Viktor standing on the stone steps. 'I get us food. You safe up here.'

'Okay, but don't be long,' said Henry quietly.

The Pole nodded.

'Viktor,' Henry said, causing his friend to turn back. 'Be careful out there.'

They waited until they heard the heavy outer door of the church close behind him.

'How are you doing, Tommy?'

'This is hopeless, Sarge. I'm fed up of waiting, my nerves are shot to pieces, and my belly feels like it hasn't seen food for a week.'

'I know what you mean, but it is going to be fine. There's not long to go now. We need to sit tight until this evening. After that, we're on the homeward straight.'

'We're so close, but I keep thinking we're not going to make it.'

'It'll be okay,' Henry said reassuringly. 'We've come this far, and we've overcome everything we've encountered.'

'I guess you're right,' Tommy said with an unconvincing smile.

'He won't be much longer. You'll feel better with some food in your belly.'

Viktor carried a brown paper bag full of bread, cut meats, and tomatoes up the stairs of the basilica tower. They sat on the steps at the top of the draughty tower, picking at the items he had brought back with him. The impromptu meal was delicious, but an unacknowledged tension hung over them.

'One thing's bothering me,' Tommy said, talking with his mouth full. 'How are we going to get into the harbour?'

'I'm not sure,' said Henry. 'You can bet your lift it will be heavily guarded. Viktor, are they any backways into the port?'

'No,' he said bluntly.

'I guess we're going to have to find a way when we're there.'

**

He woke with a start, his eyes darting around, not knowing how long he had slept for. From the poor light coming through the windows, Henry deduced it was early evening.

'What time is it?' he whispered, sitting down in front of Viktor.

'Nearly six. Did you have well sleep?'

'Yeah, thanks,' Henry blushed. 'I think it's time we left.'

He looked across at Tommy and waved him over.

'Are we going?' the blond soldier asked as he approached.

Henry nodded.

'If we don't have a chance, Viktor, I'd like to say a huge thank you. You've been really helpful, and without you, we wouldn't be here.'

'My pleasure,' he said. 'Good luck getting home.'

'Thanks.'

'What will you do now?' asked Tommy.

'Nothing here. I'll go back to Olsztyn,' he replied. 'It will take me several days.'

'I hope you make it back safely,' said Henry.

The three men exchanged hugs and handshakes.

'You have a friend in Poland,' Viktor said.

'Thank you.'

With one final goodbye, they walked out of the church and down the stone steps. At the bottom, without making eye contact, Viktor turned right and the two British soldiers turned left.

34

The Danzig trawler fleet was visible through the chain-link fence which ran between two low buildings. The few boats preparing to set out to sea had their lights on, while the rest languished in darkness. Their crews ashore were enjoying the delights of Danzig's nightlife.

'One of those must be the *Margarite*,' Henry whispered.

'I hope so,' said Tommy.

'Can you see a way in?'

Without warning, Tommy pulled him into the shadow of the nearest building as a cone of torchlight passed on the other side of the fence.

'That was close,' Tommy said once the guard had passed.

'Thanks, mate.'

Tilting his head back and letting out a sigh of relief, Henry spotted a window occupying the upper part of the whitewashed wall.

'Give me a lift up.'

Tommy cradled his hands together, giving his sergeant a boost up to the large, stone sill. From his elevated position, he had a good view of the whole expanse of the harbour. Steadying himself on a guttering bracket, he helped Tommy up before they scrambled onto the roof.

Lying face-down on the cold slates, they peered over the ridge of tiles. The numerous torches of the guards moved about, illuminating pockets of the vast complex. Once in total darkness, the two British soldiers shuffled over the apex until they lay above the quayside. Henry studied the ships with their lights on. Most were Polish, but alarmingly, quite a few bore the war ensign of the Kriegsmarine, the German Navy. He could not identify two of the fishing boats. The *Margarite* had to be one of them, but which one? With the two unidentified trawlers moored at opposite ends of the port, if they went to the wrong one, they would not have enough time to get to the *Margarite* before it set sail.

Henry scrutinised the nearest of the two ships, but frustratingly, the boat was too far away for him to read the name. A southerly wind picked up, causing a Norwegian flag to billow in the bright glow of the deck lights. That must be it.

Lowering themselves from the roof onto the quay, they were now close enough to see the warm breath of the crew making their final preparations before putting to sea. Although Tommy and Henry only had to cover a relatively short distance, the large number of guards inside the harbour complex meant they would not be able to walk to the Margarite without being seen.

A giant, rusting boom from a trawler rested against the side of the building, providing a perfect hiding place for them as another guard approached. Among the lobster pots and other discarded fishing equipment, Henry found a tiny, flat-bottomed raft, the kind used by sailors to reach their ships moored in the middle of the docks. An idea formed in his mind. If they couldn't walk there, perhaps they could paddle there. Presumably, the guards would not be expecting them to be in the water. Hopefully, they would only be looking for intruders on the land.

Henry bent over and examined the small boat in the poor light. It appeared seaworthy, as much as he was able to tell. Tucked inside was a single short-handled oar. The craft had once been painted white, but the majority of the paint had worn away, leaving the wood beneath to become heavily weathered. Once the guard had passed, the two British soldiers carried the raft down a nearby slipway, placing it at the water's edge. Tommy steadied the small vessel as Henry climbed aboard. The little boat was only designed to carry one man, so as both of them put their weight onto it, the raft became perilously low in the water. There was no time to make two trips, so they would have to hope they could stay afloat long enough to complete the short journey to the *Margarite*.

Henry knelt at the very front of the boat, while Tommy squatted on the back with the oar. As they set off, water splashed over the bow, and it started sinking. Henry carefully readjusted his weight, spreading it more evenly, causing them to rise slightly in the water. Tommy continued to paddle gently into the darkness, making as little noise as possible.

The trawler's lights shone brightly above them, its engines idling as the crew worked busily on deck. A knotted rope hung down the side, dangling into the sea. Henry checked the front of the vessel; large white letters spelt out the name *Margarite*.

He grabbed the rope, pulling them alongside, and then began to climb. As he lifted off, the craft sat considerably higher, alleviating Tommy's fears of sinking. When Henry was halfway up, a fisherman looked down and glared at him. He froze. Did the crewmen not know he and Tommy were coming?

Voices shouted in German up on the deck. Now, it made sense. The boat was being scarched by the Wehrmacht before it put out to sea. Henry tried to bring his finger to his lips, but when he took a hand off the rope, he started to sway uncontrollably.

Presently, the fisherman appeared with a much friendlier expression and waved them aboard. Once his sergeant had made it to the deck, Tommy, grabbed hold of the rope and pushed down on the raft with his foot. The small vessel disappeared beneath the surface and quickly sank to the bottom. The blond soldier nimbly clambered up the side where the fisherman helped him over the rail before promptly ushering him below.

In the cramped cabin, Henry was sitting on a bunk wrapped in a horse-hair blanket, looking relieved. The crewman returned to his duties, leaving the two British soldiers on the edge of the springy bed.

As it left the sheltered haven of the harbour, the trawler started rolling in the rougher open sea. The two men congratulated each other, before slumping on their bunks. After a quarter of an hour, a burly man knocked and entered the room.

'Good evening,' he said in perfect English with a slight Scandinavian accent. 'My name is Einar Andersen. Welcome aboard my ship, *Margarite*.'

Henry and Tommy introduced themselves, shaking the captain's hand.

'Sorry to keep you hanging around,' he said with a smile. 'But now, the Germans are searching all ships leaving Danzig. You two have caused something of a stir. Anyhow, we're already two miles out. So, you're safe now. It'll take several days for us to reach the Scottish coast. I suggest you catch up on your sleep. One of my crew will call you when it's time for breakfast.'

'Thanks, Captain,' Henry said.

'Have a good night, gentlemen.' The captain turned to leave. 'Oh, one last thing, I would appreciate it if you did not venture out on deck until morning. We can't risk either of you being seen.'

Tommy relaxed on the top bunk, smiling with a mixture of euphoria and relief.

'We made it, Sarge,' he celebrated. 'We've made it.'

Henry, yet to find his sea legs, was beginning to feel unwell. His nausea was amplified by the inescapable smell of fish which penetrated everything.

'For a while, I thought we would be stuck in Danzig forever,' said Tommy.

'I hope Viktor makes it out of the city without too much difficulty.'

'It won't be easy, but he's a wily old chap.'

'Yeah, I'm sure he'll be okay.'

Henry's seasickness subsided after forty-eight hours. By the evening of the third day, he had regained his appetite. Mealtimes were an experience; everything on the table rolled and clattered. He struggled to keep hold of his plate while he ate, causing the crewmen much amusement.

They spent the final few days either sleeping or talking on the deck while watching the crew members work. The two British soldiers had offered to help, but their strength did not match that of the fishermen, and they proved to be more of a hindrance.

'Afternoon, gentlemen,' said the bearded captain as he entered their room. 'We're about thirty minutes from Shetland. You're almost home. In a few hours, you'll be on the mainland.'

'Did you hear that, Sarge? We're nearly home,' Tommy shouted excitedly.

He embraced Henry, then went to hug the Norwegian fisherman but thought better of it.

The land was initially a blur on the horizon, and the two men stood against the rail, savouring the Scottish coastline as they approached. Eventually, the ship slowed its engines and pulled into a quaint, granite harbour. The surrounding countryside was rugged heathland except for a couple of isolated farmhouses and cottages. A single black car was parked on the quayside, looking incongruous in the rural setting.

A fisherman stepped onto the quay and secured a

rope to a capstan. Henry and Tommy climbed over the side, relieved to be back in Britain. Wearing full uniform, Major Fosdyke stood by the car.

'Welcome home, gentlemen!' he said in his gruff voice.

'Thank you, Sir,' Henry said, the two soldiers standing to attention.

'At ease, men,' the officer said. 'You two have had one hell of a journey. I'm pleased to see you back in Blighty.'

Opening the rear door, Henry slid across the back seat.

'It's good to see you again, 'Enry,' the driver said, looking over his shoulder.

Henry looked up, greeted by the round face of Alf Morrison.

'Alf! How are you?' he asked. 'How's the ankle?'

'It was only a sprain, Sarge. Thanks for getting me to the plane. I thought I was a goner.'

Before Henry could reply, Tommy got in beside him.

'Hello, Alf,' the blond soldier said exuberantly.

'I wondered if you'd ever turn up again,' Morrison said, reaching over and shaking his hand. 'Where did you get to?'

'There will be plenty of time for story-telling during our trip, but now, it's time to head back,' said the major slipping into the front seat. 'We have a very long drive ahead of us.'

***

It took Viktor seven days to complete the journey to Olsztyn on foot. He had slept rough in hedgerows and ditches, hitching lifts from farmers and salesmen. It was a glorious feeling, walking down the driveway and entering

271

the kitchen. The family were seated at the table, eating dinner as he stepped through the door.

Zofia, now in the final stages of pregnancy, had presumed her husband was dead. She leapt to her feet, rushing across the room. With tears streaming, he wrapped his arms around her, their two children cuddling around his legs while his parents watched from a distance.

'Where have you been?' Zofia kept asking, nuzzling into his chest.

'You would never believe me,' Viktor replied.

Printed in Great Britain
by Amazon